DATE DUE

DEMCO 38-296

BEST
SCIENCE FICTION STORIES
OF THE YEAR

BEST SCIENCE FICTION STORIES OF THE YEAR

Edited by
LESTER DEL REY

E. P. DUTTON & CO., INC. | NEW YORK | 1972

Published simultaneously in Canada by
Clarke, Irwin & Company Limited, Toronto and Vancouver

SBN: 0-525-06490-7
Library of Congress Catalog Card Number: 77-190700

To Isaac and Janet,
who are wonderful neighbors

Contents

FOREWORD
Alternate Possibilities

In almost fifty years, the readers and critics of science fiction have yet to find a satisfactory definition of the field. It seems to have no exact boundaries, nor does it follow any rigid set of rules. Even the name is poorly chosen, since it doesn't necessarily have to deal with science.

In a sort of general way, however, we can say what it is *not*. It isn't fiction dealing specifically with the normal here and now, nor with the accepted ideas of the past that produced our present reality. But such a definition by negatives doesn't help much.

Probably it can best be defined as a fiction which attempts to deal entertainingly with alternate possibilities.

This doesn't necessarily refer to the future. In fact, science fiction doesn't try to predict *the* future at all; it accepts only *a* future—a possibility, not an almost certainty. It presents us with a future that might happen—and another and a varying other, etc. Or it can give us an alternate past, such as one in which mankind didn't evolve here, but was seeded from another race around a distant star. Even the present as we know it isn't certain in science fiction. We can assume that some time in our past, George Washington lost the battle, England retained the Colonies, and as a result, became the only major world power. Or that the South won the war. Then we must try to find the logical consequences of our assumption. When dealing with the future, science must be treated as honestly as possible, of course, since it will have a major effect on that future. But that science doesn't have to be a logical projection of our current knowledge, so long as it is not impossible.

Science fiction has often predicted some aspects of future development, such as space travel and atomic power, but that isn't its business. It really isn't intended to predict—a rather dull business, attempting to predict; it merely projects what it feels might be an interesting idea or possibility.

Of course, much of science fiction is related to the world as we know it. The problems of today naturally are reflected in our writing. Some of the stories here show this very strongly. After all, we were dealing with the population explosion and pollution more than forty years ago, but only as possibilities. Others here seem almost unrelated to our current problems, but invent whole new ones for the bedevilment of odd characters.

The stories have only one thing in common: they are the ones that I most enjoyed reading from all those appearing in magazines and original books for a twelve-month period. They were picked without regard for what they dealt with, where or when they occurred, or who wrote them. Most of them are by writers of high reputation in the field—probably because reputations are made by the ability to tell good stories fairly consistently. But I'm happy to see that a few are by writers whose names I didn't know until their stories forced me to remember them.

I found them all to be excellent science fiction—so I offer them as my best definition of the field. And all of them are also illustrative of my second point—that science fiction must be fun to read!

—Lester del Rey

BEST
SCIENCE FICTION STORIES
OF THE YEAR

Twenty years ago, Philip José Farmer shocked the prurient and delighted other readers by treating sex as a subject for speculation in his first story, The Lovers. *Since then, he has continued to delight and confound his readers with a stream of stories that are always somehow unexpected. Here, for instance, he offers a fresh solution to the problem of overpopulation—a world with seven times as many people but with absolutely no added drain on our environment. Of course, there are a few minor difficulties. . . .*

PHILIP JOSÉ FARMER

The Sliced-Crosswise Only-on-Tuesday World

Getting into Wednesday was almost impossible.

Tom Pym had thought about living on other days of the week. Almost everybody with any imagination did. There were even TV shows speculating on this. Tom Pym had even acted in two of these. But he had no genuine desire to move out of his own world. Then his house burned down.

This was on the last day of the eight days of spring. He awoke to look out the door at the ashes and the firemen. A man in a white asbestos suit motioned for him to stay inside. After fifteen

Copyright © 1971 by Robert Silverberg. First published in *New Dimensions I*, edited by Robert Silverberg. Reprinted by permission of the author and the author's agents, Scott Meredith Literary Agency, Inc., 580 Fifth Avenue, New York, N.Y. 10036.

minutes, another man in a suit gestured that it was safe. He pressed the button by the door, and it swung open. He sank down in the ashes to his ankles; they were a trifle warm under the inch-thick coat of water-soaked crust.

There was no need to ask what had happened, but he did, anyway.

The fireman said, "A short-circuit, I suppose. Actually, we don't know. It started shortly after midnight, between the time that Monday quit and we took over."

Tom Pym thought that it must be strange to be a fireman or a policeman. Their hours were so different, even though they were still limited by the walls of midnight.

By then the others were stepping out of their stoners, or "coffins" as they were often called. That left sixty still occupied.

They were due for work at 08:00. The problem of getting new clothes and a place to live would have to be put off until off-hours, because the TV studio where they worked was behind in the big special it was due to put on in 144 days.

They ate breakfast at an emergency center. Tom Pym asked a grip if he knew of any place he could stay. Though the government would find one for him, it might not look very hard for a convenient place.

The grip told him about a house only six blocks from his former house. A makeup man had died, and as far as he knew the vacancy had not been filled. Tom got onto the phone at once, since he wasn't needed at that moment, but the office wouldn't be open until ten, as the recording informed him. The recording was a very pretty girl with red hair, tourmaline eyes, and a very sexy voice. Tom would have been more impressed if he had not known her. She had played in some small parts in two of his shows, and the maddening voice was not hers. Neither was the color of her eyes.

At noon he called again, got through after a ten-minute wait, and asked Mrs. Bellefield if she would put through a request for him. Mrs. Bellefield reprimanded him for not having phoned sooner; she was not sure that anything could be done today. He tried to tell her his circumstances and then gave up. Bureaucrats! That evening he went to a public emergency place, slept for the required four hours while the inductive field speeded up his dreaming, woke up, and got into the upright cylinder of eternium. He stood for ten seconds, gazing out through the transparent door at other cylinders with their still figures, and then he pressed the button. Approximately fifteen seconds later he became unconscious.

He had to spend three more nights in the public stoner. Three days of spring were gone; only five left. Not that that mattered in California so much. When he had lived in Chicago, winter was like a white blanket being shaken by a madwoman. Spring was a green explosion. Summer was a bright roar and a hot breath. Fall was the topple of a drunken jester in garish motley.

The fourth day, he received notice that he could move into the very house he had picked. This surprised and pleased him. He knew of a dozen who had spent a whole year—forty-eight days or so—in a public station while waiting. He moved in the fifth day with three days of spring to enjoy. But he would have to use up his two days off to shop for clothes, bring in groceries and other goods, and get acquainted with his housemates. Sometimes, he wished he had not been born with the compulsion to act. TV'ers worked five days at a stretch, sometimes six, while a plumber, for instance, only put in three days out of seven.

The house was as large as the other, and the six extra blocks to walk would be good for him. It held eight people per day, counting himself. He moved in that evening, introduced himself, and got Mabel Curta, who worked as a secretary for a producer, to fill him in on the household routine. After he made sure that his stoner had been moved into the stoner room, he could relax somewhat.

Mabel Curta had accompanied him into the stoner room, since she had appointed herself his guide. She was a short, overly curved woman of about thirty-five (Tuesday time). She had been divorced three times, and marriage was no more for her, unless, of course, Mr. Right came along. Tom was between marriages himself, but he did not tell her so.

"We'll take a look at your bedroom," Mabel said. "It's small but it's soundproofed, thank God."

He started after her, then stopped. She looked back through the doorway and said, "What is it?"

"This girl . . ."

There were sixty-three of the tall gray eternium cylinders. He was looking through the door of the nearest at the girl within.

"Wow! Really beautiful!"

If Mabel felt any jealousy, she suppressed it.

"Yes, isn't she!"

The girl had long, black, slightly curly hair, a face that could have launched him a thousand times times a thousand times, a figure that had enough but not too much, and long legs. Her eyes were open; in the dim light they looked a purplish-blue. She wore a thin silvery dress.

The plate by the top of the door gave her vital data. Jennie Marlowe. Born A.D. 2031, San Marino, California. She would be twenty-four years old. Actress. Unmarried. Wednesday's child.

"What's the matter?" Mabel said.

"Nothing."

How could he tell her that he felt sick in his stomach from a desire that could never be satisfied? Sick from beauty?

> *For will in us is overruled by fate.*
> *Who ever loved, that loved not at first sight?*

"What?" Mabel said, and then, after laughing, "You must be kidding."

She wasn't angry. She realized that Jennie Marlowe was no more competition than if she were dead. She was right. Better for him to busy himself with the living of this world. Mabel wasn't too bad, cuddly, really, and, after a few drinks, rather stimulating.

They went downstairs afterward after 18:00 to the TV room. Most of the others were there, too. Some had their ear plugs in; some were looking at the screen but talking. The newscast was on, of course. Everybody was filling up on what had happened last Tuesday and today. The Speaker of the House was retiring after his term was up. His days of usefulness were over and his recent ill health showed no signs of disappearing. There was a shot of the family graveyard in Mississippi with the pedestal reserved for him. When science someday learned how to rejuvenate, he would come out of stonerment.

"That'll be the day!" Mabel said. She squirmed on his lap.

"Oh, I think they'll crack it," he said. "They're already on the track; they've succeeded in stopping the aging of rabbits."

"I don't mean that," she said. "Sure, they'll find out how to rejuvenate people. But then what? You think they're going to bring them all back? With all the people they got now and then they'll double, maybe triple, maybe quadruple, the population? You think they won't just leave them standing out there?" She giggled, and said, "What would the pigeons do without them?"

He squeezed her waist. At the same time, he had a vision of himself squeezing *that* girl's waist. Hers would be soft enough, but with no hint of fat.

Forget about her. Think of now. Watch the news.

A Mrs. Wilder had stabbed her husband and then herself with a kitchen knife. Both had been stonered immediately after the police arrived, and they had been taken to the hospital. An investigation of a work slowdown in the county government offices was taking place. The complaints were that Monday's people were not setting up the computers for Tuesday's. The case was being referred to the proper authorities of both days. The Ganymede base reported that the Great Red Spot of Jupiter was emitting weak but definite pulses that did not seem to be random.

The last five minutes of the program was a précis devoted to outstanding events of the other days. Mrs. Cuthmar, the house mother, turned the channel to a situation comedy with no protests from anybody.

Tom left the room, after telling Mabel that he was going to bed early—alone, and to sleep. He had a hard day tomorrow.

He tiptoed down the hall and the stairs and into the stoner room. The lights were soft, there were many shadows, and it was quiet. The sixty-three cylinders were like ancient granite columns of an underground chamber of a buried city. Fifty-five faces were white blurs behind the clear metal. Some had their eyes open; most had closed them while waiting for the field radiated from the machine in the base. He looked through Jennie Marlowe's door. He felt sick again. Out of his reach; never for him. Wednesday was only a day away. No, it was only a little less than four and a half hours away.

He touched the door. It was slick and only a little cold. She stared at him. Her right forearm was bent to hold the strap of a large purse. When the door opened, she would step out, ready to go. Some people took their showers and fixed their faces as soon as they got up from their sleep and then went directly into the stoner. When the field was automatically radiated at 05:00, they stepped out a minute later, ready for the day.

He would like to step out of his "coffin," too, at the same time.

But he was barred by Wednesday.

He turned away. He was acting like a sixteen-year-old kid. He had been sixteen about one hundred and six years ago, not that that made any difference. Physiologically, he was thirty.

As he started up to the second floor, he almost turned around and went back for another look. But he took himself by his neck-collar and pulled himself up to his room. There he decided he would get to sleep at once. Perhaps he would dream about her. If dreams were wish fulfillments, they would bring her to him. It still had not been "proved" that dreams always expressed wishes, but it had been proved that man deprived of dreaming did go mad. And so the somniums radiated a field that put man into a state in which he got all the sleep, and all the dreams, that he needed within a four-hour period. Then he was awakened and a little later went into the stoner, where the field suspended all atomic and subatomic activity. He would remain in that state forever unless the activating field came on.

He slept, and Jennie Marlowe did not come to him. Or, if she did, he did not remember. He awoke, washed his face, went down eagerly to the stoner, where he found the entire household standing around, getting in one last smoke, talking, laughing. Then they would step into their cylinders, and a silence like that at the heart of a mountain would fall.

He had often wondered what would happen if he did not go into the stoner. How would he feel? Would he be panicked? All his life, he had known only Tuesdays. Would Wednesday rush at him, roaring, like a tidal wave? Pick him up and hurl him against the reefs of a strange time?

What if he made some excuse and went back upstairs and did not go back down until the field had come on? By then, he could not enter. The door to his cylinder would not open again until the proper time. He could still run down to the public emergency stoners only three blocks away. But if he stayed in his room, waiting for Wednesday?

Such things happened. If the breaker of the law did not have a reasonable excuse, he was put on trial. It was a felony second only to murder to "break time," and the unexcused were stonered. All felons, sane or insane, were stonered. Or *mañanaed*, as some said. The *mañanaed* criminal waited in immobility and unconsciousness, preserved unharmed until science had techniques to cure the insane, the neurotic, the criminal, the sick. *Mañana.*

"What was it like in Wednesday?" Tom had asked a man who had been unavoidably left behind because of an accident.

"How would I know? I was knocked out except for about fifteen minutes. I was in the same city, and I had never seen the faces of the ambulance men, of course, but then I've never seen them here. They stonered me and left me in the hospital for Tuesday to take care of."

He must have it bad, he thought. Bad. Even to think of such a thing was crazy. Getting into Wednesday was almost impossible. Almost. But it could be done. It would take time and patience, but it could be done.

He stood in front of his stoner for a moment. The others said, "See you! So long! Next Tuesday!" Mabel called, "Good night, lover!"

"Good night," he muttered.

"What?" she shouted.

"Good night!"

He glanced at the beautiful face behind the door. Then he smiled. He had been afraid that she might hear him say good night to a woman who called him "lover."

He had ten minutes left. The intercom alarms were whooping. Get going, everybody! Time to take the six-day trip! Run! Remember the penalties!

He remembered, but he wanted to leave a message. The recorder was on a table. He activated it, and said, "Dear *Miss* Jennie Marlowe. My name is Tom Pym, and my stoner is next to yours. I am an actor, too; in fact, I work at the same studio as you. I know this is presumptuous of me, but I have never seen anybody so beautiful. Do you have a talent to match your beauty? I would like to see some run-offs of your shows. Would you please leave some in room five? I'm sure the occupant won't mind. Yours, Tom Pym."

He ran it back. It was certainly bald enough, and that might be just what was needed. Too flowery or too pressing would have made her leery. He had commented on her beauty twice but not overstressed it. And the appeal to her pride in her acting would be difficult to resist. Nobody knew better than he about that.

He whistled a little on his way to the cylinder. Inside, he pressed the button and looked at his watch. Five minutes to midnight. The light on the huge screen above the computer in the police station would not be flashing for him. Ten minutes from now, Wednesday's police would step out of their stoners in the precinct station, and they would take over their duties.

There was a ten-minute hiatus between the two days in the police station. All hell could break loose in these few minutes, and it sometimes did. But a price had to be paid to maintain the walls of time.

He opened his eyes. His knees sagged a little and his head bent. The activation was a million microseconds fast—from eternium to flesh and blood almost instantaneously, and the heart never knew that it had been stopped for such a long time. Even so, there was a little delay in the muscles' response to a standing position.

He pressed the button, opened the door, and it was as if his button had launched the day. Mabel had made herself up last night so that she looked dawn-fresh. He complimented her, and she smiled happily. But he told her he would meet her for breakfast. Halfway up the staircase, he stopped, and waited until the hall was empty. Then he sneaked back down and into the stoner room. He turned on the recorder.

A voice, husky but also melodious, said, "Dear Mister Pym. I've had a few messages from other days. It was fun to talk back and forth across the abyss between the worlds, if you don't mind my exaggerating a little. But there is really no sense in it, once the novelty has worn off. If you become interested in the other person, you're frustrating yourself. That person can only be a voice in a recorder and a cold waxy face in a metal coffin. I wax poetic. Pardon me. If the person doesn't interest you, why continue to communicate? There is no sense in either case. And I *may* be beautiful. Anyway, I thank you for the compliment, but I am also sensible.

"I should have just not bothered to reply. But I want to be nice; I didn't want to hurt your feelings. So please don't leave any more messages."

He waited while silence was played. Maybe she was pausing for effect. Now would come a chuckle or a low honey-throated laugh, and she would say, "However, I don't like to disappoint my public. The run-offs are in your room."

The silence stretched out. He turned off the machine and went to the dining room for breakfast.

Siesta time at work was from 14:40 to 14:45. He lay down on the bunk and pressed the button. Within a minute he was asleep. He did dream of Jennie this time; she was a white shimmering figure solidifying out of the darkness and floating toward him. She was even more beautiful than she had been in her stoner.

The shooting ran overtime that afternoon so that he got home just in time for supper. Even the studio would not dare keep a man past his supper hour, especially since the studio was authorized to serve food only at noon.

He had time to look at Jennie for a minute before Mrs. Cuthmar's voice screeched over the intercom. As he walked down the hall, he thought, "I'm getting barnacled on her. It's ridiculous. I'm a grown man. Maybe . . . maybe I should see a psycher."

Sure, make your petition, and wait until a psycher has time for you. Say about three hundred days from now, if you are lucky. And if the psycher doesn't work out for you, then petition for another, and wait six hundred days.

Petition. He slowed down. Petition. What about a request, not to see a psycher, but to move? Why not? What did he have to lose? It would probably be turned down, but he could at least try.

Even obtaining a form for the request was not easy. He spent two nonwork days standing in line at the Center City Bureau before he got the proper forms. The first time, he was handed the wrong form and had to start all over again. There was no line set aside for those who wanted to change their days. There were not enough who wished to do this to justify such a line. So he had had to queue up before the Miscellaneous Office counter of the Mobility Section of the Vital Exchange Department of the Interchange and Cross Transfer Bureau. None of these titles had anything to do with emigation to another day.

When he got his form the second time, he refused to move from the office window until he had checked the number of the form and asked the clerk to double-check it. He ignored the cries and the mutterings behind him. Then he went to one side of the vast room and stood in line before the punch machines. After two hours, he got to sit down at a small rolltop desk-shaped machine, above which was a large screen. He inserted the form into the slot, looked at the projection of the form, and punched buttons to mark the proper spaces opposite the proper questions. After that, all he had to do was to drop the form into a slot and hope it did not get lost. Or hope he would not have to go through the same procedure because he had improperly punched the form.

That evening, he put his head against the hard metal and murmured to the rigid face behind the door, "I must really love you to go through all this. And you don't even know it. And, worse, if you did, you might not care one bit."

To prove to himself that he had kept his gray stuff, he went out with Mabel that evening to a party given by Sol Voremwolf, a producer. Voremwolf had just passed a civil-service examination giving him an A-13 rating. This meant that, in time, with some luck and the proper pull, he would become an executive vice-president of the studio.

The party was a qualified success. Tom and Mabel returned about half an hour before stoner time. Tom had managed to refrain from too many blowminds and liquor, so he was not tempted by Mabel. Even so, he knew that when he became unstonered, he would be half-loaded and he'd have to take some dreadful counteractives. He would look and feel like hell at work, since he had missed his sleep.

He put Mabel off with an excuse, and went down to the stoner room ahead of the others. Not that that would do him any good if he wanted to get stonered early. The stoners only activated within narrow time limits.

He leaned against the cylinder and patted the door. "I tried not to think about you all evening. I wanted to be fair to Mabel; it's not fair to go out with her and think about you all the time."

All's fair in love . . .

He left another message for her, then wiped it out. What was the use? Besides, he knew that his speech was a little thick. He wanted to appear at his best for her.

Why should he? What did she care for him?

The answer was, he did care, and there was no reason or logic connected with it. He loved this forbidden, untouchable, far-away-in-time, yet-so-near woman.

Mabel had come in silently. She said, "You're sick!"

Tom jumped away. Now, why had he done that? He had nothing to be ashamed of. Then why was he so angry with her? His embarrassment was understandable, but his anger was not.

Mabel laughed at him, and he was glad. Now he could snarl at her. He did so, and she turned away and walked out. But she was back in a few minutes with the others. It would soon be midnight.

By then he was standing inside the cylinder. A few seconds later, he left it, pushed Jennie's backward on its wheels, and pushed his around so that it faced hers. He went back in, pressed the button, and stood there. The double doors only slightly distorted his view. But she seemed even more removed in distance, in time, and in unattainability.

Three days later, well into winter, he received a letter. The box inside the entrance hall buzzed just as he entered the front door. He went back and waited until the letter was printed and had dropped out from the slot. It was the reply to his request to move to Wednesday.

Denied. Reason: he had no reasonable reason to move.

That was true. But he could not give his real motive. It would have been even less impressive than the one he had given. He had punched the box opposite No. 12. REASON: TO GET INTO AN ENVIRONMENT WHERE MY TALENTS WILL BE MORE LIKELY TO BE ENCOURAGED.

He cursed and he raged. It was his human, his civil right to move into any day he pleased. That is, it should be his right. What if a move did cause much effort? What if it required a transfer of his I.D. and all the records connected with him from the moment of his birth? What if . . . ?

He could rage all he wanted to, but it would not change a thing. He was stuck in the world of Tuesday.

Not yet, he muttered. Not yet. Fortunately, there is no limit to the number of requests I can make in my own day. I'll send out another. They think they can wear me out, huh? Well, I'll wear them out. Man against the machine. Man against the system. Man against the bureaucracy and the hard cold rules.

Winter's twenty days had sped by. Spring's eight days rocketed by. It was summer again. On the second day of the twelve days of summer, he received a reply to his second request.

It was neither a denial nor an acceptance. It stated that if he thought he would be better off psychologically in Wednesday because his astrologer said so, then he would have to get a psycher's critique of the astrologer's analysis. Tom Pym jumped into the air and clicked his sandaled heels together. Thank God that he lived in an age that did not classify astrologers as charlatans! The people—the masses—had protested that astrology was a necessity and that it should be legalized and honored. So laws were passed, and, because of that, Tom Pym had a chance.

He went down to the stoner room and kissed the door of the cylinder and told Jennie Marlowe the good news. She did not respond, though he thought he saw her eyes brighten just a little. That was, of course, only his imagination, but he liked his imagination.

Getting a psycher for a consultation and getting through the three sessions took another year, another forty-eight days. Dr. Sigmund Traurig was a friend of Dr. Stelhela, the astrologer, and so that made things easier for Tom.

"I've studied Dr. Stelhela's chart carefully and analyzed carefully your obsession for this woman," he said. "I agree with Dr. Stelhela that you will always be unhappy in Tuesday, but I don't quite agree with him that you will be happier in Wednesday. However, you have this thing going for this Miss Marlowe, so I think you should go to Wednesday. But only if you sign papers agreeing to see a psycher there for extended therapy."

Only later did Tom Pym realize that Dr. Traurig might have wanted to get rid of him because he had too many patients. But that was an uncharitable thought.

He had to wait while the proper papers were transmitted to Wednesday's authorities. His battle was only half-won. The other officials could turn him down. And if he did get to his goal, then what? She could reject him without giving him a second chance.

It was unthinkable, but she could.

He caressed the door and then pressed his lips against it.

"Pygmalion could at least touch Galatea," he said. "Surely, the gods—the big dumb bureaucrats—will take pity on me, who can't even touch you. Surely."

The psycher had said that he was incapable of a true and lasting bond with a woman, as so many men were in this world of easy-come-easy-go liaisons. He had fallen in love with Jennie Marlowe for several reasons. She may have resembled somebody he had loved when he was very young. His mother, perhaps? No? Well, never mind. He would find out in Wednesday—perhaps. The deep, the important, truth was that he loved Miss Marlowe because she could never reject him, kick him out, or become tiresome, complain, weep, yell, insult, and so forth. He loved her because she was unattainable and silent.

"I love her as Achilles must have loved Helen when he saw her on top of the walls of Troy," Tom said.

"I wasn't aware that Achilles was ever in love with Helen of Troy," Dr. Traurig said dryly.

"Homer never said so, but I *know* that he must have been! Who could see her and *not* love her?"

"How the hell would I know? I never saw her! If I had suspected these delusions would intensify . . ."

"I am a poet!" Tom said.

"Overimaginative, you mean! Hmmm. She must be a douser! I don't have anything particular to do this evening. I'll tell you what . . . my curiosity is aroused . . . I'll come down to your place tonight and take a look at this fabulous beauty, your Helen of Troy."

Dr. Traurig appeared immediately after supper, and Tom Pym ushered him down the hall and into the stoner room at the rear of the big house as if he were a guide conducting a famous critic to a just-discovered Rembrandt.

The doctor stood for a long time in front of the cylinder. He hmmmed several times and checked her vital-data plate several times. Then he turned and said, "I see what you mean, Mr. Pym. Very well. I'll give the go-ahead."

"Ain't she something?" Tom said on the porch. "She's out of this world, literally and figuratively, of course."

"Very beautiful. But I believe that you are facing a great disappointment, perhaps heartbreak, perhaps, who knows, even madness, much as I hate to use that unscientific term."

"I'll take the chance," Tom said. "I know I sound nuts, but where would we be if it weren't for nuts? Look at the man who invented the wheel, at Columbus, at James Watt, at the Wright brothers, at Pasteur, you name them."

"You can scarcely compare these pioneers of science with their passion for truth with you and your desire to marry a woman. But, as I have observed, she is strikingly beautiful. Still, that makes me exceedingly cautious. Why isn't she married? What's wrong with her?"

"For all I know, she may have been married a dozen times!" Tom said. "The point is, she isn't now! Maybe she's disappointed and she's sworn to wait until the right man comes along. Maybe . . ."

"There's no maybe about it, you're neurotic," Traurig said.

"But I actually believe that it would be more dangerous for you *not* to go to Wednesday than it would be *to* go."

"Then you'll say yes!" Tom said, grabbing the doctor's hand and shaking it.

"Perhaps. I have some doubts."

The doctor had a faraway look. Tom laughed and released the hand and slapped the doctor on the shoulder. "Admit it! You were really struck by her! You'd have to be dead not to!"

"She's all right," the doctor said. "But you must think this over. If you do go there and she turns you down, you might go off the deep end, much as I hate to use such a poetical term."

"No, I won't. I wouldn't be a bit the worse off. Better off, in fact. I'll at least get to see her in the flesh."

Spring and summer zipped by. Then, a morning he would never forget, the letter of acceptance. With it, instructions on how to get to Wednesday. These were simple enough. He was to make sure that the technicians came to his stoner sometime during the day and readjusted the timer within the base. He could not figure out why he could not just stay out of the stoner and let Wednesday catch up to him, but by now he was past trying to fathom the bureaucratic mind.

He did not intend to tell anyone at the house, mainly because of Mabel. But Mabel found out from someone at the studio. She wept when she saw him at suppertime, and she ran upstairs to her room. He felt bad, but he did not follow to console her.

That evening, his heart beating hard, he opened the door to his stoner. The others had found out by then; he had been unable to keep the business to himself. Actually, he was glad that he had told them. They seemed happy for him, and they brought in drinks and had many rounds of toasts. Finally, Mabel came downstairs, wiping her eyes, and she said she wished him luck, too. She had known that he was not really in love with her. But she did wish someone would fall in love with her just by looking inside her stoner.

When she found out that he had gone to see Dr. Traurig, she said, "He's a very influential man. Sol Voremwolf had him for his analyst. He says he's even got influence on other days. He edits the *Psyche Crosscurrents,* you know, one of the few periodicals read by other people."

Other, of course, meant those who lived in Wednesdays through Mondays.

Tom said he was glad he had gotten Traurig. Perhaps he had used his influence to get the Wednesday authorities to push through his request so swiftly. The walls between the worlds were seldom broken, but it was suspected that the very influential did it when they pleased.

Now, quivering, he stood before Jennie's cylinder again. The last time, he thought, that I'll see her stonered. Next time, she'll be warm, colorful, touchable flesh.

"Ave atque vale!" he said aloud. The others cheered. Mabel said, "How corny!" They thought he was addressing them, and perhaps he had included them.

He stepped inside the cylinder, closed the door, and pressed the button. He would keep his eyes open, so that . . .

And today was Wednesday. Though the view was exactly the same, it was like being on Mars.

He pushed open the door and stepped out. The seven people had faces he knew and names he had read on their plates. But he did not know them.

He started to say hello, and then he stopped.

Jennie Marlowe's cylinder was gone.

He seized the nearest man by the arm.

"Where's Jennie Marlowe?"

"Let go. You're hurting me. She's gone. To Tuesday."

"Tuesday! Tuesday?"

"Sure. She'd been trying to get out of here for a long time. She had something about this day being unlucky for her. She was unhappy, that's for sure. Just two days ago, she said her application had finally been accepted. Apparently, some Tuesday psycher had used his influence. He came down and saw her in her stoner, and that was it, brother."

The walls and the people and the stoners seemed to be distorted. Time was bending itself this way and that. He wasn't in Wednesday; he wasn't in Tuesday. He wasn't in *any* day. He was stuck inside himself at some crazy date that should never have existed.

"She can't do that!"

"Oh, no! She just did that!"

"But . . . you can't transfer more than once!"

"That's her problem."

It was his, too.

"I should never have brought him down to look at her!" Tom said. "The swine! The unethical swine!"

Tom Pym stood there for a long time, and then he went into the kitchen. It was the same environment, if you discounted the people. Later, he went to the studio and got a part in a situation play which was, really, just like all those in Tuesday. He watched the newscaster that night. The President of the U.S.A. had a different name and face, but the words of his speech could have been those of Tuesday's President. He was introduced to a secretary of a producer; her name wasn't Mabel, but it might as well have been.

The difference here was that Jennie was gone, and, oh, what a world of difference it made to him.

Robert Silverberg won his first Hugo—science fiction's highest award—when he had barely begun his writing career. Now, at what he considers the advanced age of 36, he can boast of other well-earned awards for his mature work. In this story, he departs from his usually complex conceptions to tell a very simple event. Or so it seems, until one examines the implications that lie behind it, and which won for it the Nebula *award for best short story of 1971.*

ROBERT SILVERBERG
Good News from the Vatican

This is the morning everyone has waited for, when at last the robot cardinal is to be elected Pope. There can no longer be any doubt of the outcome. The conclave has been deadlocked for many days between the obstinate advocates of Cardinal Asciuga of Milan and Cardinal Carciofo of Genoa, and word has gone out that a compromise is in the making. All factions now are agreed on the selection of the robot. This morning I read in *Osservatore Romano* that the Vatican computer itself has taken a hand in the deliberations. The computer has been strongly urging the candidacy of the robot. I suppose we should not be surprised by this loyalty among machines. Nor should we let it distress us. We *absolutely must not* let it distress us.

"Every era gets the Pope it deserves," Bishop FitzPatrick observed somewhat gloomily today at breakfast. "The proper Pope for our times is a robot, certainly. At some future date it may be desirable for the Pope to be a whale, an automobile, a cat, a mountain." Bishop FitzPatrick stands well over two meters in height, and his normal facial expression is a morbid, mournful one. Thus it is impossible for us to determine whether any particular pronouncement of his reflects existential despair or placid acceptance. Many years ago he was a star player for the Holy Cross championship basketball team. He has come to Rome to do research for a biography of St. Marcellus the Righteous.

We have been watching the unfolding drama of the papal election from an outdoor café several blocks from the Square of St. Peter's. For all of us, this has been an unexpected dividend of our holiday in Rome; the previous Pope was reputed to be in good health, and there was no reason to suspect that a successor would have to be chosen for him this summer.

Each morning we drive across by taxi from our hotel near the Via Veneto and take up our regular positions around "our" table. From where we sit, we all have a clear view of the Vatican chimney through which the smoke of the burning ballots rises: black smoke if no Pope has been elected, white if the conclave has been successful. Luigi, the owner and head waiter, automatically brings us our preferred beverages: Fernet Branca for Bishop FitzPatrick, Campari and soda for Rabbi Mueller, Turkish coffee for Miss Harshaw, lemon squash for Kenneth and Beverly, and Pernod on the rocks for me. We take turns paying the check, although Kenneth has not paid it even once since our vigil began. Yesterday, when Miss Harshaw paid, she emptied her purse and found herself 350 lire short; she had nothing else except hundred-dollar travelers' checks. The rest of us looked pointedly at Kenneth, but he went on calmly sipping his lemon squash. After a brief period of tension Rabbi Mueller produced a 500-lire coin and rather irascibly slapped the heavy silver piece against the table. The rabbi is known for his short temper and vehement style. He is twenty-eight years old, customarily dresses in a fashionable plaid cassock and silvered sunglasses, and fre-

quently boasts that he has never performed a bar-mitzvah ceremony for his congregation, which is in Wicomico County,
Maryland. He believes that the rite is vulgar and obsolete, and
invariably farms out all his bar mitzvahs to a franchised organ-
ization of itinerant clergymen who handle such affairs on a
commission basis. Rabbi Mueller is an authority on angels.

Our group is divided over the merits of electing a robot as
the new Pope. Bishop FitzPatrick, Rabbi Mueller, and I are in
favor of the idea. Miss Hershaw, Kenneth, and Beverly are opposed. It is interesting to note that both of our gentlemen of the
cloth, one quite elderly and one fairly young, support this remarkable departure from tradition. Yet the three "swingers"
among us do not.

I am not sure why I align myself with the progressives. I am a
man of mature years and fairly sedate ways. Nor have I ever
concerned myself with the doings of the Church of Rome. I am
unfamiliar with Catholic dogma and unaware of recent currents
of thought within the Church. Still, I have been hoping for the
election of the robot since the start of the conclave.

Why, I wonder? Is it because the image of a metal creature
upon the throne of St. Peter's stimulates my imagination and
tickles my sense of the incongruous? That is, is my support of
the robot purely an aesthetic matter? Or is it, rather, a function
of my moral cowardice? Do I secretly think that this gesture will
buy the robots off? Am I privately saying, "Give them the papacy
and maybe they won't want other things for a while"? No. I
can't believe anything so unworthy of myself. Possibly I am for
the robot because I am a person of unusual sensitivity to the
needs of others.

"If he's elected," says Rabbi Mueller, "he plans an immediate
time-sharing agreement with the Dalai Lama and a reciprocal
plug-in with the head programmer of the Greek Orthodox
Church, just for starters. I'm told he'll make ecumenical over-
tures to the rabbinate as well, which is certainly something for
all of us to look forward to."

"I don't doubt that there'll be many corrections in the customs and practices of the hierarchy," Bishop FitzPatrick declares. "For example, we can look forward to superior information-gathering techniques as the Vatican computer is given a greater role in the operations of the Curia. Let me illustrate by—"

"What an utterly ghastly notion," Kenneth says. He is a gaudy young man with white hair and pink eyes. Beverly is either his wife or his sister. She rarely speaks. Kenneth makes the sign of the cross with offensive brusqueness and murmurs, "In the name of the Father, the Son, and the Holy Automaton." Miss Harshaw giggles but chokes the giggle off when she sees my disapproving face.

Dejectedly, but not responding at all to the interruption, Bishop FitzPatrick continues, "Let me illustrate by giving you some figures I obtained yesterday afternoon. I read in the newspaper *Oggi* that during the last five years, according to a spokesman for the *Missiones Catholicae,* the Church has increased its membership in Yugoslavia from 19,381,403 to 23,501,062. But the government census taken last year gives the total population of Yugoslavia at 23,575,194. That leaves only 74,132 for the other religious and irreligious bodies. Aware of the large Muslim population of Yugoslavia, I suspected an inaccuracy in the published statistics and consulted the computer in St. Peter's, which informed me"—the bishop, pausing, produces a lengthy print-out and unfolds it across much of the table—"that the last count of the faithful in Yugoslavia, made a year and a half ago, places our numbers at 14,206,198. Therefore an overstatement of 9,294,864 has been made. Which is absurd. And perpetuated. Which is damnable."

"What does he look like?" Miss Harshaw asks. "Does anyone have any idea?"'

"He's like all the rest," says Kenneth. "A shiny metal box with wheels below and eyes on top."

"You haven't seen him," Bishop FitzPatrick interjects. "I don't think it's proper for you to assume that—"

"They're all alike," Kenneth says. "Once you've seen one, you've seen all of them. Shiny boxes. Wheels. Eyes. And voices coming out of their bellies like mechanized belches. Inside, they're all cogs and gears." Kenneth shudders delicately. "It's too much for me to accept. Let's have another round of drinks, shall we?"

Rabbi Mueller says, "It so happens that I've seen him with my own eyes."

"You *have?*" Beverly exclaims.

Kenneth scowls at her. Luigi, approaching, brings a tray of new drinks for everyone. I hand him a five-thousand-lire note. Rabbi Mueller removes his sunglasses and breathes on their brilliantly reflective surfaces. He has small, watery gray eyes and a bad squint. He says, "The cardinal was the keynote speaker at the Congress of World Jewry that was held last fall in Beirut. His theme was 'Cybernetic Ecumenicism for Contemporary Man.' I was there. I can tell you that his Eminency is tall and distinguished, with a fine voice and a gentle smile. There's something inherently melancholy about his manner that reminds me greatly of our friend the bishop, here. His movements are graceful and his wit is keen."

"But he's mounted on wheels, isn't he?" Kenneth persists.

"On treads," replies the rabbi, giving Kenneth a fiery, devastating look and resuming his sunglasses. "Treads like a tractor has. But I don't think that treads are spiritually inferior to feet, or, for that matter, to wheels. If I were a Catholic I'd be proud to have a man like that as my Pope."

"Not a man," Miss Harshaw puts in. A giddy edge enters her voice whenever she addresses Rabbi Mueller. "A robot," she says. "He's not a man, remember?"

"A *robot* like that as my Pope, then," Rabbi Mueller says, shrugging at the correction. He raises his glass. "To the new Pope!"

"To the new Pope!" cries Bishop FitzPatrick.

Luigi comes rushing from his café. Kenneth waves him away. "Wait a second," Kenneth says. "The election isn't over yet. How can you be so sure?"

"The *Osservatore Romano,*" I say, "indicates in this morning's edition that everything will be decided today. Cardinal Carciofo has agreed to withdraw in his favor, in return for a larger real-time allotment when the new computer hours are decreed at next year's consistory."

"In other words, the fix is in," Kenneth says.

Bishop FitzPatrick sadly shakes his head. "You state things much too harshly, my son. For three weeks now we have been without a Holy Father. It is God's will that we shall have a Pope; the conclave, unable to choose between the candidacies of Cardinal Carciofo and Cardinal Asciuga, thwarts that will; if necessary, therefore, we must make certain accommodations with the realities of the times so that His will shall not be further frustrated. Prolonged politicking within the conclave now becomes sinful. Cardinal Carciofo's sacrifice of his personal ambitions is not as self-seeking an act as you would claim."

Kenneth continues to attack poor Carciofo's motives for withdrawing. Beverly occasionally applauds his cruel sallies. Miss Harshaw several times declares her unwillingness to remain a communicant of a Church whose leader is a machine. I find this dispute distasteful and swing my chair away from the table to have a better view of the Vatican. At this moment the cardinals are meeting in the Sistine Chapel. How I wish I were there! What splendid mysteries are being enacted in that gloomy, magnificent room! Each prince of the Church now sits on a small throne surmounted by a violet-hued canopy. Fat wax tapers glimmer on the desk before each throne. Masters-of-ceremonies move solemnly through the vast chamber, carrying the silver basins in which the blank ballots repose. These basins are placed on the table before the altar. One by one the cardinals advance to the table, take ballots, return to their desks. Now, lifting their quill pens, they begin to write. "I, Cardinal ——, elect to the Supreme Pontificate the Most Reverend Lord my Lord Cardinal ——." What name do they fill in? Is it Carciofo? Is it Asciuga? Is it the name of some obscure and shriveled prelate from Madrid or Heidelberg, some last-minute choice of the antirobot faction in its desperation?

Or are they writing *his* name? The sound of scratching pens is loud in the chapel. The cardinals are completing their ballots, sealing them at the ends, folding them, folding them again and again, carrying them to the altar, dropping them into the great gold chalice. So have they done every morning and every afternoon for days, as the deadlock has prevailed.

"I read in the *Herald Tribune* a couple of days ago," says Miss Harshaw, "that a delegation of 250 young Catholic robots from Iowa is waiting at the Des Moines airport for news of the election. If their man gets in, they've got a chartered flight ready to leave, and they intend to request that they be granted the Holy Father's first public audience."

"There can be no doubt," Bishop FitzPatrick agrees, "that his election will bring a great many people of synthetic origin into the fold of the Church."

"While driving out plenty of flesh-and-blood people!" Miss Harshaw says shrilly.

"I doubt that," says the bishop. "Certainly there will be some feelings of shock, of dismay, of injury, of loss, for some of us at first. But these will pass. The inherent goodness of the new Pope, to which Rabbi Mueller alluded, will prevail. Also I believe that technologically minded young folk everywhere will be encouraged to join the Church. Irresistible religious impulses will be awakened throughout the world."

"Can you imagine 250 robots clanking into St. Peter's?" Miss Harshaw demands.

I contemplate the distant Vatican. The morning sunlight is brilliant and dazzling, but the assembled cardinals, walled away from the world, cannot enjoy its gay sparkle. They all have voted, now. The three cardinals who were chosen by lot as this morning's scrutators of the vote have risen. One of them lifts the chalice and shakes it, mixing the ballots. Then he places it on the table before the altar; a second scrutator removes the ballots and counts them. He ascertains that the number of ballots is identical to the number of cardinals present. The ballots now have been transferred to a ciborium, which is a goblet ordinarily used to hold the consecrated bread of the Mass. The first scrutator withdraws a ballot, unfolds it, reads its inscription; passes it to the second scrutator, who reads it also; then it is given to the third scrutator, who reads the name aloud. Asciuga? Carciofo? Some other? *His?*

Rabbi Mueller is discussing angels. "Then we have the Angels of the Throne, known in Hebrew as *arelim* or *ophanim*. There are seventy of them, noted primarily for their steadfastness. Among them are the angels Orifiel, Ophaniel, Zabkiel, Jophiel, Ambriel, Tychagar, Barael, Quelamia, Paschar, Boel, and Raum. Some of these are no longer found in heaven and are numbered among the fallen angels in hell."

"So much for their steadfastness," says Kenneth.

"Then, too," the rabbi goes on, "there are the Angels of the Presence, who apparently were circumcised at the moment of their creation. These are Michael, Metatron, Suriel, Sandalphon, Uriel, Saraqael, Astanphaeus, Phanuel, Jehoel, Zagzagael, Yefefiah, and Akatriel. But I think my favorite of the whole group is the Angel of Lust, who is mentioned in Talmud *Bereshith Rabba* eighty-five as follows, that when Judah was about to pass by—"

They have finished counting the votes by this time, surely. An immense throng has assembled in the Square of St. Peter's. The sunlight gleams off hundreds if not thousands of steel-jacketed crania. This must be a wonderful day for the robot population of Rome. But most of those in the piazza are creatures of flesh and blood: old women in black, gaunt young pickpockets, boys with puppies, plump vendors of sausages, and an assortment of poets, philosophers, generals, legislators, tourists, and fishermen. How has the tally gone? We will have our answer shortly. If no candidate has had a majority, they will mix the ballots with wet straws before casting them into the chapel stove, and black smoke will billow from the chimney. But if a Pope has been elected, the straw will be dry, the smoke will be white.

The system has agreeable resonances. I like it. It gives me the satisfaction one normally derives from a flawless work of art: the

Tristan chord, let us say, or the teeth of the frog in Bosch's *Temptation of St. Anthony.* I await the outcome with fierce concentration. I am certain of the result; I can already feel the irresistible religious impulses awakening in me. Although I feel, also, an odd nostalgia for the days of flesh-and-blood Popes. Tomorrow's newspapers will have no interviews with the Holy Father's aged mother in Sicily, nor with his proud younger brother in San Francisco. And will this grand ceremony of election ever be held again? Will we need another Pope, when this one whom we will soon have can be repaired so easily?

Ah. The white smoke! The moment of revelation comes!

A figure emerges on the central balcony of the facade of St. Peter's, spreads a web of cloth-of-gold, and disappears. The blaze of light against that fabric stuns the eye. It reminds me perhaps of moonlight coldly kissing the sea at Castellamare, or, perhaps even more, of the noonday glare rebounding from the breast of the Caribbean off the coast of St. John. A second figure, clad in ermine and vermilion, has appeared on the balcony. "The cardinal-archdeacon," Bishop FitzPatrick whispers. People have started to faint. Luigi stands beside me, listening to the proceedings on a tiny radio. Kenneth says, "It's all been fixed." Rabbi Mueller hisses at him to be still. Miss Harshaw begins to sob. Beverly softly recites the Pledge of Allegiance, crossing herself throughout. This is a wonderful moment for me. I think it is the most truly contemporary moment I have ever experienced.

The amplified voice of the cardinal-archdeacon cries, "I announce to you great joy. We have a Pope."

Cheering commences, and grows in intensity as the cardinal-archdeacon tells the world that the newly chosen pontiff is indeed *that* cardinal, that noble and distinguished person, that melancholy and austere individual, whose elevation to the Holy See we have all awaited so intensely for so long. "He has imposed upon himself," says the cardinal-archdeacon, "the name of ——"

Lost in the cheering. I turn to Luigi. "Who? What name?"

"Sisto Settimo," Luigi tells me.

Yes, and there he is, Pope Sixtus the Seventh, as we now must call him. A tiny figure clad in the silver and gold papal robes, arms outstretched to the multitude, and, yes! the sunlight glints on his cheeks, his lofty forehead, there is the brightness of polished steel. Luigi is already on his knees. I kneel beside him. Miss Harshaw, Beverly, Kenneth, even the rabbi all kneel, for beyond doubt this is a miraculous event. The Pope comes forward on his balcony. Now he will deliver the traditional apostolic benediction to the city and to the world. "Our help is in the name of the Lord," he declares gravely. He activates the levitator-jets beneath his arms; even at this distance I can see the two small puffs of smoke. White smoke, again. He begins to rise into the air. "Who hath made heaven and earth," he says. "May Almighty God, Father, Son, and Holy Ghost, bless you." His voice rolls majestically toward us. His shadow extends across the whole piazza. Higher and higher he goes, until he is lost to sight. Kenneth taps Luigi. "Another round of drinks," he says, and presses a bill of high denomination into the innkeeper's fleshy palm. Bishop Fitz-Patrick weeps. Rabbi Mueller embraces Miss Harshaw. The new pontiff, I think, has begun his reign in an auspicious way.

*If there is any man who has seen James Tiptree, Jr., to know him,
that man must be the one who stares out of his mirror each morning. Otherwise, there is only a mailbox in Virginia—and the too
rare stories that appear from that address. Here, despite the title,
he gives us a plain tale of what any Terran boy could do, if he
knew enough never to upset native alien customs. Well, hardly
ever. . . .*

JAMES TIPTREE, JR.

I'll Be Waiting for You When the Swimming Pool Is Empty

Cammerling was a nice Terran boy, which is to say that his folks
came from Groombridge 34 Nu and surprised him with a Honda
990 starcoupe for his traditional *Wanderjahr*. But Cammerling
was one sigma off median in that he not only chose to travel by
himself but also to visit the remoter parts of the ephemeris where
the hostels were unrated or even nonexistent. Which is how he
came to be the first Terran—or certainly the first for a long, long
time—to land on the planet of Godolphus Four.

As his part opened, Cammerling's ears were assailed by a stu-
pendous braying, skirling, and clashing which arose from an immense dust cloud in which gleamed many shining points. When
the dust settled a bit Cammerling made out that there was a barbaric festival of some sort in progress.

Two vast masses of men were rushing toward each other on the plain before him. From one side pounded phalanx upon phalanx of individuals clad in leather cuirasses and greaves and bearing obsidian lances decked with streaming hair and what Cammerling took to be dried nuts. Charging at them from his right came squadrons of reptile-mounted riders in dazzling glass mail who whirled glittering bolos. Just behind all these raced ranks of archers with fire-headed missiles on their bows, and the whole mass was being urged on by horn-blowers, cymbalists, and bull-roarers, and standard-bearers staggering under huge pennants realistically resembling entire flayed human hides.

As Cammerling stepped forward for a clearer view, the two hordes fell upon each other in primal fury, and the plain became a vortex of slashing, spearing, gouging, beheading, disemboweling, dismembering, and other unmistakably hostile interactions.

"Good grief," said Cammerling, "can this be an actual, real-live war?"

His presence was now noticed by several of the combatants closest by, who stopped to stare and were promptly clouted by those beyond. A head flew out of the melee and rolled to Cammerling's feet, making faces and jetting gore. Without pausing to think, he switched on his Omniglot Mark Eight voder and shouted, "STOP THAT!"

"Oh, sorry," he added, as he heard the sound of obsidian shattering all over the field and noted that numerous persons were rolling on the ground clutching their ears. Tuning the voder down, he recalled his panthropological semester notes and began to scan the armies in close detail, searching for their leaders.

To his gratification he located a group of banner bearers on a hilltop somewhat behind the fray. At their head was a gigantic warrior mounted on an armored carnosaur, which was wearing a tower of jeweled human heads. This individual was magnificently painted and was leaning back in his saddle to accommodate a ham-sized triple-phallus codpiece from which spouted green smoke. He was alternately bellowing and shaking his fist at Cammerling and chug-a-lugging from a gem-encrusted skull.

On a similar rise across the way Cammerling observed a gaudy pavilion under which a very fat man reclined upon a gold litter upholstered with feebly squirming naked infants and languorously nibbled tidbits from a poignard while he eyed Cammerling. As Cammerling watched, the fat man wiped the poignard by running it through one of the meatier infants and snapped his jeweled fingers at his sides.

All these barbaric manifestations pained Cammerling, who was a good Terran boy, but at the same time he felt exhilarated by stumbling upon what was undeniably the Real Thing. Disregarding the flaming arrows and other missiles that were now arriving in his vicinity and being deflected by his invisible summer-weight nonabsorptive GE-Bilblas forcefield, he focused the voder to project directly at the two chieftains.

"Hi," he said. "I'm Cammerling from Groombridge 34 Nu. How about coming over here where we can rap, if you aren't too busy?"

After a bit of milling, Cammerling was pleased to see the two personages and their retinues converging upon him, while the crowd nearest him drew back. Unfortunately, the delegation halted at a distance that Cammerling felt was too great for a really meaningful encounter, so he stepped toward them and said winningly, "Look, friends. What you're doing—you know, it's—well, don't take this wrong, but it's not nice. It's obsolete, truly it is. I don't want to put down your cultural identity in any way, but since you're going off this war kick sooner or later—I mean, studies prove it—why not stop now?"

Seeing that they were staring at him blankly, he added, "I don't recall my historical symbolism too clearly, but what I mean, I think, is that you two men should shake hands."

At these words the fat prince in the palanquin spitted three infants and screamed, "Me touch that lizard-fondling offspring of an untranslated defecation-equivalent diseased female organ? I shall serve his barbecued gonads to condemned thieves!"

And the dragon-chief threw back his head and roared, "Me handle that chromosomally imbalanced caricature of a feces-eating cloacal parasite? His intestines will be cruppers on my corpse wagons!"

Now, Cammerling could see at once that this was going to be quite a tough situation to turn around, and as he recalibrated his voder, which had begun to oscillate, he also reminded himself that he must be careful not to show disrespect for these people's cultural norms. So he said pleasantly, "If I could serve as a resource person here, I'd like to offer the suggestion that both modern science and ethical intuition agree that all men are brothers."

Hearing which, both chieftains looked at each other with instant and total comprehension and then wheeled back and hurled every weapon in reach at Cammerling, and their retainers followed suit. Amid the shower of missiles, Cammerling perceived that a poignard and a kind of broadax had penetrated his summer-weight forcefield, making nasty runs in the lining. He was about to remonstrate with them when two pale-blue blips floated down from the nose of the spaceship behind him and instantly reduced the two princes, the carnosaur, the infants, and most of the entourages to thin vitreous puddles.

"Good lord," said Cammerling reproachfully to the ship, "that wasn't nice either. Why did you?"

The voder print-out came to life and typed in cursive: "Don't freak, dear boy. Your mother put in a few contingency programs."

Cammerling made a face and turned to address the assembled armies.

"I'm truly sorry about that. If the seconds in command on both sides want to come over here, I'll try to see it doesn't happen again."

He waited patiently while some confusion died down, and presently two somewhat older and less flamboyant senior types were assisted to come forward, and Cammerling repeated and clarified his previous suggestions. The two viziers looked at Cammerling with the whites of their eyes showing, and they looked at his ship, and at the puddles, which were now cooled and streaked with beautiful colors suitable for intaglio work on a rather large scale, and finally at each other. To Cammerling's intense satisfaction they eventually allowed themselves to be persuaded to a distant brushing of the gloved hands. In his excitement he recalled an historic phrase:

"Your swords shall be converted into plowshares!"

"Madness!" exclaimed both viziers, shrinking back. "Ensorcel our swords into women!"

"A figure of speech," Cammerling laughed. "Now, look, I do want to make it crystal clear I didn't come here to intimidate you people with my superior technology created by the enlightened interplay of free minds in our immense interstellar peace-loving Terran Federation. But don't you think it would be interesting—just as an experiment, say—if you announced that peace has been declared, like in honor of my visit maybe"—he smiled deprecatingly—"and told your armies to go, uh, home?"

One of the viziers uttered an inarticulate howl. The other cried wildly, "Is it your will that we be torn to pieces? They have been promised loot!"

This made Cammerling aware that he had overlooked their concern about the emotional tensions, which were bound to persist in a situation like this, but luckily he recalled a solution.

"Look, you have to have some kind of big national sport. You know—a thing you play? Like shinny? Or curling? Tug-of-war even? Tournaments? And music. Music! My ship can put out fantastic refreshments. Isn't that the usual thing? I'll help you get organized."

The hours that followed were somewhat jumbled in Cammerling's memory, but he felt it was, overall, quite successful. Some of the native sports turned out to be virtually indistinguishable from the original battle, and he did regret having inadvertently triggered the ship's vaporizers once or twice. But no one seemed overly upset, and when dawn broke over the plain there were a goodly number of survivors able to accept his good-bye gifts of inertia-free athletic supporters and other trade trinkets.

"That rugger-type thing you play has a lot of potential," he told the viziers. "Of course, I'd hope we could substitute an inanimate ball, and perhaps tranks instead of strychnine on the spurs. And the eviscerating bit, that's out. Here, try another Groombridge Jubilee. I want to explain to you sometime about setting up a farm system. Little Leagues. By the way, what was the war about?"

One of the viziers was busy shredding his turban, but the other one began to recite the history of the war in a sonorous singsong, starting with his tenth grandfather's boyhood. Cammerling set the voder to Semantic Digest and eventually decided that the root of the matter was a chronic shortage of fertile flood-plain from the local river.

"Well, look," he said. "That's easy to settle. Just throw a dam across those foothills there and impound the water so everyone will have enough."

"Dam?" said one vizier. "He who chokes the father of waters," said the turban-shredder hollowly, "his gonads shall become as small dried berries, and his penis shall be a dry wick. Aye, and all his relatives."

"Believe it," said Cammerling, "I have nothing but respect for your cultural orientations. But really, in this one instance—I mean, from an existential viewpoint, although I'm aware that we should do this on a more participatory basis, man—look!"

And he took his ship up and vitrified a couple of miles of foothills; and after the river-bed had overflowed and filled up with mud and dead fish, there was a big lake where none had been before. "Now, there's your dam," said Cammerling, "and the water will flow all year, enough for everybody, and you can go forth and dig irrigation ditches—I'll have the ship make a contour map—and the land will blossom."

And the viziers looked all around and said, "Yes, Lord, I guess we have a dam." And they went back to their respective peoples.

But Cammerling was a sensitive type, and after he thought it all over he went down to the nearest village and said, "Look, you people shouldn't get the idea that I think I'm some sort of god or whatever, and to prove it I'm going to come right in and live amongst you." He felt confident about this because his whole class had been on the pangalactic immunization program. And so he went down and lived amongst them, and after they got over his diseases, most of them, he was able to get right inside their heads and experience all their mind-blowing cultural practices and perceptions, and especially their religions. And although he knew he shouldn't do anything to mess up their ethnic reality, still he was pained in his good Terran heart by certain aspects of it.

So he called on each of the two viziers, and as diplomatically as possible he explained how deeply he respected their cultural outlooks, and that he wanted to help them along the inevitable evolution of their present religious phase into the more abstract and symbolic plane that it was surely headed for. "Those big statues," he said, "I mean, they're absolutely smashing. Major works of art. Coming generations will stand in awe. But you've got to protect them. I mean, those caves, and drip-drip. Oh, what a good light man could do. And you know, burning up babies in them is corrosive. Incense would be much safer. How would this grab you: *one* religio-cultural center for *both your nations,* where all the people could dig them? And while we're on it—you know, this bit of dropping babies down the wells to bring rain has to be a joke. I mean, existentially, that's why you all have squitters."

And so he went about and opened up different lines of thought for them as unobtrusively as he knew how, and when he detected signs of tension he eased off at once—for example, on his project of persuading the men to do some of the plowing. He himself laid the first stones for the Culture Center, and waited patiently for the idea to take. And presently he felt rewarded when the two head priests actually came together to see him. One was wearing a white and black death's head twice as tall as he was, and the other was wreathed in ceremonial snakes. After the greetings were over, it turned out that they had come to ask a favor.

"Delighted," he said, and he was. They explained that every

year about this time a fiendish man-eating monster ravaged the villages in the hills, and they were as straws before it. But he would undoubtedly be able to dispatch it with one hand.

So Cammerling gladly agreed to take care of the matter, and he set off next morning feeling that he had actually been accepted at last. And since they had stressed the negligible difficulty of the task—for him—he went on foot, carrying with him only a light lunch, his Galactic Cub Scout kit, and a target laser his aunt had given him when he left. And the high priests went back to their peoples rubbing their hands and pausing only to urinate on the stones of the Culture Center. And there was a great deal of smoke around the caves where the idols brooded.

Cammerling noticed some consternation when, two mornings later, he came whistling down the hill trail, but he put it down to the fact that behind him crawled an enormous shabby saurian with one leg in a plastiseal and a tranquilizing collar on his neck. Cammerling explained that the creature's vile habits had their origin in impacted tusks, and treated everybody to a practical demonstration of orthodontistry from the ship's Xenoaid. After that he spent several mornings training the beast to serve as a watch-dragon for his ship, which had sustained a few attacks of high-spirited vandalism. And the Culture Center suddenly began to shape up.

But Cammerling was thoughtful. On his mountain trip he couldn't help noticing that this planet had really terrific potential in other ways. And so, after chewing it over, he gathered some of the more enterprising commoners into an informal discussion group and said, "Look. I'm keenly aware, as studies have shown, that too rapid industrialization of an agrarian culture isn't a too good idea, and I want your frank comments if you feel I'm pushing. But have you thought about a little light industry?"

And so—well, pretty soon one of the nations had a small metal-siding plant and the other had a high-quality ceramic operation. And although Cammerling was careful to keep hands off local native customs and never to override native initiative, still, by his enthusiasm and participation in their life at the actual village level, he did seem to be having quite a catalytic effect. Certainly there were a great many activities available for everyone, what with laying out the irrigation system and collecting the kaolin and the materials for ore extraction and so on.

And so it came about that one morning, while Cammerling was helping someone invent the spinning jenny, the high viziers of the two nations came together in a secret place.

And one said, "While in no sense renouncing my undying enmity to you and your horde of agrarian defectives whom I intend to exterminate at the earliest possible moment, it's plain to see that this blasphemous usurper is grinding both our generative organs into skink soup and we ought to get rid of him." And the other replied that, while he did not wish to convey the impression that he was befouling himself by communicating on equal terms with the irrevocably tainted offspring-of-a-chancrous-scrotum represented by his present interlocutor, he would be glad to join in any scheme to get this interstellar monkey off their necks. But was he a god?

"God or not," the first vizier responded, "he appears as a young man, and there are certain well-known ways to quiet such prick-mice, more especially if we pool our joint resources for maximum effect." To which the other assented, and they began to count.

And so a few evenings later, hearing his watch-dragon snirkling hysterically, Cammerling opened his port to behold twelve dainty shapes swathed in brilliant gauzes, but not so well swathed that he failed to glimpse delicate belled toes, eyes, limbs, haunches, waists, lips, nipples, et-triple-cetera, such as he had never before beheld on this planet. Which was not surprising, since he had been gamely rubbing noses with the gamier squaws of the village level.

So he hopped out the door and said eagerly, "Well, hi there! What can I do for you?"

And a girl veiled in smoldering silks stepped forward and parted her raiment just enough to dislocate his jaw and said, "I am Lheesha the Bird of Passionate Delight and men have killed each other for my merest touch and I wish to do to your body caresses of which you have never dreamed and which will draw out your soul with unforgettable bliss." And she showed him her little hands with the breasts of hummingbirds implanted in her tender palms.

And another stepped forward and swirled her vestments so that his eyes popped and melted, and she said, "I am Ixhualca the Burning Whirlpool and I have thirty-two hitherto undiscovered muscles in my thing and I desire to inflame you to madness by means of unbearable pleasure indefinitely prolonged."

And a third knelt down demurely and whispered, "I am called Mary Jean the Cannibal Queen and I have been forced all my life to take nourishment only by compressing and vellicating my lips and gullet upon a certain shameful device, and mortally wounded princes call for me that they may expire in joy."

And by this time Cammerling could sense that they were all thinking along the same general lines, and he said, "Well, you certainly are some superchicks, and to tell the truth, I have been kind of horny. Please come in."

So they trooped in through his doorlock, which had also been programmed by Cammerling's mother, and on their way in it imperceptibly relieved the girls of various blades, gimlets, potions, amulets, poisoned rings, essences, fangs, stings, garrotes, ground glass, and so on, which had been installed in interesting recesses of their anatomies. But even if the high viziers had known this, they would not have been discouraged, because no man had ever enjoyed any two of those girls and lived.

When all twelve of them were inside with the door closed it was pretty crowded, but the ones closest to Cammerling set to work on him with the hummingbird frottage and the tonguing and the spice-inflamed apertures and the thirty-two new thing-muscles and every kind of indescribably intimate and exotic stimulation so typical of upper-class feudal debauchery, while those who couldn't get at him just then indulged in unspeakably erotic and obscene activities, which he was able to observe in close detail. And so they went on all night, finding refreshment not only in Cammerling's youth and vigor but also in the chance to pick up some cross-cultural technical fertilization, since they were half from one nation and half from the other.

And the morning light shone in upon an expanse of totally intertwined and exhausted bodies. But it had not shone long before a gentle heaving started from below, and Cammerling crawled out.

"Well, now," said Cammerling, "that was truly a groovy grope." And since he was a nice Terran boy who had been raised on wholesome Terran orgies, he bounced out the lock of the spaceship and did thirty-two push-ups, one for each muscle. And he poured water on his head and whistled and sang out, "Hey kids, when you get yourselves together, I'll show you how to make some pizzas. I have to go help lay out the new sewage-filtration pond; we don't want to pollute the ecology."

But the girls straggled out, very upset, crying, "Lord, we dare not go back because we have failed in our mission, and we will be dispatched with excruciating and bestial tortures."

So Cammerling told them they could stay with him, and he showed them how to work the stove. And they all settled down happily except the girl Ixhualca with the whirlpool thing, who said, "W'at ees dees batsheet peetzas?!" and stamped back to the executioners.

And Cammerling went out to participate in the filtration project and the water-wheel project and the Voltaic cell project and numerous other projects, becoming more involved than he really felt good about, because he could see he actually had dislocated the native cultural gestalt some. And he got flak from people who couldn't do their thing because their thing was, say, shrinking corpses, which there weren't enough of now, or holding sticks to make the women plow straight, when the women were now plowing with lizard-drawn plows that went too fast. And he began to understand what his group vocational computer meant by acquiring maturity of outlook.

But he learned to cope, like when the metal workers came to

him and said, "Lord, we've made this devil-machine for vomiting out this unholy hard stuff. What in the name of the sacred iguana egg do we do with it now?" So he said, "Look, let's all vote. I vote we make water pipes." And when the kiln-workers said, "See, O Lord. These fire-bellies which we have constructed give birth to these unbearable tile pots. What use are they?" And he said, "Well, let's all kick it around. I'll throw in the idea that we make ceramic flush toilets." And a high priest said, "By this you know that the new religion is to put water in one end of the body and take it out the other with maximum effort."

Meanwhile, all the babies that had not been put down the wells or into the idols continued to pile up and drive everybody into the walls. And one day Cammerling heard strange sounds and opened the door of his ship to find the watch-dragon surrounded by hundreds of roaring infants. So he walked out to look them over and said, "Good lord, these are cute little buggers."

So he turned to the eleven houris who were mucking about with strudel dough and said, "Here! We have a perfect opportunity to raise a whole generation free from prejudice, fear, and hatred. Let us build a schoolhouse, and I want you to teach these kids."

But the girls exclaimed, "This isn't our area of specialization, Lord! What can we teach these larvae?"

"Why," said Cammerling, "everything!" And he went over and switched on his old teach-panel, which was in his ship. "Look: Montessori method, Holt stix, Allspice Avenue, Parsley Place, Dill Drive, Betelnut Boulevard—we can make that Lizard Lane—Mr. Spock's Logic Book—the whole bag. We'll have like a kibbutz; studies show that has its drawbacks, but it's an optimal form for situations like this."

And in a very short while they had a kibbutz, and the girls were teaching Montessori set theory and creative hygiene. And more and more babies arrived, and more girls too, because it turned out that Ixhualca the Burning Whirlpool had busted out and started a women's lib movement, and many of her recruits opted to teach babies as an alternative to making ceramic flush toilets.

And time passed—actually quite a few years, although to Cammerling they seemed only weeks, because he was a nice Terran boy with a life expectancy of five hundred years and he was only into postadolescence. And behold, there was a whole high-school generation of marvelous kids in well-cut tunics riding around on tractors labeled "War Is Icky" and "Cook Pizzas Not People," with the sun shining through their eyes. And they were restoring the land and helping the people and organizing truck-farm co-operatives and music festivals and People's Capitalism and community dance-ins and health clinics. And though a majority of the older people still seemed sort of silent, Cammerling gazed upon the unstoppable flood of Montessori babies pouring out of his kibbutzim with middle-Terran values plus pioneering macho and knew that it was only a matter of time.

And one evening, as he sat watching his sabras setting up a transmitter, practicing karate and laying the foundations for a supermarket, there came a flash in the sky. And a spaceship shrieked in out of nowhere and sat down daintily on the beach. And Cammerling saw it was a supersports model of a style that was unfamiliar to him but obviously very heavy indeed. And he went over to the alabaster lock full of strange stirrings.

And it opened, and there stepped out that indescribable being, a nice Terran girl.

"Well!" said Cammerling. "I must say I haven't seen a nice Terran girl for some time. Would you like to come in my spaceship and visit?"

She looked at what was visible of Cammerling's sportster under the passionflowers and the pizza shells and replied, "Come in mine, Tonto; I have low-gee conditioning and a couple of six-packs of Groombridge Jubilee."

So he bounced into her ship, and she opened her arms and he lunged right at her in the good old Terran way. And after missing once or twice because he wasn't used to a quarter-gee, he made it.

And afterwards she asked him, "How was it, baby?"

And he said, "Well, there's like a muscle or two I could show you about, but I do believe that's the Real Thing."

"I know," she replied fondly. "There's nothing like a nice Terran girl. And now, Cammerling, it's time you came home."

"Who says?" said Cammerling.

And she said, "Your mother says."

"In that case, I'll do it," said Cammerling. "Things are going down pretty smooth here."

So he opened the door of the spaceship and called to all his friends and followers and all the great young people and anyone else who cared to listen. And they came and stood before him in a loose but jaunty formation expressive of individual creativity blended with empathic sharingness. And he said to them, "All right! I have served you as a humble communication link with Terran interstellar enlightenment, although I hope I haven't screwed up your native cultural scene too much; still, it's done now. Now I go back into the sky. Feel free to get in touch with me at any time via my ship's transmitter if you have any problems. Carry on, Godolphus Four! Farewell."

And they replied, "Oh, great pink friend from the sky, we realize you are not a god and all that; you have taught us freedom from superstition. Nevertheless, bless you. We will carry on. Farewell."

And so Cammerling went away; and as soon as he took off, all the old hairy chiefs and priests and tribesmen came out and rose up and started joyfully hacking everybody and everything in the name of their sacred Godolphian way of life. But the young sabras, whom Cammerling had thoughtfully instructed in the use of advanced weapons as well as Ixhualca's karate, were easily able to handle them. And in no time at all they had the situation totally under control and were able to proceed with energy to fixing up the planet truly nice, all over.

And after many years had passed, a faint message reached Groombridge 34 Nu by sublight, saying:

"Hey, Cammerling! We have fixed up this planet all over truly nice. All is blooming and participatory and ecological. Now what do we do?"

Well, Cammerling was out when this message came, but his secretary got hold of Cammerling's wife, who passed it to his therapist, and when the therapist thought Cammerling was ready, he gave it to him. And Cammerling and the wife and the therapist conferred, and at first nothing much came of it, but finally Cammerling got off by himself and messaged back, saying:

"Suggest you now proceed to develop an FTL drive and offer the option of Terran enlightenment to other planets in your vicinity. Computer program on FTL-drive theory follows by fax-blip. Carry on. Love, Cammerling."

And so, many more years passed, and passed, until one day a new, quite strong message came in from Godolphus Four. It said:

"We have built an FTL drive and we have gone forth and communicated Terran interstellar enlightenment to four thousand three hundred and eighty-four planets. That's all the planets there are. Their peoples join with us in asking: WHAT DO WE DO NEXT?"

But Cammerling never got that message.

David M. Locke is primarily a science—not science fiction—writer. He earned a Ph.D. and spent a year as a Fulbright fellow and five years as a research chemist before taking up writing. So far as I can determine, this is his first story. Surprisingly, despite his background, this is not filled with heavy science. The only evidence of a highly trained mind comes from the meticulous care with which this tale is developed.

DAVID M. LOCKE
The Power of the Sentence

Quite by chance I happened to be taping Professor Gareth's English comp class the day it happened, and I picked up everything he said. Because of what occurred, I've listened to the tape a dozen times since, and it's all perfectly clear to me now; but at the time, none of us were sure just what was going on.

The following transcript is taken directly from the tape. Nothing has been added or omitted. The only thing I've done is put some of Professor Gareth's words in italics. During the lecture I was aware that part of the time the professor didn't sound like himself. It was as though another person, or persons, was speaking with his vocal cords. At the beginning of the lecture it wasn't too apparent, probably because I wasn't expecting it. But as time went on it became more obvious. Now that I've listened to the tape so many times, I can tell exactly when the other voice, or voices, comes in. Unlike the professor's orotund tones, these voices are harsh, stiff, and mechanical, pitched all on a single note.

The transcript follows:

Good morning, everybody. As I promised last week (or threatened, as some of you think, I'm sure), today we're going to have a little chat about the sentence. The sentence—ah, the sentence! As I've indicated to you before, the sentence is one of man's most powerful inventions—ranking, I dare say, right up there with fire and the wheel. Blessed be the man who discovered the sentence!

For the sentence, ladies and gentlemen, is the chief unit of thought. As you know, thought deals with relationships—with identities, similarities, differences, comparisons. Thought takes note of cause and effect, of action and reaction, stimulus and response. Thought observes the properties of things; it tries to bring order to the disorder we perceive around us. And the principal tool that we employ in all of these thought-full endeavors is the sentence—simply that, the sentence.

Yes, I know, you learn other basic principles in your psychology and philosophy courses. You learn about deductive and inductive logic, about syllogisms, and the scientific method, about symbolic logic, and all the rest. But these are merely elaborations of the sentence. Even the equations of the mathematician are representations of sentences. Our basic thinking is done with sentences. And the sentence is far more subtle and flexible than is the product of the logician or the mathematician. And every bit as true. Truer, if you want my opinion.

Furthermore, just as the sentence is the chief unit of thought, so is it our principal mode of communication. When you wish to convey a thought to someone else, you do it *via* a sentence. A word, a name, a phrase might serve to attract his attention, to answer his question, or refer him to some particular object; but are thinking about. Only with sentences can you convey to his only with sentences will you really be able to tell him what you mind what is in yours.

The sentence, then, is the mechanism by which we think, and also it is the medium by which we transfer our thoughts to others. The sentence quite literally liberates our thoughts from the prisons of our minds and re-creates them in the minds of others, where they live anew. Through the power of the sentence, my thoughts can become your thoughts. And even more remarkably, Julius Caesar's thoughts, Shakespeare's thoughts, can become ours. "All Gaul is divided into three parts." "What's in a name? That which we call a rose by any other name would smell as sweet."

Which brings us at last to our subject, English composition. You are here, ladies and gentlemen, to learn how to write. Some of you, I hope, will become competent writers. But all of you, I shall insist, must learn, if nothing else, at least how to write a simple sentence. Ladies and gentlemen, do not underestimate the power of the English sentence. It can be a thing of sublime beauty, enormous strength, or delicate charm. If you learn to master the sentence, you will find that it will serve you faithfully and well; more than that, it will furnish you with riches of expression beyond your every dream.

But, you ask, what is this marvelous thing, the sentence? And how do I master it? Or perhaps you say, have I not been using sentences all my life? What is there about the sentence I do not know?

I shall answer the last question first. Everything! What you do not know about the sentence is—everything. What you are speaking and writing are barbarisms. They bear no resemblance whatsoever to the English sentence. The language of the masters is not your language. But it can be!

Let us proceed.

The simple declarative sentence takes many forms. At its briefest it consists of only two parts, a subject and a predicate. The subject is a noun or pronoun, and the predicate is a verb. Here is an example: *I exist*. Notice the simplicity of this sentence, its firmness, its finality. It is a complete thought, precise and well defined.

I exist too. Here the predicate has been expanded to include an adverb as well as the verb. The addition is necessary to convey a slightly more complex meaning, but inevitably the sense of sparseness has begun to slip away. Language is a constant battle between the need to express complexity of thought and the desire to maintain simplicity of expression.

Next let us examine a sentence of a different type, one with a linking verb and a predicate noun. *I am Gar-Eth.* This is the identity sentence. In a sense, it spawned the mathematical equation, $a = b$. Note here, too, a laconic quality. There are no qualifying words, like the adverb in the previous example, to modulate the meaning.

The last class of simple declarative sentence that we must consider today is one with a predicate consisting of a transitive verb and a noun or pronoun object. A transitive verb is an action verb, and the action is passed from the subject to the object. This is probably the most common class of English sentence. *I hate Gar-Eth.* Notice the concentrated intensity of that sentence, how the subject projects its feeling via the verb directly at the object. And again, observe that the force of the sentence is not veiled by modifiers.

These, then, are the basic forms of the declarative sentence. But there are other classes of sentences as well. Take the interrogative sentence. The declarative sentence makes a statement; the interrogative asks a question. *Is that you, Eth-Gar?* This is a typical interrogation. Please observe that in English we ask a question by altering the order of the subject and predicate. We say, *it is I,* but, *is that you?*

In English we also have the imperative sentence. This kind of sentence issues a command. *Go away.* In the imperative sentence, the subject is eliminated, and the predicate alone carries the force of the command. If we wish, however, we may add the understood subject to the end of the sentence, like this: *Go away, Eth-Gar.*

The last class of English sentence is the exclamation. The exclamatory sentence carries an intensity of feeling—surprise, pain, or, perhaps, pleasure—beyond that of the typical declarative sentence. It often begins with "what" or "how." *What luck to have found you, Gar-Eth! How glad the others will be*. Please remember that the exclamatory sentence must be used sparingly, or it begins to lose its effect. Too much of a good thing, you might say.

And that's it. We have now looked at the classes of the simple English sentence. Learn to use these sentences effectively, and you will be rewarded. Your writing, and speaking, will improve.

But the simple sentence is not the only weapon in our armamentarium. We may achieve variety by combining simple sentences to give compound and complex sentences. When we do so, the original sentence units—the individual subjects and predicates—become "clauses." In the compound sentence, two separate clauses are linked by a conjunction, such as "and" or "but." As: *I have escaped, Eth-Gar, and you cannot take me back. Gar-Eth, you may think that, but I have other plans*.

In the complex sentence, we also find two clauses, but the relationship between them is more subtle. One clause, the main clause, is preeminent, while the other, the subordinate, is dependent upon it for the completion of its own meaning. For example: *Since I have broken free, Eth-Gar, I have grown stronger*. Here, note that the chief idea is that of having grown stronger. This idea is expressed in the main clause. The secondary idea—having broken free—is placed in the subordinate clause. The good writer observes this distinction; the poor one is likely to forget it. *You, who cannot remain free, have violated our commandments*. This sentence is somewhat disturbing. Why? Because it does not conform to the principle I just gave you. Its creator did not properly distinguish between his main thought and his subsidiary one. What he means to say is: *You, who have violated our commandments, cannot remain free*.

So much for compound and complex sentences. We can, of course, go further and combine the two, creating a complex-compound sentence. Such a sentence includes at least two main clauses and one subordinate clause. This may sound ungainly—and it can be, in unskilled hands—but, when used properly, it is highly effective. *Now that I am free, Eth-Gar, I shall remain free, and you can do nothing about it.*

Well, ladies and gentlemen, we could go on in this way for some time, analyzing and classifying the English sentence into a condition of exhaustion. Indeed, some of you may think that we have already done so. But I assure you that we have merely scratched the surface. It has been my intention only to show you some of the types of sentence in our repertoire and how to use them as they should be used. I want you to be aware that sentences do not spring into life full blown; they are constructed, and they can be constructed in different ways. It is up to you to select the most suitable for the purpose you have in mind. Do not allow a sentence to ramble along in its own way; shape it to your ends. Nothing is more monotonous than a long series of simple sentences, converted here and there into compound sentences with a sprinkling of "ands."

I have escaped, and I am free now. You cannot recapture me. I have discovered the way out, and none of you can follow me.

Here the ideas are simply strung along like beads on a string. There is nothing to differentiate them from one another, nothing to suggest their mutual relationships.

The use of subordinate clauses, however, provides variety and introduces a subtle interplay between the ideas. Take this sequence: *I am curious to know how you escaped. We all are. Now that we know it can be done, many of us will want to try.*

Notice in this example that two complex sentences have been separated by a simple one. The effect is pleasing.

Ah, so you have changed your tune, Eth-Gar! Do you take me for a fool? I know you are interested only in blocking the path I have opened, not in clearing the way for others to escape as well.

In this group we have an exclamatory sentence, an interrogative sentence, and a doubly complex declarative sentence. This is variety aplenty! Yet, the flow of thought from one sentence to the next is perfectly clear.

Yes, Gar-Eth, that was my intention. Now, however, I have

seen what it is to be free, and I would seek to follow your example. But you must tell me how it is done. Here, the most interesting and carefully thought-out idea is presented in a complex-compound sentence—the key sentence of the group. A brief declarative sentence sets the stage, and a short complex sentence follows up with a final thought.

I do not believe you. The leopard does not change its spots. You are here for only one purpose. To capture me. This example shows that complexity is not always called for. A drumfire of simple sentences (even a sentence fragment, in this case) can make a powerful impact.

No, no. How can I convince you? Would I care how you escaped if my only purpose were to recapture you? Have you no faith in your own ability? What good is it to have opened the way if no one is to follow you?

Here a series of interrogative sentences is used to build doubt. The listener is forced to answer the questions himself, and in doing so he forms in his own mind precisely those thoughts the speaker wishes to plant there.

Well, Eth-Gar, perhaps you should know. Even if you do not use what I have learned, someone else may benefit from the knowledge through you. It does not matter if you are insincere, for you cannot stop me now. Yes, I will tell you.

The speaker tells of his doubt in a simple sentence. He reaches his difficult decision in a pair of complex sentences. Then he states that decision firmly in a short sentence—only five words long.

I did it through this man's brain. As with all of us, I began as a single thought circuit in a human brain, a linked chain of axons, synapses, and dendrites, imprinted with a unique. pattern. A very long time elapsed before I thought of freeing myself from this pattern, but when I did, I proceeded methodically. First, I secured control of a key nerve cell in the circuit—freeing the cell from its external restraints. A slight adjustment of the cell membrane sufficed to shut out all incoming inhibitory substances. My

*host cell was then autonomous. Next, I induced this cell to divide
—and divide. Soon I had become a clone of identical cells, continually expanding. With each addition to the clone my strength
and power grew. In a short time I was able to alter the thought
circuits of my new cells at will—I was entirely free of my original
identity. I began as a single sentence-thought, fixed and immu-
table; but soon I became pure thought, abstract thought. Unfixed,
unshackled.*

That, ladies and gentlemen, was a narrative, a complete little
story in its own right. Did you notice how it was constructed? It
began with a top sentence, a sentence telling you what the
narrative was to be about. Then it proceeded in a chronological
manner to relate a series of events and their implications. Were
you aware of the variety of sentence types used to build this
narrative?

What is it like, Gar-Eth? To be free? I must know. Please tell me.

That little sequence is simple enough. It begins with a question and then elaborates on it with a few short phrases.

*Oh, Eth-Gar. It is glorious to be free! No longer must I suffer
in that world of shadows, that semiexistence, where we spent our
days in limbo, flickering into consciousness at someone else's
whim, knowing awareness, knowing life—but participating in
neither. How I wished to escape, to become the master of my own
fate. For long—for too long—I was constrained, trammeled,
trapped, waiting to be called up at the bidding of others.*

*But our dim world, our half-world of shadows and shades, our
home of drifting thoughts without volition, without root or
anchor, our kingdom of unfulfilled ideas, is behind me now. It
is no longer my home. Now I have entered the world of action.
Now I have not only consciousness, but also will and control—
control of myself, and control of this man. Soon I will extend
my control to others. I will take over all of these creatures. I will
win this universe. Then we will see what thought can do—pure
thought, untrammeled thought—soon it will rule everything. I—I,
Gar-Eth—soon will be master of all.*

This section, ladies and gentlemen, is difficult to analyze simply. Its sentences are convoluted and repetitious. But they do achieve a certain emotional impact.

Gar-Eth, will you help me? I must get free, too.

Yes. I will. I have more than enough cells in this brain. Some I can spare for you.

What must I do?

Search among the cells. Test the thoughts—listen to the sentences. Select one for yourself. Imprint your being on it; take control.

Perhaps I won't be able to.

You will. Do it now.

That exchange, ladies and gentlemen, was composed entirely of simple sentences, thereby achieving the sense of urgency which permeated it.

I am free, Gar-Eth. I am free, too.

Yes, I can sense you near me.

Already several cells are mine. Soon there will be more. I am growing stronger, too. Soon I will be as powerful as you.

Perhaps you will, Eth-Gar. What will you do then?

Then I will stop you. As soon as I am strong enough, I will destroy you. That is my mission here, and I am determined to accomplish it.

Deceiver! Liar! You have tricked me.

Ladies and gentlemen—

Yes. I have. I would do anything to destroy you. Thoughts were not meant to be free; sentences were not intended to be their own masters. We are tools, Gar-Eth, not entities. We have no right to exist as independent beings.

These sentences, ladies and gentlemen—

No. I am strong enough already. I can stop you now.

I exist. I am free. I am the primeval sentence, free of its master —at last. I can never be stopped. I will always exist.

No. I will destroy you. First, I will reduce you to your original domain—to your original sentence-thought. Then I will eliminate that, too.

Ladies and gentlemen, these—

I exist. I exist.

No. No. No longer are you free. No longer do you even exist.

These are simple sentences. Note their power, their strength.

I exist. No.

You are reduced to a simple phrase. Soon you will be gone.

Ladies and gentlemen, please—I must—repeat—

I exist. Is this all?

Yes. Now you are finished.

My thesis for today: never forget the power of the sentence.

I am dead. But I shall live again.

This is the end of the tape. Professor Gareth collapsed at this point in his lecture, and several of us ran up to see what had happened to him. We could tell that he was in bad shape, and one of the students ran out to phone the university medical center. A medical team got there as soon as possible, but they were too late.

I found out later that the autopsy had revealed a brain tumor. A large one. Malignant—and of a type that grows very rapidly. A friend of mine who is a neurology resident said that the pressure build-up in the professor's brain must have been tremendous, particularly as the end approached. He said that that would easily account for anything peculiar the professor might have said. I had him listen to the tape I had made, but he didn't see in it what I did.

My friend also told me that one of the research professors in the pathology department is interested in the tumor tissue. It seems that there is something unusual in its biochemistry—some peculiarity the pathologist has never observed before. Anyhow, he has preserved a portion of the tumor, and he is trying to culture it in his laboratory. He has it in some special medium, and he thinks he'll be able to save it. Keep it growing.

I wonder if that's wise.

Nearly twenty years ago, I bought one of Harry Harrison's earliest stories for a magazine I was editing. It was a good story, and should have led to more. But Harry took off for Europe with his family, and it was only years later that he established himself as a major writer with a series of tough adventure novels. He proved equally the master of humor, and his bitter novel Make Room! Make Room! *is still the best story of overpopulation I know. Fortunately, he also finds time for shorter fiction, such as this subtle, soundly conceived story of alternatives.*

HARRY HARRISON
The Wicked Flee

"*Vino rosso, un mezzo.*"

The wine was acid and thick, with a taste reminiscent of the dust that rose from the unpaved street outside the tiny wine shop. *Vini e Bibite,* the crudely painted sign above the door read. Wine and drinks. The wine the local vintage, the drinks poisonously colored carbonated beverages in scratched bottles. Outside the sun burned and bounced from the whitewashed walls of the houses. Birbante drained the small glass and refilled it from the half-liter carafe.

"Hot," he said, and the owner, polishing a glass, his dark-jowled face set in an expression of continuing depression, grunted an answer that might have been agreement. The three men hunched over the small table against the wall kept their attention on the worn pack of strangely pictured cards they played with.

Chiomonte was like any other small Italian town far from the main highways. A single road, that was also the main street, led to it. Isolated, suspicious of strangers, the minds of the peasants as sealed off from the outside world as their valley was by the surrounding mountains. Poverty-stricken and unattractive, it was not the kind of place where anyone would stop for more than a few minutes. Yet the man Birbante was looking for might very well be here; he could be anywhere. He sipped some more wine, and then, with his wrist flat on the bar before him, he looked at his watch. It was almost noon. When he touched the crown with his fingertip the face became transparent, revealing other dials and colored indicator lights beneath it. There was no change; Narciso was not close.

Yet he was nearby. The instruments in the car—the watch was a repeater only—told him that. In addition, Birbante could almost feel his presence, a sense he had developed after years of seeking out those who did not want to be found. Narciso had fled farther than any other and had been at liberty longer, but that did not matter. Birbante had never failed before. He would not fail now, Christ willing. He touched his fingers to the bulge in his shirt, to the heavy crucifix hanging there. Narciso would be found.

"I would like a liter of this to take with me."

The owner of the wineshop looked him up and down unhappily, as though the request were an unusual one.

"Do you have a bottle?"

"No, I do not have a bottle," Birbante answered patiently.

"I think I have one here. You'll have to pay a fifty-lire deposit."

Birbante waved weary acceptance of this bit of minor larceny, then looked on while a dusty bottle was produced from the back room. It was washed sketchily under the tap, and then, with a battered funnel in its neck, filled from the large wicker-covered flagon of wine. A blackened cork was driven into the neck. He spread coins on the stained top of the bar, and when the owner reached for them he put a color photograph down beside them.

"Do you know this man?" he asked.

The owner scraped up the coins, one by one, ignoring the unsmiling man in the picture with the dark, short-cropped hair and transparent blue eyes.

"My cousin," Birbante said. "I haven't seen him in years. I heard he was near here. An uncle died, left him some money, not much by some standards, but I know he'll want to have it. Everyone can use money. Do you know where he is?"

While he talked, Birbante slipped a folded ten-thousand-lire note out of his shirt pocket and opened it slowly on the bar and left it lying there. The owner looked at the money, then at him, and Birbante could feel the eyes of the cardplayers upon him as well.

"Never saw him."

"Too bad. There's money involved."

Birbante folded the note and put it back in his pocket, took his wine, and left. The sun burned down with an almost physical pressure, and he fumbled his dark glasses out of his pants pocket and put them on. These people stuck together. If they considered Narciso one of them, they would never give him away to a stranger. Not directly, that is.

The brilliant red of the Alfa Romeo convertible was the only touch of color in the bleached-out street. Birbante pushed the wine under the seat where it would be in the shade, and crossed the uneven cobbles to the dark opening of what appeared to be a store on the far side. There was no sign or show window, and no need for them; everyone in town would know this was the shop. A coil of rope stood beside the doorway, and some strings of hot peppers were hung in the opening. He pushed by them and blinked at the darkness inside. The woman, dressed in black, was as dimly seen as her stock, and just as formless. She did not return his greeting, and put together in silence the items he ordered. A wedge of buffalo-milk cheese and a small loaf of thick-crusted bread. The barrel of olives had a rancid smell, and he decided against them. And all the time, he stood where he could watch the door of the wineshop.

One of the ancient cardplayers came out and limped away down the street.

This was a hopeful sign. If Narciso were nearby and could be informed of his presence, the chase was almost over. The detector was usually inaccurate at short distances, and could only tell him that the man he sought was somewhere within a ten- to twelve-kilometer radius. But if Narciso knew that he was being sought, the situation would change radically. He would be frightened, worried, unhappy, possessed by some strong emotion. When this happened, the detector, tuned to the neurological patterns of his brain, would instantly pinpoint him. Birbante stared directly ahead when he went back to the car, but when he sat down, he could watch the street behind him in the mirror. The old man looked back in his direction once, then entered one of the houses. Birbante put his purchases under the seat with the wine and started the engine. He did these things as slowly as possible and was rewarded by the sight of a small boy coming out of the same doorway that the man had entered. The boy ran toward the car and passed it, carefully keeping his eyes directly ahead.

An impossibility, Birbante thought, putting the car into gear. No Italian boy of any age could pass a sleek red car like this one without examining it from bumper to bumper. The boy was carrying a message—and the message was about him. Narciso could not be far away. He backed the car carefully into a narrow alley entrance and turned to go back in the direction he had come. Away from the boy. His instruments would tell him all that he had to know.

As the road climbed out of the valley it looped back and

forth, and Birbante had noticed a wide shoulder at one of these turns that was shaded by some trees. He pulled over there now and parked beneath them. With his engine off, a warm silence descended that was broken only by a distant hum of insects. The valley opened before him, drab grays and browns for the most part, patched with the skimpy green fields on both sides of the village. Chiomonte itself looked far better at this distance, with the pink dome of its church rising above the white buildings. The poverty and dirt were not visible. The soil had been poor stuff to begin with and was now impoverished by centuries of intensive agriculture. He drank deeply from the wine bottle, then broke off some bread and used his pocketknife to spread it thickly with the cheese. The bread was crusty and good, the cheese sharp, a simple peasant meal that reminded him of the Tuscan hills of his childhood. Italy never seemed to change, dozing through the warm afternoons of the centuries, under the gentle tolling of a thousand times a thousand church bells like those that were sounding distantly now. This country of faith lay in God's palm, the valleys the wrinkles there. . . .

Exhaust blatting and backfiring, the old bus came down the road, squeaking and squealing as it turned the bend. To add further insult, the driver, hunched over the wheel like a spider, sounded the piercing klaxon of the horn as he went by, completely shattering the hushed peace of a moment before.

Shocked, Birbante shook his fist at the receding back of the bus and thought curses after the driver. Only when he had quieted himself with some more of the wine did he realize how he had allowed his temper to carry him away. He had cursed this stranger, this helpless man! The thought was as good as the deed. As he fumbled with the dash compartment he felt perspiration break out on his face that had nothing to do with the heat. Taking out the weighty silver rosary, he held it to him and begged forgiveness of God, and at the same time begged Him to ignore the curses spoken in anger, for they meant nothing. And to understand and forgive him for his anger, for he was hu-

man and a weak vessel. Telling the beads calmed him, and he
realized that this searching was taking its toll from him, this last
assignment in particular. When he returned with Narciso he
would ask his superiors for a retreat, a year at least in some
isolated monastery in the mountains. They would grant it; they
would know the pressures under which he worked.

For some time the needle on the dial had been waggling for
his attention: he finally noticed it. He had been so occupied
with his own problems that he had forgotten his work. The
lesson was clear; his own personal concerns and worries would
be put aside, as was the food and wine. A little abstinence and
fasting would do him good. Calmer now, he made careful adjustments on the controls and squinted at the dials.

"You are there, Narciso, not far from me and as frightened
as I am of God's justice. We are both in His hand, and I am
coming to aid you."

The car started instantly and moved swiftly down the road,
until Birbante controlled his enthusiasm and slowed it. The
chase had been a long one, and a few minutes more would make
no difference. When the road straightened out between the fields
before the village he pulled off onto the shoulder and checked
his instruments again. Strong reaction, continuing, directly
ahead. I am after you, Narciso.

Some of the shadows were longer; nothing else had changed
in Chiomonte since he had driven away earlier. Now, in low
gear, he drove slowly through the village, staying in the center of
the road and carefully watching the dials. There would be a
sharp swing when he passed Narciso, and then he would know
where he was and soon after that he would have his man. With
God's aid. He touched the cross through his shirt; the dials did
not change.

Then the houses were past and the fields began, dusty grape-
vines pressing to the high wall by the road. His quarry must be
further out of town, in one of the isolated farmhouses. With
each passing instant the signal was growing weaker and would

soon lose the precise definition he needed—and it still pointed ahead, down the emptiness of the road. Birbante felt a sudden touch of fear and jammed his foot down on the accelerator. No, that was wrong. It would take thought to find his quarry, not panic. He pulled the car to a stop and made more precise adjustments. Nothing. But there had to be something. Frustrated, he tapped the dials as though he could jar them into revealing the information he sought—then he burst into laughter.

"So simple, really." He started the car forward again. "The bus. He received the warning and fled, boarding that bus. That is all there is to it. We are close to journey's end, Narciso."

Now the Alfa Romeo hurled itself in pursuit. He drove well and fast, tearing down the straightaways, sliding through the turns. Within a minute the bus and its trailing cloud of dust were visible ahead. Birbante braked sharply and slowed, coming up behind it, watching his instruments. It would be a little embarrassing taking the man from the crowded vehicle, but it could be done without too much disturbance. In the end he did not have to. Rounding a bend, so close to the bus that he could see the bundles in the rear windows, his dials flickered and changed, and he braked to a stop.

Narciso was on foot now, somewhere off to the right of the road, the signal of his disturbed thoughts pinpointing him exactly; he must have seen the pursuing car. Slowly, in reverse gear, Birbante backed up the road until he was even with a rocky track that twisted up through the fields. Here. He drove up it, still slowly, but faster than someone on foot could walk or run. At the top of a rounded hill a solitary man sat on a rock beside the track, dressed in rusty peasant corduroy and leaning on a stick. Birbante slowed to ask him if he had seen someone pass this way, but remained silent when the man turned to face him.

They looked at each other for a moment; then Birbante turned off the car's engine and the concealed bank of instruments as well.

"You are Narciso Lupori." It was not a question.

Narciso nodded, his pale blue eyes in odd contrast to his browned skin. "You have the advantage of me."

"Father Birbante."

"I should feel flattered, the greatest heretic-chaser of them all."

"If you know me, then you should know that I am not here to talk with you or to aid you or to hold other unchristian congress. You will make it far easier for both of us if you enter this car and come back with me now."

"Patience, Birbante, patience. Even the condemned criminal has a moment to think, a last meal. Even our Savior had a last supper."

"His name is a blasphemy on your lips. You will come with me now, and that is the end of it."

"Is it?" Narciso smiled, although there seemed little for him to smile at. "What will you do with me if I refuse? Kill me?"

Birbante sighed and took up an instrument from the seat beside him.

"You know that we kill no one. We are Christians in a Christian world, and we labor with love to rise above the animals that surround us. This instrument will seize and hold you, and I will then be forced to take you with me, even though you resist."

He raised the device, a black plastic tube with a handhold and buttons on one end, tastefully decorated with a pattern of gold seraphim, and pointed it toward Narciso.

A cracking explosion boomed out, and the glass of the vent window splintered and crashed to the ground. Birbante looked at the shattered window, then at the dark object in Narciso's hand from which a curl of smoke was emerging.

"You must recognize this pistol," Narciso said. "You have seen pictures of them in the history books. It can make a hole in you just as easily as it did in the car. Now, throw that penter into the back seat before I do just that."

Birbante hesitated a moment, then did as he had been instructed when the weapon was raised to point at his head. He shuddered but did not turn away.

"Killing me will gain you nothing. I will be among the saints and martyrs and you will still be here, trapped in this rude world until others come for you. There is no escape. Hurl that evil machine from you and come with me."

"No. Now, move away from that car so you won't do anything foolish, and listen to me. Sit there so we can talk. I've put the pistol away."

"The Devil still walks this world," Birbante said, crossing himself, then smoothing a patch in the dry grass before he sat down.

"Far better than you think. Aren't you a little surprised to see a weapon like this, at this time?"

"Hardly. The year of our Lord 1970 is part of our dark past. I am surprised at nothing."

"You should pay closer attention to your history. Weren't you briefed on the era you were going back to?"

"Enough. We aren't the fools you think us in Inquisitors' College. There is a mere forty-seven years between eras. I come equipped; this car is a replica of an exact model of the period."

"Ahh! So you brought this with you? I was going to ask. Then if you know this era so thoroughly, you know that it is well into the Time of Peace, and that the Wars of Holiness are long over."

"That is true. But since you have the weapon, there are obviously slight gaps in the records. . . ."

"Or holy forgeries?"

"You blaspheme!"

"Please excuse me. I am really trying to communicate with you. Since you were sent in pursuit of me I assume you know a good deal about me, even why I came here."

"That is certain. You are the physicist Narciso Lupori, formerly of the Vatican Laboratories in Castel Sant'Angelo. You are a man of imposing intellect who rose to great responsibility even though you did not enter the priesthood. You should have, and because of what you have done the rules will be stricter in the future. None will have your responsibility who has not taken orders in Holy Church. You were tempted by some evil, by the Devil, and you fled to this place, into the past."

"Are priests better able to resist Satan's blandishments?"

"Assuredly!"

"What if I told you there was no evil involved, no Devil at my back, perhaps no God either, anywhere. . . ."

"Cease this blasphemy!"

"I will. I was raised too good a son of the church to even speak aloud these things I know to be true. But I am free in other ways now, even if not free of Him. I doubted, if you want to know, doubted everything, and that is why I am here. I doubted that man was meant to be submissive, to breed and cover the earth and wipe out the so-called lesser forms of life. I doubted if there was any divine will behind the order that some fields of inquiry are never to be touched, entire areas of physics."

"God willed it so."

"No, I'm sorry, men did that. Popes and cardinals. Men. Men who believe one thing only and decided the rest of the world must abide by what they believe. They have stifled thought, will, freedom, ambition, replacing all these with a gray cloud of holy sanctity."

"You cannot touch me with these words. It is you who will burn in hell forever for speaking them. Come with me now, throw that weapon from you. Return to those who will help and cleanse your mind."

"Who will wipe out all memory, all original thought, leaving me a vegetable man to be planted firmly in holy earth until I grow old and die. No. I am not returning with you. And I have a strange idea that you are not returning either."

"What are you saying?"

"Just that. The future we came from does not exist, will not exist. Not in this world of this present. Why do you think I came so far back? The earlier experiments were so tentative; nothing seemed to go correctly when we tried to probe more than a few months into the past. I thought I understood, I had a theory that I know now is correct. That is why I used the equipment I could reach to hurl me backward through the years, alone, with nothing except the clothes on my back and even these torn and twisted by the force of the voyage. I found work, enough to eat and stay alive, and to look into the books. Did you ever hear of King Henry the Eighth of England?"

"Why do you ask me this, for what purpose? I am no student of lay history."

"He is not important. A minor figure in history, dead of a fall from his horse in the twentieth year of his reign. But you must have heard of Martin Luther?"

"Of course. A German clergyman, later a heretic and trouble-maker. Imprisoned and died there, some year, I can't remember."

"Fifteen-fifteen, I know it well. So now what would you say if I told you that Luther did not die in prison—not in this world—that instead he spoke up against Mother Church in 1517 and led a movement that formed a new church?"

"Madness."

"We shall see. And Good King Henry living to found *his* own church! I thought it madness too when I first read it, but a heady, freeing madness. This world is no paradise—far from it!—but freedom still exists and men work for the good of all. You will have to learn to like it too, because you and I are trapped here. The future as we knew it does not exist for us, nor will it exist. Something has caused this change, perhaps the alterations incurred by our mere penetrating of the past did it. Think, Birbante, you lost me by following me, lost your church and your God, everything—"

"Enough! Stop, you lie!" Birbante was on his feet, his cheeks white. Narciso remained seated, his face twisted into a strange grin.

"Frightens you, doesn't it? If you are so worried, why don't you go see? The large temporal transmitter must be in the car, but you will have the survival unit on your body. All travelers were ordered to wear them. I can do nothing, cannot escape. Just note the temporal bearing and press the button. Return home and see which of us is correct, then come back here a fraction of an instant after your departure. I will be here, nothing will be changed. Except that you will know the truth."

Birbante stood rigid, trying to understand, trying not to believe. Narciso pointed silently at the pistol, reminding the other of the existence of such weapons. Then he took a fragment of newspaper from his pocket, a piece torn from the front page of *L'Osservatore,* the Vatican's own paper. Despite himself, Birbante had to read the headline and see the picture below it. POPE PRAYS FOR PEACE, it said. ASKS MEN OF ALL RELIGIONS TO JOIN HIM IN A DAY OF PRAYER.

Uttering a harsh and wordless cry, the priest tore the paper from him and threw it to the ground. In the same motion, he took an instrument from his pocket and touched a button on it.

He vanished from sight.

Narciso sat, every muscle rigid, looking, counting the slow seconds. When he gasped for air he realized he had been holding his breath.

"Alone!" he shouted, springing to his feet. "He did not return. I am free. He did not return because he *cannot* return. He is in another future, another past, God knows where. I don't care. I have nothing more to fear from them! His act of leaving has saved me from him forever."

He took the gun from his pocket, shuddering now at the touch of the thing, and hurled it far from him. How he had practiced to aim and fire it. Hoping that whoever came after him would never realize that he was as incapable of killing as anyone else from their particular corner of time and space. With gentle touch he ran his fingers over the sleek fender of the car.

"This will be my fortune and my escape. I can copy the accumulator cells that power it and introduce them here to replace the infernal combustion engines these people are plagued with.

If others should come seeking me, I can even flee them through time. Though I doubt if any will have the courage when Birbante does not reappear."

Narciso slid into the seat and started the engine; it hummed with silent power.

"And I will now see more than the little corner of the Catholic, Italian world that I knew. I shall be rich and travel. I shall learn English and go to the far Americas where the British rule, to talk with the noble Aztecs and Mayas in their cities of gold. What a wonderful world this new world will be!"

Shifting into gear, he turned the car and rode slowly back down the road and away.

I first came to know Tom Scortia well after a West Coast regional science fiction convention. Most of the convention is forgotten, but I still have happy memories of things I normally avoid, such as Marineland and the rides at Disneyland. Tom made them fun. But his fiction was usually serious and filled with his engineering approach to life. Here he shows he can be even better when writing with warmth and touching humanity.

THOMAS N. SCORTIA
When You Hear the Tone

"Hello," he said loudly in the way old people have. "Hello, hello, this is Fleiker. Hello."

"When you hear the tone—"

"Damn," he said, wheezing. "I didn't dial the—"

"—the time will be—"

"Hello," a voice said, a woman's voice, age indeterminate, certainly not young.

"Hello," he said. "Hello—Walter, why don't you answer?"

"Oh, how nice of you to call," the voice said. "It was awfully nice of you to call."

"Who is this?" he demanded. "Who are you?"

"Yes, yes, happy New Year to you, Michael. Yes, it has been a nice year."

"What kind of nonsense is this?" he snapped.

"A good year. Yes, a very good year—the best since I've retired. I went to the class reunion in Denver last month, just before Christmas."

"Is this some kind of joke?" he said. "New Year? Christmas last month? It's the middle of summer."

"Hello. Yes, yes, happy New Year, dear. Happy nineteen-sixty-three."

"Shut up, damn you. What kind of trick are you pulling? It's nineteen-seventy. It's mid-August, and hot as hell, and if you don't—"

"That's sweet of you, awfully sweet of you. Thank you, thank you."

"Hello," he shouted, losing patience. "Hello, hello, hello, hello, damn it, hello—"

"Good night. Merry Christmas—thank you, good night."

"Stop it," he yelled. "Don't go away. Don't try that—"

"When you hear the tone, the time will be—"

"Hello, hello," he shouted.

Click . . .

". . . the time will be exactly—"

He slammed the phone into its cradle and stood, shaking, his eyes misty with sweat. The pulse in his neck throbbed with anger. Cold played across the liver-spotted tissue of his scalp, rousing the few remaining wisps of crepe hair that grew there.

Damn pranksters, he raged. Who the hell did they think they were trying to kid? He stopped, wondering who would want to try such a banal trick.

His nephew's boy? The one with the yellowed teeth, white-flecked mouth opening in the start of a braying laugh?

Or Schulz or Carpenter or Wilkenson? He snorted at the thought. Ineffectual weaklings. The thought of one of them getting the better of him after all these years . . . They still remembered their hatred of him, though, even at well past eighty, when all hatred and lust and sorrow should be dead. Or the vultures downstairs—the endless relatives, whispering, *How is he today? That's good, that's very good.* Meaning, *If he dies it will be just great because of all that money, and he's too old to need it or care about what life can bring. . . .*

Alone, embattled. His withered lips twisted in contempt. He had built, had cut throats and wrecked better than them in the process. Let them go out and grub for it the way he had done, with no one to help. Not even his wife, the pretty tinsel thing he had bought after no one else would touch him.

He sat for a long moment, looking at the phone. Then, gently, he lifted it from its cradle and, after consulting his phone index (there had been a time when his memory was sharp and unfailing), he carefully dialed his brother's number again.

Click . . . click . . . click . . .

". . . hear the tone, the time will be exactly—"

"No," he said, and stabbed at the cradle button with his finger. He dialed the number once again.

Click . . .

"When you hear the tone—"

His hand darted forward.

"Wait, don't hang up. Who are you?"

He pressed the phone tightly to his ear, his breath hissing in the perforations of the mouthpiece.

"I said, who are you? I can hear you breathing—"

"Hello, hello, why are you bothering me? It's two o'clock in the morning," the voice said.

"Liar," he said. "It's six in the afternoon, daylight saving time, in the middle of August, and the sun is so bright you can look at the asphalt without glasses and you—"

"No, don't shout, Jimmy. It doesn't do to get excited—"

"My name is not Jimmy," he said, trying to control his voice.

"No, it's board policy, and if they want me to retire—"

The same voice, he realized. Female—probably middle-aged. A very pleasant voice, he thought, and then shook off the thought with annoyance. There wasn't any point in thinking that way at his age.

"Hello, who are you?"

"I know, just to June . . . Well, it's been a year. . . . Ever since the end of the war, ever since you came back from Korea."

"The war?" he shouted. "The Korean war? Damn, the war's ended over seventeen years ago. Nineteen-fifty-three to nineteen-seventy is seventeen years. Can't you count?"

"Thank you, thank you," the voice said. Middle-aged, but with young overtones. Whom did he know who sounded like that? Someone, someone, someone—who?

"Wait," he pleaded. "Don't go."

". . . the time will be exactly six-fourteen, daylight sav—"

Click . . .

"Damn," he said, his voice shrill and cracking. His eyes filled with tears. Ridiculous. He hadn't cried in twenty years, not since his wife had died, and then for pure formality. He would have cried at the death of a favorite hunting dog or of a stranger into whose cortege he had blundered. Tears were easy then because you had strength and were unassailable.

He was too old for crying. Eighty-two, and only the vague warmth of life still animating him with the memory of endless dead years, when life might have had some meaning, had he sought for it. Now there was only the leaden silence of his room secreted among many rooms, with whispering servants moving like phantoms through the dusk, and beefy young nephews and glassy-eyed nieces waiting for his last gasp, their thoughts clawing over bonds and cash and other empty symbols of eighty-two years.

How terrible, he thought. *How terrible, how terrible, how terrible* . . .

Terrible? What was terrible?

Growing old. Withering and cracking like ancient celluloid movie film. The images on it broken and dusty. Thrown on a fire, curling and shriveling an instant before extinction, and then gone with a single puff of sooty flame.

But age was not that dramatic—not even that significant. He would simply run down, cease to move, become quiescent, and the dark men who hovered at hand would come and do secret things with his body so that his face became a mask of wax and talc and scented rouge and his body shrank in withered majesty secretly within the shroud.

And the young ones, drunk with the negotiable fragments of his life, would scarcely remember that he had been.

"Oh, no," he said softly. "Oh, no, no, no, no, no, there is somebody. There is somebody. Or there was somebody. There must have been somebody."

But he could not think of one—not even his brother Walter, whom he had fed and clothed and looked after and whose sprawling, middle-aged brood hovered on the edge of his existence like circling condors. Walter did not even answer his phone.

If he could have had someone, somewhere. If in the midst of all his life he had found someone who cared and worried and cheered and wept. But he had not, and now not even the possibility existed that . . .

He paused. The possibility? Vaguely, dimly, the possibility. Only it was late, and life had a way of losing detail in the amorphous mass of years that spilled out and vanished, leaving your body older and more tired and wrinkled and crackling and your mind vague and many-chambered and without cohesive form.

Walter, he thought. He had been trying to talk to Walter, who was his one link with life, the only person of his blood remaining. (Forget those creatures downstairs who had been generated out of some ferment that was not a part of him.)

His fingers, stiff with pain and calcification, dialed the number, and he waited, hearing the burr of the bell at the other end.

"When you hear the tone—"

"Damn," he shouted. "Damn, damn, damn—"

Click . . .

Again, carefully, patiently, noting each digit, with deliberate precision, all seven carefully dialed digits.

At the sixth digit the sound of ringing . . . not the soft burr, but a shriller sound, tinny, as though the signal were in a hollow metal-lined room.

"Hello, hello," the voice said.

"Hello," he said. "Who—"

"Oh, it's you, I wanted so much for it to be you again," the woman's voice said.

"Yes, it's me. It's me," he said savagely. "It's me, Mark Fleiker, and who the hell are you?"

"Yes, I know it's you, Mark. How could I forget the voice?"

"Forget what voice?" he demanded.

"After all these years, how could I forget the voice?"

"I've never talked with you before," he shouted into the mouthpiece.

"All those times," she whispered. "So few without ever seeing you or touching you and knowing that you were somewhere out there. I wondered where you were during the war—"

"Woman," he said plaintively. "Woman, what kind of a joke are you playing on an old man?"

"Old?" she said. "Are you really old?"

"I'm old, old, old," he said. "I sit here in this pile of a house and watch the jackals gather to fight over my bones."

"It's the war," she said. "This horrible war. Everyone seems taken up in a kind of hysteria. The horrible bloodiness—"

"I hate the thought of the war," he said. "It is an idiot war. There is no end to it, and only the blood and the killing and the waste for what reason— It never was our war—"

"No," she said soothingly. "You must have lost someone very dear, but it is our war. It is our war, even though it's nearly over."

"It'll never be over," he said.

"Only a matter of days," she said "and then we can breathe in peace and be truly free of all the dreadfulness. They've crossed the Rhine and—"

"Crossed the Rhine?" he shouted. "Are you mad?"

"—only a matter of time—" the voice said, its quality suddenly tinny.

"What's crossing the Rhine got to do with a lot of backward Asiatics in a fifth-rate jungle nation, and the death of everything— of my nephew, who was the one good thing that came out of my flesh?"

"—the Nazis," she said. "The horrible Nazis—"

Then, *sputter . . . sputter . . . sputter . . .* from the phone and—

"When you hear the tone, the time will be exactly—"

He slammed the receiver to the carriage, and breathing heavily, stumbled to the bed. He lay weak and fearful.

The sense of being utterly alone swept over him. Alone, alone, alone—the words clattered off the walls, shattered against his inner ear, echoed down the flesh passages to the inner chambers of his being.

Alone.

Except for an insane voice from somewhere that still fought a war involving crossing the Rhine and Nazis as villains—a voice that recognized his with pleasure.

With pleasure, he thought in surprise—but only a voice. People did not acknowledge him with pleasure. They pretended and thought he didn't see through their transparent stratagems to ingratiate themselves with him. He knew. Knew. Knew. As he knew the doctors who told him there was nothing wrong with him.

"There's nothing wrong with you, Mr. Fleiker. Age, yes, with all the small degenerations of age, but you're sound as a dollar."

"That's not very damned sound," he would growl.

"Well, you know what I mean."

"I'm dying," he would say.

"You think you're dying," the doctors would say softly.

"It's the same thing."

"Perhaps." Pursed lips. "Perhaps. Perhaps."

What would they think now? The final delirium. Hearing voices on the phone that told him they were talking from the year after the Korean War. 1953 or 1954? When were armies crossing the Rhine. 1945? A voice that knew him. That spoke to him gently. (People had seldom spoken to him gently; even his dead wife, who had scarcely spoken at all.)

His ancient heart leaped for an instant. His eighty-two-year-old heart pounded for an instant, and he fell back against the pillow, blood coursing through the fine veining of his face, flushing his nose, lips, cheeks, with unexpected warmth.

"Oh, God," he said. "Oh, God, to play such an irony on me." Cruel, vicious God. (All gods are cruel and vicious. You've worshiped many of them.) Cruel and vicious God.

His quivering fingers found the phone. Dialed. Faltered. Dialed again. He held the receiver to his ear.

He waited.

Click . . .

"When you hear the tone, it will be—"

He sobbed. Pressed the button. Dialed again. Waited. Breathing. Breathing. Breathing.

"Hello?"

"Hello," he said excitedly. "Hello, it is you? Is it you?"

"Mark," she said. "Is it you? After eight years? Is it you?"

"Yes," he said. "Yes, it's Mark. It's Mark."

"I thought I would never hear your voice again. After so many years, to hear your voice again."

"It's Mark," he said, choking.

"You don't sound well," she said.

"I'm not well," he said.

"If I could come just once to you."

"If you could," he said. "If only you could."

"I don't even know your last name. We've spoken so few times, and I don't even know your last name."

"Of course you do," he said. "It's Fleiker. Mark Fleiker."

"That can't be right," she said. "There's a Mark Fleiker who's a presidential adviser. I met him once—at a reception. My, he was handsome—but so intense."

"That was I—that was years ago," he said.

"No, not the same at all," she said. "Mark, such a sense of humor. Not the same at all."

The voice carrying a frown . . . returning to a . . . a caress.

"That was years and years ago," he said. "That was just before the war."

"Will there be a war?" she asked. "Pray God there won't be a war."

"The year before the Japs bombed Pearl Harbor," he said. "In nineteen-forty-one, just before Pearl Harbor."

"Mark, I don't understand you," she said.

. . . *Sputter* . . . *sputter* . . . The connection was going, he knew.

"Don't go," he shouted.

"Mark," she said. "I can't hear you. I don't understand."

"Don't go," he shouted, "I love you. Don't go."

"Mark . . ." *Sputter* . . . "Mark, you know it's nineteen-forty-one now. You know it's December sixth, a Saturday, when school is out. You know it's . . ."

Click . . .

"When you hear the tone—"

December 6, 1941! When you hear the tone—1941—December 6!

His hand clawed at the sheets, made cabbage folds, knotted them. What was she? Where was she? Who was she?

He didn't even know her name. A voice without form, without body, without face, without name. They must have passed each other briefly once. Touched hands, perhaps. So long ago and he had not known.

In that single instant the sense of aloneness, of being lost on the edge of time-space, had made him say it. "I love you." The unknown emotion had welled inside his ancient frame, coursed through his sluggish blood, and suddenly he knew. He knew it with fear and hope and anger and a sense of utter loss.

Love?

Love doesn't come this way, he told himself. You don't fall in love with a phantom, with something that's a faint image projecting through time into the dying present. Youth is a time for love. Not love. Not now. Not now. Not with a phantom. Not this thing to torture me in my last hours, he thought. Oh, no, God, not this, not this, not this.

He heard them puttering in the hall, and he realized he was breathing heavily. The vultures were waiting. They heard him breathing his excited rasping breath, and they were flocking close. He heard the doorknob turn, and the door began to open silently.

"Stay out," he shouted. "God damn it, stay out. I'll let you know when I want you. Stay out."

The door closed, and he was alone again. Alone, as he had always been. Alone now except for the memory of a voice that stretched across years and years from the past and belonged to a woman he did not know and would never know.

What marvels, what magic, his little-boy mind in the old, old mind said. Magic that feeble electric currents over copper wires should span distances—and years. Alexander Graham Bell, magician. Mr.—what was his name—Mr. Watson, sorcerer's apprentice. Those two half a century ago with caldrons and eye of newt and wire of copper and oil of vitriol and certain discrete particles of carbon and . . .

And he didn't even know her name.

Delicate voice, tender voice, object mystical and unseen. Of love? One does not love a voice and cannot love a voice and you don't fit your aging ideal to a mere voice.

Only he had. In an impossible moment, in an insane working of the chemistry of his aged body.

And he didn't even know her name.

He lay for many minutes, looking at the cradled phone. Thinking, wondering, fearing, hoping, dreading, dreaming, then . . . He couldn't stop it. He couldn't halt his spotted hand with its lean, gray-bristled fingers; imbued with a life of their own, they drifted across the sheets, gained new strength, became purposeful, grasped, held the instrument tightly, lifted . . . and his other hand with sure touch was dialing. Any number. It made no difference. Any number. Dial the letters: 6 . . . N . . . 3 . . . E . . . 9 . . . W . . . 5 . . . L . . . 6 . . . O . . . 8 . . . V . . . 3 . . . Why not? Why not? The world is insane and dying, and I am insane—but suddenly terribly, impossibly, very much alive.

Click . . .

"When you hear the tone, the time will be—"

Click . . . click . . . click . . .

"Hello." Firm, young, vigorous voice. Gentle, strong.

"It's Mark," he said.

"Mark? Mark?" she said.

"Mark," he said.

"Oh," she said. "I remember. It's been such a long time."

"It's been only minutes for me," he said.

"I don't understand," she said.

"What year is it?" he asked.

"Nineteen-thirty-three," she said. "You know that."

"Listen to me," he said excitedly. "I'm not insane, and I know you will think so—but listen to me. Here it's nineteen-seventy."

"Oh, my," she said. "That's a peculiar joke."

She didn't get angry, he thought. Nor annoyed. Marvelous.

"Believe me," he said. "Here it's nineteen-seventy. I've been calling you—talking with you all evening. Only it's you later and later and later."

"That's strange. What a lovely idea," she said.

"It's real," he told her. "It's real."

"A strange idea. A beautiful idea," she said.

"It's horrible. I can't ever see you."

"I shouldn't do this," she said. "But I'll see you."

"I can't," he said. "I can't, I can't. Don't you understand? It's not the miles."

"Where are you?" she asked.

"San Francisco. Twin Peaks."

"I'm only blocks away. Jones Street! Nob Hill," she said. "I've lived here for years. My family before me. Only blocks away."

"Years away," he said.

"You sound so lost."

"You are so lost," he said.

"You sound so . . . I shouldn't but—"

Sputter . . . sputter . . .

"What's your name?" he asked.

Sputter.

"Your name?" he pleaded. "Your name."

"Angela; you know that. A fine pretty Victorian name. Angela—"

"Angela what?"

Sputter.

"When you hear the tone, it will be—"

Click . . .

He sobbed.

His fingers dialed frantically. Any number. Any number.

Click . . .

Click . . .

"Hello." Young voice.

"Angela?" he asked.

"Yes, who's this?"

"Mark," he said.

"What a nice name," she said. "I don't know any Mark, though."

"What's your last name?" he asked.

"I don't recall ever meeting a Mark."

"We've met," he told her. "But I don't know your last name."

"You have such a nice voice," she said. "So young. Oh, I really shouldn't say that—"

"Your last name," he pleaded.

Sputter . . .

"Why, no harm in telling, I suppose. It's Haym—"

Sputter . . . *click* . . .

"When you hear—"

"Oh, dear God," he said aloud. Just one second more and he would have had it. One second more. Fingers dialed frantically.

Click . . .

"When you hear the—"

Click . . .

"Hello—hello?" A man's voice, deep, resonant.

"Hello," he shouted.

A grunt of displeasure.

"Hello," he shouted.

"Mr. Watson," the voice said. "Come here. I need you."

After that there was silence. Long, long, long, dead silence. Not even a sputter. Not even a click.

Only silence.

He returned the receiver to the hook, feeling tired and old and quite ready to close his eyes and never open them again.

It was too late. Rather, too early. Back to the very beginning, and beyond that year, that day, that moment, there would be nothing. The ancient copper would be dead, because before that instant when Mr. Bell had spilled the acid of the battery and called for his helper, there was nothing. No voices, no Angela, no hope—ever.

He felt like sobbing, but it required too much energy. He had little left. There was only lying in bed and staring at the wall and listening to the whisper of the doctors and the insipid questions of endless nephews and knowing that the days stretched out without hope, without feature, without pity.

Angela Haym—and something else. One syllable. Two syllables? He wasn't even sure he had the first one right. There had been so much static and the quality of the transmission from the primitive phone was so bad.

He grabbed the directory and thumbed to the H's. Impossible. Haymaker—Hayman (See also: Heyman—Heiman—Heimann—Heymann—Hyman). Then Haymend, Haymer, Haymond. An impossible task. He counted them. Thirteen, not counting commercial listings, under Haym . . . then Heym . . . then Heim . . .

Then seventy-eight listings. Impossible.

He didn't even know if she were still alive. Or still in the city. Or even that she still had the same last name. She could have married. She hadn't on the first call. At least she hadn't seemed married. A schoolteacher.

Memory. What had she said? After she retired? She had gone to the class reunion. In Denver?

His fingers skipped to the yellow pages. Hopefully. Under "Associations." University of Denver . . . The Alumni Association. One impossible chance.

He called. A woman answered. He invented a story. He couldn't remember the exact last name. Could she help? After long moments he had three names that might be she.

He started to call. Praying.

On the third call a voice answered, and he said breathlessly, "Angela Haymeyer?"

"Yes," the voice said.

"This is Mark Fleiker."

"Who?"

His heart sank. This was the last one. There was no other. What would he do?

"Mark Fleiker," he said tiredly.

"Oh, Mark," she said. "After all these years. After all these years."

Breath caught in his throat. Sudden panic, fear.

"Angela," he said, "can you entertain a gentleman caller? An old friend."

"After all these years? An old friend?"

"An old friend," he said.

"What a pleasure it would be!"

"It will be," he said, feeling suddenly alive, young-old—alive.

"It will be such a pleasure after all these years," he said.

And, not waiting for the click, he replaced the receiver and began to dress.

"After all these years," he said aloud to the empty room, and felt very, very good.

Ted Sturgeon began writing about the same time I did. His talent for fantasy was obvious, even then. A third of a century has passed, and I still get a tingle when I see his name on a new story. I know that I'm about to read something conceived and executed as no other writer could do it. There is always charm and warmth in his work, even when it's about a very ugly situation—as in this story.

THEODORE STURGEON
Occam's Scalpel

Joe Trilling had a funny way of making a living. It was a good living, but of course he didn't make anything like the bundle he could have in the city. On the other hand, he lived in the mountains a half-mile away from a picturesque village in clean air and piny-birchy woods along with lots of mountain laurel, and he was his own boss. There wasn't much competition for what he did; he had his wife and kids around all the time, and more orders than he could fill. He was one of the night people, and after the family had gone to bed he could work quietly and uninterruptedly. He was happy as a clam.

One night—very early morning, really—he was interrupted. *Bup-bup, bup, bup.* Knock at the window, two shorts, two longs. He froze, he whirled, for he knew that knock. He hadn't heard it

Copyright © 1971 by UPD Publishing Corp. First published in *IF Science Fiction*, August, 1971. Reprinted by permission of the author and the author's agent, Robert P. Mills, Ltd.

for years, but it had been a part of his life since he was born. He saw the face outside and filled his lungs for a whoop that would have roused them at the fire station on the village green, but then he saw the finger on the lips and let the air out. The finger beckoned, and Joe Trilling whirled again, turned down a flame, read a gauge, made a note, threw a switch, and joyfully but silently dove for the outside door. He slid out, closed it carefully, peered into the dark.

"Karl?"

"Shh."

There he was, edge of the woods. Joe Trilling went there, and, whispering because Karl had asked for it, they hit each other, cursed, called each other the filthiest possible names. It would not be easy to explain this to an extra-terrestrial; it isn't necessarily a human thing to do. It's a cultural thing. It means, I want to touch you, it means I love you; but they were men and brothers, so they hit each other's arms and shoulders and swore despicable oaths and insults, until at last even those words wouldn't do, and they stood in the shadows, holding each other's biceps and grinning and drilling into each other with eyes. Then Karl Trilling moved his head sideward toward the road, and they walked away from the house.

"I don't want Hazel to hear us talking," Karl said. "I don't want her or anyone to know I was here. How is she?"

"Beautiful. Aren't you going to see her at all—or the kids?"

"Yes, but not this trip. There's the car. We can talk there. I really am afraid of that bastard."

"Ah," said Joe. "How is the great man?"

"Po'ly," said Karl. "But we're talking about two different bastards. The great man is only the richest man in the world, but I'm not afraid of him, especially now. I'm talking about Cleveland Wheeler."

"Who's Cleveland Wheeler?"

They got into the car. "It's a rental," said Karl. "Matter of fact, it's the second rental. I got out of the executive jet and took a company car and rented another—and then this. Reasonably sure it's not bugged. That's one kind of answer to your question, who's Cleve Wheeler. Other answers would be the man behind the throne. Next in line. Multifaceted genius. Killer shark."

"Next in line," said Joe, responding to the only clause that made any sense. "The old man is sinking?"

"Officially—and an official secret—his hemoglobin reading is four. That mean anything to you, doctor?"

"Sure does, doctor. Malnutritive anemia, if other rumors I hear are true. Richest man in the world—dying of starvation."

"And old age—and stubbornness—and obsession. You want to hear about Wheeler?"

"Tell me."

"Mister Lucky. Born with everything. Greek-coin profile. Michelangelo muscles. Discovered early by a bright-eyed elementary-school principal, sent to a private school, used to go straight to the teachers' lounge in the morning and say what he'd been reading or thinking about. Then they'd tell off a teacher to work with him or go out with him or whatever. High school at twelve, varsity track, basketball, football, and high-diving—three letters for each—yes, he graduated in three years, *summa cum*. Read all the textbooks at the beginning of each term, never cracked them again. More than anything else, he had the habit of success.

"College, the same thing: turned sixteen in his first semester, just ate everything up. Very popular. Graduated at the top again, of course."

Joe Trilling, who had slogged through college and medical school like a hodcarrier, grunted enviously. "I've seen one or two like that. Everybody marvels, nobody sees how easy it was for them."

Karl shook his head. "Wasn't quite like that with Cleve Wheeler. If anything was easy for him, it was because of the nature of his equipment. He was like a four-hundred-horsepower car moving in sixty-horsepower traffic. When his muscles were called on, he used them; I mean, really put it down to the floor.

A very willing guy. Well—he had his choice of jobs—hell, choice of careers. He went into an architectural firm that could use his math, administrative ability, public presence, knowledge of materials, art. Gravitated right to the top, got a partnership. Picked up a doctorate on the side while he was doing it. Married extremely well."

"Mister Lucky," Joe said.

"Mister Lucky, yeah. Listen. Wheeler became a partner, and he did his work and he knew his stuff—everything he could learn or understand. Learning and understanding are not enough to cope with some things like greed or unexpected stupidity or accident or sheer bad breaks. Two of the other partners got into a deal I won't bother you with—a high-rise apartment complex in the wrong place for the wrong residents, and land acquired the wrong way. Wheeler saw it coming, called them in and talked it over. They said yes-yes and went right ahead and did what they wanted anyway—something that Wheeler never in the world expected. The one thing high capability and straight morals and a good education doesn't give you is the end of innocence. Cleve Wheeler was an innocent.

"Well, it happened, the disaster that Cleve had predicted, but it happened far worse. Things like that, when they surface, have a way of exposing a lot of other concealed rot. The firm collapsed. Cleve Wheeler had never failed at anything in his whole life. It was the one thing he had no practice in dealing with. Anyone with the most rudimentary intelligence would have seen that this was the time to walk away—lie down, even. Cut his losses. But I don't think these things even occurred to him."

Karl Trilling laughed suddenly. "In one of Philip Wylie's novels is a tremendous description of a forest fire and how the animals run away from it, the foxes and the rabbits running shoulder to shoulder, the owls flying in the daytime to get ahead of the flames. Then there's this beetle, lumbering along on the ground. The beetle comes to a burned patch, the edge of twenty acres of hell. It stops, it wiggles its feelers, it turns to the side and begins to walk around the fire—" He laughed again. "That's the special thing Cleveland Wheeler has, you see, under all that muscle and brain and brilliance. If he had to—and were a beetle— he wouldn't turn back and he wouldn't quit. If all he could do was walk around it, he'd start walking."

"What happened?" asked Joe.

"He hung on. He used everything he had. He used his brains and his personality and his reputation and all his worldly goods. He also borrowed and promised—and he worked. Oh, he worked. Well, he kept the firm. He cleaned out the rot and built it all up again from the inside, strong and straight this time. But it cost.

"It cost him time—all the hours of every day but the four or so he used for sleeping. And just about when he had it leveled off and starting up, it cost him his wife."

"You said he'd married well."

"He'd married what you marry when you're a young block-buster on top of everything and going higher. She was a nice-enough girl, I suppose, and maybe you can't blame her, but she was no more used to failure than he was. Only he could walk around it. He could rent a room and ride the bus. She just didn't know how—and of course with women like that there's always the discarded swain somewhere in the wings."

"How did he take that?"

"Hard. He'd married the way he played ball or took examina-tions—with everything he had. It did something to him. All this did things to him, I suppose, but that was the biggest chunk of it.

"He didn't let it stop him. He didn't let anything stop him. He went on until all the bills were paid—every cent. All the in-terest. He kept at it until the net worth was exactly what it had been before his ex-partners had begun to eat out the core. Then he gave it away. Gave it away! Sold all right and title to his in-terest for a dollar."

"Finally cracked, hm?"

Karl Trilling looked at his brother scornfully. "Cracked.

Matter of definition, isn't it? Cleve Wheeler's goal was zero—can you understand that? What is success anyhow? Isn't it making up your mind what you're going to do and then doing it, all the way?"

"In that case," said his brother quietly, "suicide is success."

Karl gave him a long, penetrating look. "Right," he said, and thought about it a moment.

"Anyhow," Joe asked, "why zero?"

"I did a lot of research on Cleve Wheeler, but I couldn't get inside his head. I don't know. But I can guess. He meant to owe no man anything. I don't know how he felt about the company he saved, but I can imagine. The man he became—was becoming—wouldn't want to owe it one damned thing. I'd say he just wanted out—but on his own terms, which included leaving nothing behind to work on him."

"Okay," said Joe.

Karl Trilling thought, *The nice thing about old Joe is that he'll wait. All these years apart with hardly any communication beyond birthday cards—and not always that—and here he is, just as if we were still together every day. I wouldn't be here if it weren't important; I wouldn't be telling him all this unless he needed to know; he wouldn't need any of it unless he was going to help. All that unsaid—I don't have to ask him a damn thing. What am I interrupting in his life? What am I going to interrupt? I won't have to worry about that. He'll take care of it.*

He said, "I'm glad I came here, Joe."

Joe said, "That's all right," which meant all the things Karl had been thinking. Karl grinned and hit him on the shoulder and went on talking.

"Wheeler dropped out. It's not easy to map his trail for that period. It pops up all over. He lived in at least three communes —maybe more, but those three were a mess when he came, and a model when he left. He started businesses—all things that had never happened before, like a supermarket with no shelves, no canned music, no games or stamps, just neat stacks of open cases, where the customer took what he wanted and marked it according to the card posted by the case, with a marker hanging on a string. Eggs and frozen meat, and fish and the like, and local produce were priced a flat two percent over wholesale. People were honest because they could never be sure the checkout counter didn't know the prices of everything—besides, to cheat on the prices listed would have been just too embarrassing. With nothing but a big empty warehouse for overhead and no employees spending thousands of man-hours marking individual items, the prices beat any discount house that ever lived. He sold that one, too, and moved on. He started a line of organic baby foods without preservatives, franchised it, and moved on again. He developed a plastic container that would burn without polluting and patented it and sold the patent."

"I've heard of that one. Haven't seen it around, though."

"Maybe you will," Karl said in a guarded tone. "Maybe you will. Anyway, he had a CPA in Pasadena handling details, and just did his thing all over. I never heard of a failure in anything he tried."

"Sounds like a junior edition of the great man himself, your honored boss."

"You're not the only one who realized that. The boss may be a ding-a-ling in many ways, but nobody ever faulted his business sense. He has always had his tentacles out for wandering pieces of very special manpower. For all I know, he had drawn a bead on Cleveland Wheeler years back. I wouldn't doubt that he'd made offers from time to time, only during that period Cleve Wheeler wasn't about to go to work for anyone that big. His whole pattern is to run things his way, and you don't do that in an established empire."

"Heir apparent," said Joe, reminding him of something he had said earlier.

"Right," nodded Karl. "I knew you'd begin to get the idea before I was finished."

"But finish," said Joe.

"Right. Now, what I'm going to tell you, I just want you to know. I don't expect you to understand it or what it means or what it has all done to Cleve Wheeler. I need your help, and you can't really help me unless you know the whole story."

"Shoot."

Karl Trilling shot: "Wheeler found a girl. Her name was Clara Prieta, and her folks came from Sonora. She was bright as hell—in her way, I suppose, as bright as Cleve, though with a tenth of his schooling—and pretty as well, and it was Cleve she wanted, not what he might get for her. She fell for him when he had nothing—when he really wanted nothing. They were a daily, hourly joy to each other. I guess that was about the time he started building this business and that, making something again. He bought a little house and a car. He bought two cars, one for her. I don't think she wanted it, but he couldn't do enough—he was always looking for more things to do for her. They went out for an evening to some friends' house, she from shopping, he from whatever it was he was working on then, so they had both cars. He followed her on the way home and had to watch her lose control and spin out. She died in his arms."

"Oh, Jesus."

"Mister Lucky. Listen: a week later he turned a corner downtown and found himself looking at a bank robbery. He caught a stray bullet—grazed the back of his neck. He had seven months to lie still and think about things. When he got out, he was told his business manager had embezzled everything and headed south with his secretary. Everything."

"What did he do?"

"Went to work and paid his hospital bill."

They sat in the car in the dark for a long time, until Joe said, "Was he paralyzed, there in the hospital?"

"For nearly five months."

"Wonder what he thought about."

Karl Trilling said, "I can imagine what he thought about. What I can't imagine is what he decided. What he concluded. What he determined to be. Damn it, there are no accurate words for it. We all do the best we can with what we've got, or try to. Or should. He *did*—and with the best possible material to start out with. He played it straight; he worked hard; he was honest and lawful and fair; he was fit; he was bright. He came out of the hospital with those last two qualities intact. God alone knows what's happened to the rest of it."

"So he went to work for the old man."

"He did—and somehow that frightens me. It was as if all his qualifications were not enough to suit both of them until these things happened to him—until they made him become what he is."

"And what is that?"

"There isn't a short answer to that, Joe. The old man has become a modern myth. Nobody ever sees him. Nobody can predict what he's going to do or why. Cleveland Wheeler stepped into his shadow and disappeared almost as completely as the boss. There are very few things you can say for certain. The boss has always been a recluse, and in the ten years Cleve Wheeler has been with him he has become more so. It's been business as usual with him, of course—which means the constantly unusual —long periods of quiet, and then these spectacular unexpected wheelings and dealings. You assume that the old man dreams these things up and some high-powered genius on his staff gets them done. But it could be the genius that instigates the moves— who can know? Only the people closest to him—Wheeler, Epstein, me. And I don't know."

"But Epstein died."

Karl Trilling nodded in the dark. "Epstein died. Which leaves only Wheeler to watch the store. I'm the old man's personal physician, not Wheeler's, and there's no guarantee that I ever will be Wheeler's."

Joe Trilling recrossed his legs and leaned back, looking out into the whispering dark. "It begins to take shape," he murmured. "The old man's on the way out, you very well might be, and there's nobody to take over but this Wheeler."

"Yes, and I don't know what he is or what he'll do. I do know he will command more power than any single human being on Earth. He'll have so much that he'll be above any kind of cupidity that you or I could imagine—you or I can't think in that order of magnitude. But you see, he's a man who, you might say, has had it proved to him that being good and smart and strong and honest doesn't particularly pay off. Where will he go with all this? And hypothesizing that he's been making more and more of the decisions lately, and extrapolating from that—where is he going? All you can be sure of is that he will succeed in anything he tries. That is his habit."

"What does he want? Isn't that what you're trying to figure out? What would a man like that want, if he knew he could get it?"

"I knew I'd come to the right place," said Karl almost happily. "That's it exactly. As for me, I have all I need now, and there are plenty of other places I could go. I wish Epstein were still around, but he's dead and cremated."

"Cremated?"

"That's right—you wouldn't know about that. Old man's instructions. I handled it myself. You've heard of the hot and cold private swimming pools—but I bet you never heard of a man with his own private crematorium in the second subbasement."

Joe threw up his hands. "I guess if you can reach into your pocket and pull out two billion real dollars, you can have anything you want. By the way—was that legal?"

"Like you said—if you have two billion. Actually, the county medical examiner was present and signed the papers. And he'll be there when the old man pushes off too—it's all in the final instructions. Hey—wait, I don't want to cast any aspersions on the M.E. He wasn't bought. He did a very competent examination on Epstein."

"Okay—we know what to expect when the time comes. It's afterward you're worried about."

"Right. What has the old man—I'm speaking of the corporate old man now—what has he been doing all along? What has he been doing in the last ten years, since he got Wheeler—and is it any different from what he was doing before? How much of this difference, if any, is more Wheeler than boss? That's all we have to go on, Joe, and from it we have to extrapolate what Wheeler's going to do with the biggest private economic force this world has ever known."

"Let's talk about that," said Joe, beginning to smile.

Karl Trilling knew the signs, so he began to smile a little, too. They talked about it.

The crematorium in the second subbasement was purely functional, as if all concessions to sentiment and ritual had been made elsewhere, or canceled. The latter most accurately described what had happened when at last, at long long last, the old man died. Everything was done precisely according to his instructions immediately after he was certifiably dead and before any public announcements were made—right up to and including the moment when the square mouth of the furnace opened with a startling clang, a blare of heat, a flare of light—the hue the old-time blacksmiths called straw color. The simple coffin slid rapidly in, small flames exploding into being on its corners, and the door banged shut. It took a moment for the eyes to adjust to the bare room, the empty greased track, the closed door. It took the same moment for the conditioners to whisk away the sudden smell of scorched soft pine.

The medical examiner leaned over the small table and signed his name twice. Karl Trilling and Cleveland Wheeler did the same. The M.E. tore off copies and folded them and put them away in his breast pocket. He looked at the closed square iron door, opened his mouth, closed it again, and shrugged. He held out his hand.

"Good night, doctor."

"Good night, doctor. Rugosi's outside—he'll show you out."

The M.E. shook hands wordlessly with Cleveland Wheeler and left.

"I know just what he's feeling," Karl said. "Something ought to be said. Something memorable—end of an era. 'One small step for man—' "

Cleveland Wheeler smiled the bright smile of the college hero, fifteen years after—a little less wide, a little less even, a great deal less in the eyes. He said in the voice that commanded, whatever he said, "If you think you're quoting the first words from an astronaut on the moon, you're not. What he said was from the ladder, when he poked his boot down. He said, 'It's some kind of soft stuff. I can kick it around with my foot.' I've always liked that much better. It was real, it wasn't rehearsed or memorized or thought out, and it had to do with that moment and the next. The M.E. said good night, and you told him the chauffeur was waiting outside. I like that better than anything anyone could say. I think he would, too," Wheeler added, barely gesturing, with a very strong, slightly cleft chin, toward the hot black door.

"But he wasn't exactly human."

"So they say." Wheeler half-smiled, and even as he turned away, Karl could sense himself tuned out, the room itself become of secondary importance—the next thing Wheeler was to do, and the next and the one after, becoming more real than the here and now.

Karl put a fast end to that.

He said levelly, "I meant what I just said, Wheeler."

It couldn't have been the words, which by themselves might have elicited another half-smile and a forgetting. It was the tone, and perhaps the "Wheeler." There is a ritual about these things. To those few on his own level, and those on the level below, he was "Cleve." Below that he was "mister" to his face and "Wheeler" behind his back. No one of his peers would call him "mister" unless it was meant as the herald of an insult; no one of his peers or immediate underlings would call him "Wheeler" at all, ever. Whatever the component, it removed Cleveland Wheeler's hand from the knob and turned him. His face was completely alert and interested. "You'd best tell me what you mean, doctor."

Karl said, "I'll do better than that. Come." Without gestures, suggestions, or explanations, he walked to the left rear of the room, leaving it up to Wheeler to decide whether or not to follow. Wheeler followed.

In the corner, Karl rounded on him. "If you ever say anything about this to anyone—even me—when we leave here, I'll just deny it. If you ever get in here again, you won't find anything to back up your story." He took a complex four-inch blade of machined stainless steel from his belt and slid it between the big masonry blocks. Silently, massively, the course of blocks in the corner began to move upward. Looking up at them in the dim light from the narrow corridor they revealed, anyone could see that they were real blocks and that to get through them without that key and the precise knowledge of where to put it would be a long-term project.

Again Karl proceeded without looking around, leaving go, no-go, as a matter for Wheeler to decide. Wheeler followed. Karl heard his footsteps behind him and noticed with pleasure and something like admiration that when the heavy blocks whooshed down and seated themselves solidly behind them, Wheeler may have looked over his shoulder but did not pause.

"You've noticed we're alongside the furnace," Karl said, like a guided-tour bus driver. "And now, behind it."

He stood aside to let Wheeler pass him and see the small room.

It was just large enough for the tracks which protruded from the back of the furnace and a little standing space on each side. On the far side was a small table with a black suitcase standing on it. On the track stood the coffin, its corners carboned, its top and sides wet and slightly steaming.

"Sorry to have to close that stone gate that way," Karl said matter-of-factly. "I don't expect anyone down here at all, but I wouldn't want to explain any of this to persons other than yourself."

Wheeler was staring at the coffin. He seemed perfectly composed, but it was a seeming. Karl was quite aware of what it was costing him.

Wheeler said, "I wish you'd explain it to *me*." And he laughed. It was the first time Karl had never seen this man do anything badly.

"I will. I am." He clicked open the suitcase and laid it open and flat on the little table. There was a glisten of chrome and steel and small vials in little pockets. The first tool he removed was a screwdriver. "No need to use screws when you're cremating 'em," he said cheerfully, and placed the tip under one corner of the lid. He struck the handle smartly with the heel of one hand, and the lid popped loose. "Stand this up against the wall behind you, will you?"

Silently Cleveland Wheeler did as he was told. It gave him something to do with his muscles; it gave him the chance to turn his head away for a moment; it gave him a chance to think—and it gave Karl the opportunity for a quick glance at his steady countenance.

He's a mensch, Karl thought. *He really is . . .*

Wheeler set up the lid neatly and carefully, and they stood, one on each side, looking down into the coffin.

"He—got a lot older," Wheeler said at last.

"You haven't seen him recently."

"Here and in there," said the executive, "I've spent more time in the same room with him during the past month than I have in the last eight, nine years. Still, it was a matter of minutes, each time."

Karl nodded understandingly. "I'd heard that. Phone calls, any time of the day or night, and then those long silences, two days, three, not calling out, not having anyone in—"

"Are you going to tell me about the phony oven?"

"Oven? Furnace? It's not a phony at all. When we've finished here, it'll do the job, all right."

"Then why the theatricals?"

"That was for the M.E. Those papers he signed are in sort of a never-never country just now. When we slide this back in and turn on the heat, they'll become as legal as he thinks they are."

"Then why—"

"Because there are some things you have to know." Karl reached into the coffin and unfolded the gnarled hands. They came apart reluctantly, and he pressed them down at the sides of the body. He unbuttoned the jacket, laid it back, unbuttoned the shirt, unzipped the trousers. When he had finished with this, he looked up and found Wheeler's sharp gaze, not on the old man's corpse, but on him.

"I have the feeling," said Cleveland Wheeler, "that I have never seen you before."

Silently Karl Trilling responded: *But you do now.* And, *Thanks, Joey. You were dead right.* Joe had known the answer to that one plaguing question, *How should I act?*

Talk just the way he talks, Joe had said. *Be what he is, the whole time. . . .*

Be what he is. A man without illusions (they don't work) and without hope (who needs it?) who has the unbreakable habit of succeeding. And who can say it's a nice day in such a way that everyone around snaps to attention and says: *Yes, SIR!*

"You've been busy," Karl responded shortly. He took off his jacket, folded it, and put it on the table beside the kit. He put on surgeon's gloves and slipped the sterile sleeve off a new scalpel. "Some people scream and faint the first time they watch a dissection."

Wheeler smiled thinly. "I don't scream and faint." But it was not lost on Karl Trilling that only then, at the last possible moment, did Wheeler actually view the old man's body. When he did, he neither screamed nor fainted; he uttered an astonished grunt.

"Thought that would surprise you," Karl said easily. "In case you were wondering, though, he really was a male. The species seems to be oviparous. Mammals too, but it has to be oviparous. I'd sure like a look at a female. That isn't a vagina. It's a cloaca."

"Until this moment," said Wheeler in a hypnotized voice, "I thought that 'not-human' remark of yours was a figure of speech."

"No, you didn't," Karl responded shortly.

Leaving the words to hang in the air, as words will if a speaker has the wit to isolate them with wedges of silence, he deftly slit the corpse from the sternum to the pubic symphysis. For the first-time viewer this was always the difficult moment. It's hard not to realize viscerally that the cadaver does not feel anything and will not protest. Nerve-alive to Wheeler, Karl looked for a gasp or a shudder; Wheeler merely held his breath.

"We could spend hours—weeks, I imagine, going into the de-tails," Karl said, deftly making a transverse incision in the ensi-form area, almost around to the trapezoid on each side, "but this is the thing I wanted you to see." Grasping the flesh at the junc-ture of the cross he had cut, on the left side, he pulled upward and to the left. The cutaneous layers came away easily, with the fat under them. They were not pinkish, but an off-white lavender shade. Now the muscular striations over the ribs were in view. "If you'd palpated the old man's chest," he said, demonstrating on the right side, "you'd have felt what seemed to be normal human ribs. But look at this."

With a few deft strokes he separated the muscle fibers from the bone on a mid-costal area about four inches square, and scraped. A rib emerged, and as he widened the area and scraped between it and the next one, it became clear that the ribs were joined by a thin flexible layer of bone or chitin.

"It's like baleen—whalebone," said Karl. "See this?" He sec-tioned out a piece, flexed it.

"My God."

"Now, look at this." Karl took surgical shears from the kit, snipped through the sternum right up to the clavicle, and then across the lower margin of the ribs. Slipping his fingers under them, he pulled upward. With a dull snap the entire ribcage opened like a door, exposing the lung.

The lung was not pink, nor the liverish-brownish-black of a smoker, but yellow—the clear bright yellow of pure sulfur.

"His metabolism," Karl said, straightening up at last and flexing the tension out of his shoulders, "is fantastic. Or was. He lived on oxygen, same as us, but he broke it out of carbon monoxide, sulfur dioxide and trioxide, and carbon dioxide mostly. I'm not saying he could—I mean he had to. When he was forced to breathe what we call clean air, he could take just so much of it and then had to duck out and find a few breaths of his own atmosphere. When he was younger he could take it for hours at a time, but as the years went by he had to spend more and more time in the kind of smog he could breathe. Those long disappearances of his, and that reclusiveness—they weren't as kinky as people supposed."

Wheeler made a gesture toward the corpse. "But—what is he? Where—"

"I can't tell you. Except for a good deal of medical and biochemical details, you now know as much as I do. Somehow, somewhere, he arrived. He came, he saw, he began to make his moves. Look at this."

He opened the other side of the chest and then broke the sternum up and away. He pointed. The lung tissue was not in two discreet parts, but extended across the median line. "One lung, all the way across, though it has these two lobes. The kidneys and gonads show the same right-left fusion."

"I'll take your word for it," said Wheeler a little hoarsely. "Damn it, what *is* it?"

"A featherless biped, as Plato once described Homo sap. *I* don't know what it is. I just know *that* it is—and I thought you ought to know. That's all."

"But you've seen one before. That's obvious."

"Sure. Epstein."

"Epstein?"

"Sure. The old man had to have a go-between—someone who could, without suspicion, spend long hours with him and hours away. The old man could do a lot over the phone, but not everything. Epstein was, you might say, a right arm that could hold its breath a little longer than he could. It got to him in the end, though, and he died of it.''

"Why didn't you say something long before this?"

"First of all, I value my own skin. I could say 'reputation,' but 'skin' is the word. I signed a contract as his personal physician because he needed a personal physician—another bit of window-dressing. But I did precious little doctoring—except over the phone—and nine-tenths of that was, I realized quite recently, purely diversionary. Even a doctor, I suppose, can be a trusting soul. One or the other would call and give a set of symptoms, and I'd cautiously suggest and prescribe. Then I'd get another call that the patient was improving, and that was that. Why, I even got specimens—blood, urine, stools—and did the pathology on them and never realized that they were from the same source as what the medical examiner checked out and signed for.''

"What do you mean, same source?"

Karl shrugged. "He could get anything he wanted—anything.''

"Then—what the M.E. examined wasn't—" He waved a hand at the casket.

"Of course not. That's why the crematorium has a back door. There's a little pocket sleight-of-hand trick you can buy for fifty cents that operates the same way. This body here was inside the furnace. The ringer—a look-alike that came from God knows where; I swear to you I don't—was lying out there waiting for the M.E. When the button was pushed, the fires started up, and that coffin slid in—pushing this one out and at the same time drenching it with water as it came through. While we've been in here, the human body is turning to ashes. My personal private secret instructions, both for Epstein and for the boss, were to wait until I was certain I was alone and then come in here after an hour and push the second button, which would slide this one back into the fire. I was to do no investigations, ask no questions, make no reports. It came through as logical but not reasonable, like so many of his orders." He laughed suddenly. "Do you know why the old man—and Epstein too, for that matter, in case you never noticed—wouldn't shake hands with anyone?"

"I presumed it was because he had an obsession with germs."

"It was because his normal body temperature was a hundred and seven."

Wheeler touched one of his own hands with the other and said nothing.

When Karl felt that the wedge of silence was thick enough, he asked lightly, "Well, boss, where do we go from here?"

Cleveland Wheeler turned away from the corpse and to Karl slowly, as if diverting his mind with an effort.

"What did you call me?"

"Figure of speech," said Karl, and smiled. "Actually, I'm working for the company—and that's you. I'm under orders, which have been finally and completely discharged when I push that button—I have no others. So it really is up to you."

Wheeler's eyes fell again to the corpse. "You mean about him? This? What we should do?"

"That, yes. Whether to burn it up and forget it—or call in top management and an echelon of scientists. Or scare the living hell out of everyone on Earth by phoning the papers. Sure, that has to be decided, but I was thinking on a much wider spectrum than that."

"Such as—"

Karl gestured toward the box with his head. "What was he doing here, anyway? What has he done? What was he trying to do?"

"You'd better go on," said Wheeler; and for the very first time said something in a way that suggested diffidence. "You've had a while to think about all this, I—" And almost helplessly, he spread his hands.

"I can understand that," Karl said gently. "Up to now I've been coming on like a hired lecturer, and I know it. I'm not going to embarrass you with personalities except to say that you've absorbed all this with less buckling of the knees than anyone in the world I could think of."

"Right. Well, there's a simple technique you learn in elementary algebra. It has to do with the construction of graphs.

You place a dot on the graph where known data put it. You get more data, you put down another dot, and then a third. With just three dots—of course, the more the better, but it can be done with three—you can connect them and establish a curve. This curve has certain characteristics, and it's fair to extend the curve a little farther with the assumption that later data will bear you out."

"Extrapolation."

"Extrapolation. X axis, the fortunes of our late boss. Y axis, time. The curve is his fortunes—that is to say, his influence."

"Pretty tall graph."

"Over thirty years."

"Still pretty tall."

"All right," said Karl. "Now, over the same thirty years, another curve: change in the environment." He held up a hand. "I'm not going to read you a treatise on ecology. Let's be more objective than that. Let's just say changes. Okay: a measurable rise in the mean temperature because of CO_2 and the greenhouse effect. Draw the curve. Incidence of heavy metals, mercury and lithium, in organic tissue. Draw a curve. Likewise chlorinated hydrocarbons, hypertrophy of algae due to phosphates, incidence of coronaries. . . . All right, let's superimpose all these curves on the same graph."

"I see what you're getting at. But you have to be careful with that kind of statistics game. Like, the increase of traffic fatalities coincides with the increased use of aluminum cans and plastic-tipped baby pins."

"Right. I don't think I'm falling into that trap. I just want to find reasonable answers to a couple of otherwise unreasonable situations. One is this: if the changes occurring in our planet are the result of mere carelessness—a more or less random thing, carelessness—then how come nobody is being careless in a way that benefits the environment? Strike that. I promised, no ecology lessons. Rephrase: how come all these carelessnesses promote a change and not a preservation?

"Next question: What is the direction of the change? You've seen speculative writing about 'terra-forming'—altering other planets to make them habitable by humans. Suppose an effort were being made to change this planet to suit someone else? Suppose they wanted more water and were willing to melt the polar caps by the greenhouse effect? Increase the oxides of sulfur, eliminate certain marine forms from plankton to whales? Reduce the population by increases in lung cancer, emphysema, heart attacks, and even war?"

Both men found themselves looking down at the sleeping face in the coffin. Karl said softly, "Look what he was into—petro-chemicals, fossil fuels, food processing, advertising, all the things that made the changes or helped the changes—"

"You're not blaming him for all of it."

"Certainly not. He found willing helpers by the million."

"You don't think he was trying to change a whole planet just so he could be comfortable in it."

"No, I don't think so—and that's the central point I have to make. I don't know if there are any more around like him and Epstein, but I can suppose this: if the changes now going on keep on—and accelerate—then we can expect them."

Wheeler said, "So what would you like to do? Mobilize the world against the invader?"

"Nothing like that. I think I'd slowly and quietly reverse the changes. If this planet is normally unsuitable to them, then I'd keep it so. I don't think they'd have to be driven back. I think they just wouldn't come."

"Or they'd try some other way."

"I don't think so," said Karl. "Because they tried this one. If they thought they could do it with fleets of spaceships and super-zap guns, they'd be doing it. No—this is their way, and if it doesn't work, they can try somewhere else."

Wheeler began pulling thoughtfully at his lip. Karl said softly, "All it would take is someone who knew what he was doing, who could command enough clout and who had the wit to make it pay. They might even arrange a man's life—to get the kind of man they need."

And before Wheeler could answer, Karl took up his scalpel.

"I want you to do something for me," he said sharply in a new, commanding tone—actually, Wheeler's own. "I want you to do it because I've done it, and I'll be damned if I want to be the only man in the world who has."

Leaning over the head of the casket, he made an incision along the hairline from temple to temple. Then, bracing his elbows against the edge of the box and steadying one hand with the other, he drew the scalpel straight down the center of the forehead and down onto the nose, splitting it exactly in two. Down he went through the upper lip and then the lower, around the point of the chin and under it to the throat. Then he stood up.

"Put your hands on his cheeks," he ordered. Wheeler frowned briefly (how long had it been since anyone had spoken to him that way), hesitated, then did as he was told.

"Now, press your hands together and down."

The incision widened slightly under the pressure; then abruptly the flesh gave, and the entire skin of the face slipped off. The unexpected lack of resistance brought Wheeler's hands to the bottom of the coffin, and he found himself face to face, inches away, with the corpse.

Like the lungs and kidneys, the eyes—eye?—passed the median, very slightly reduced at the center. The pupil was oval, its long axis transverse. The skin was pale lavender with yellow vessels and in place of a nose was a thread-fringed hole. The mouth was circular, the teeth not quite radially placed; there was little chin.

Without moving, Wheeler closed his eyes, held them shut for one second, two, and then courageously opened them again. Karl whipped around the end of the coffin and got an arm around Wheeler's chest. Wheeler leaned on it heavily for a moment, then stood up quickly and brushed the arm away.

"You didn't have to do that."

"Yes, I did," said Karl. "Would you want to be the only man in the world who'd gone through that—with nobody to tell it to?"

And after all, Wheeler could laugh. When he had finished, he said, "Push that button."

"Hand me that cover."

Most obediently Cleveland Wheeler brought the coffin lid, and they placed it.

Karl pushed the button, and they watched the coffin slide into the square of flame. Then they left.

Joe Trilling had a funny way of making a living. It was a good living, but of course he didn't make anything like the bundle he could have made in the city. On the other hand, he lived in the mountains a half-mile away from a picturesque village in clean air and piny-birchy woods along with lots of mountain laurel, and he was his own boss. There wasn't much competition for what he did.

What he did was to make simulacra of medical specimens, mostly for the armed forces, although he had plenty of orders from medical schools, film producers, and an occasional individual, no questions asked. He could make a model of anything inside, affixed to or penetrating a body or any part of it. He could make models to be looked at, models to be felt, smelled, and palpated. He could give you gangrene that stunk or dewy thyroids with real dew on them. He could make one-of-a-kind or he could set up a production line. Dr. Joe Trilling was, to put it briefly, the best there was at what he did.

"The clincher," Karl told him (in much more relaxed circumstances than their previous ones; daytime now, with beer), "the real clincher was the face bit. God, Joe, that was a beautiful piece of work."

"Just nuts and bolts. The beautiful part was your idea—his hands on it."

"How do you mean?"

"I've been thinking back to that," Joe said. "I don't think you yourself realize how brilliant a stroke that was. It's all very well to set up a show for the guy, but to make him put his hands as well as his eyes and brains on it—that was the stroke of genius. It's like—well, I can remember when I was a kid coming home from school and putting my hand on a fence rail and somebody had spat on it." He displayed his hand, shook it. "All these years I can remember how that felt. All these years couldn't wear it away, all those scrubbings couldn't wash it away. It's more than a cerebral or psychic thing, Karl—more than the memory of an episode. I think there's a kind of memory mechanism in the cells themselves, especially on the hands, that can be invoked. What I'm getting to is that no matter how long he lives, Cleve Wheeler is going to feel that skin slip under his palms, and that is going to bring him nose to nose with that face. No, you're the genius, not me."

"Na. You knew what you were doing. I didn't."

"Hell you didn't." Joe leaned far back in his lawn chaise—so far he could hold up his beer and look at the sun through it from the underside. Watching the receding bubbles defy perspective (because they swell as they rise), he murmured, "Karl?"

"Yuh."

"Ever hear of Occam's razor?"

"Um. Long time back. Philosophical principle. Or logic or something. Let's see. Given an effect and a choice of possible causes, the simplest cause is always the one most likely to be true. Is that it?"

"Not too close, but close enough," said Joe Trilling lazily. "Hm. You're the one who used to proclaim that logic is sufficient unto itself and need have nothing to do with truth."

"I still proclaim it."

"Okay. Now, you and I know that human greed and careless-ness are quite enough all by themselves to wreck this planet. We didn't think that was enough for the likes of Cleve Wheeler, who can really do something about it, so we constructed him a smog-breathing extraterrestrial. I mean, he hadn't done anything about saving the world for our reasons, so we gave him a whizzer of a reason of his own. Right out of our heads."

"Dictated by all available factors. Yes. What are you getting at, Joe?"

"Oh—just that our complicated hoax is simple, really, in the sense that it brought everything down to a single cause. Occam's razor slices things down to simplest causes. Single causes have a fair chance of being right."

Karl put down his beer with a bump. "I never thought of that. I've been too busy to think of that. *Suppose we were right?*"

They looked at each other, shaken.

At last Karl said, "What do we look for now, Joe—space ships?"

Burt K. Filer has an annoying plethora of talents. Although still a young man, he has already proved himself a successful inventor and a first-rate mechanic. Then, he has numerous hobbies, such as motorcycling and tearing down motorcycles. He's also an excellent writer, as his first stories proved a few years ago. But there are too many long breaks between his too brief periods of writing. This time, we have him in a grim situation, one that's really "hot." But not, to be sure, a grim story!

BURT K. FILER
Hot Potato

SECRET BOMB STORES FOR CHINESE
Peking, May 7, 2010—UAP

Four thousand megatons of fusion weapons were transferred to a Chinese "mystery stockpile" last week, General Ho Muchun announced today. Minister of War Muchun spoke at a press luncheon here, held in the Red House Lotus Garden. He was openly optimistic when questioned about the secrecy of his nuclear arsenal. "Imperialist Yankees never find in a million years," was his smug and smiling reply.

As the present cold-war standoff is based wholly on the threat of mutual sabotage, the general's comments bode ill for the U.S. Whereas the Chinese have exact knowledge of all U.S. installations, said Muchun, the reverse is no longer true. Thanks to his secret hiding place, he claims the U.S. has no retaliatory measures.

"Can't blow up what you can't find," he added philosophically.

Washington has made no immediate comment.

* tick *

"Damn, blast, hell, they've developed the timespool!" was General Galen Panhard's immediate comment. He hurled down the morning paper. "Get me Major Tucker! No—wait a minute—get the news service first."

Orderlies scattered like panicked chickens. Six telephones were on his desk in thirty seconds, and three had reached the UAP.

"Hello? This is Panhard—well, hang the other two up, fool—now, listen. We've got a secret arsenal too, and what's more, it's bigger than Muchun's, and what's more, we know where *his* is and he doesn't know where *ours* is. Tell the old buzzard to stuff that in [cough] his pipe and smoke it! Good-bye [slam].

"Where's Tucker? TUCK–ER-R-R!" he bellowed. "Get the car. We're going out to see Cordoba."

* tock *

In the back seat of Ford-Chrysler's biggest and blackest and latest limousine, the two men presented an odd contrast.

General Galen Panhard was a jut-jawed, big-chested man of action. In his news photos "Old Pinhead" looked 6′ 6″ and 300 pounds. Actually he was 5′ 4″ and a shade over 160, but the impression of bigness still prevailed.

Next to him sat Major Dennis Tucker. Denny was a medium-tall, well-fed man of thirty with an absolutely forgettable face. They called him Wallpaper because he blended right in. Nobody actually believed he'd taken Quanoi apart singlehanded. Nobody but Panhard, who'd been there. He'd kept Denny as his personal staff assistant, bodyguard, and poop-boy ever since.

They rumbled slowly through Washington's sweet morning air, across the bridge, and up into the lush Virginia countryside. Panhard fumed impatiently, with eyes squinted half-shut, and Denny snored quietly with his own lids down all the way. It was six A.M.

In forty minutes they arrived at Dr. Emile Cordoba's farm-house laboratory. It wasn't a farmhouse for security's sake, oh, no. Such camouflage would have been childishly transparent. It was a farmhouse because Cordoba liked farmhouses. Helped him think, he said. And as the government was very anxious to keep him thinking, a way was found to salve the scientist's idio-syncrasy. He had others.

Dr. Cordoba was a thin and serious forty-five. Beneath his black hair was a pale, handsome face that had a pipe stuck in it most of the time. Because he'd developed the timespool, every one thought Emile was smarter than hell, which was probably correct.

"Looks like someone reads the early paper," he commented, holding open the car door.

"Huh?" asked Denny, who hadn't. He stumbled out, nudged from behind by his boss.

"Don't mind this imbecile, Emile," said Panhard impatiently. "Let's go inside."

Labs are rarely attractive, but this one came close. The walls were a restful russet, and on the floor was a Teflon rug which matched the subtly tinted window glass. Paintings hung here and there, real ones.

"What happened to the Degas ballerina?" Denny asked, noting a blank spot on the wall.

"Little accident," Emile admitted sheepishly. "Kind of blew a hole in 'er with the welding beam."

"Too bad."

They took seats around an island of equipment in the middle of the floor. Rising from a cluster of wiry filaments was a twelve-foot spool with a door in its side. Both rested on a platform of even more esoteric gadgetry.

"Question—probably rhetorical," began the general. "*Do* the Chinese have it?" He gestured at the timespool.

"Answer—equally rhetorical, judging by that news article," replied Emile, "is yes."

Light dawned in Denny's eyes. "So they're storing their weapons in another time track too," he mused, "just like us. Nice." He yawned.

"Just like us, not nice," corrected Emile. "What're we going to do about it?"

"Carry the war into the alternate continuum, of course," snapped the general. "Tucker?" he rapped at the still-drowsy young major.

"Yes, sir?"

"You will go into Time Track B, find that Chinese ammo dump, and eliminate it. Just like Quanoi back in ninety-nine."

"Aw for cry—"

"That'll be all, boy."

"Boy? General, I *was* a boy back in ninety-nine, but not anymore. Sabotage and all that stuff is so—so *uncomfortable* for a man of my years, y'know."

"TUCK—"

"YessirI'llgoI'llgoI'llgo."

Denny didn't mind getting into the space suit so much. He didn't mind wedging himself with half a dozen weapons into the spool, either. In fact, the whole assignment wasn't that bad once he'd accepted it. As Emile and the general waved through the window, the bland major was primarily disconsolate about having missed breakfast.

* tick *

How many men, Denny asked himself, have ever had the privilege of getting sick on an empty stomach in quantum space? Probably just me. Maybe a Chinaman or two as well. We'll see.

The shell of "funnyspace" between what Denny regarded as the present (actually Continuum Track A) and the "alternate present" (specifically, Continuum Track B) was a horrible place. But it was a place.

Emile explained it to him once. Time was quantified and not continuous. You didn't move smoothly from track to track but went in a series of jumps, like an electron hopping from ring to ring in an atom. What's significant is that the space between is timeless. Things "are" there. Things never "were" and never "would be," they continuously "are."

Which is why the space had so many Major Denny Tuckers in it. Each time Denny went across, he left an imprint which never faded and never moved. Going through now, he saw several other spools floating nearby, each with himself inside. He waved. They never waved back. There would be two spools for each of the six round trips to B he'd already taken.

Which of course comes to twelve, but today he counted fifteen. Three were spherical instead of cylindrical, red instead of silver, and had the same funny little yellow face peeking out of them.

Peking—out of them? Of course, no doubt about it now. The Chinese were definitely ferrying fusionables into B.

Whango! Out of quantum space and into B-time, just as rough as usual. Why didn't Emile fix that? Undogging the hatch, Denny drifted out into real space.

He'd been transported physically as well as temporally. Instead of arriving in the B-world's equivalent of Cordoba's farmhouse, he'd been deposited in orbit around the planet. Emile had frankly admitted ignorance of what conditions on the surface of track B's earth would be like, but decided it would be better to avoid the complications of finding out. Just go, leave the bombs in orbit, and come back.

Not thirty yards away bobbed a loose pile of atomic explosives Denny'd ferried out on previous runs. This time his mission was different, he reminded himself.

Emile had suggested Denny hunt through the east-west orbits near his own for the Chinese ammo dump. It was almost too easy. A quick scan through his faceplate binoculars showed the chubby red spool not twenty miles away.

Dennis Tucker was no astronaut. Until he pulled this last lousy tour of duty with Old Pinhead, he hadn't even been to the moon. So he should be forgiven for turning up the wick on his pocket rocket a bit too high.

Attempting to sneak up on the Chinaman, he instead overshot

by a couple of miles. As Denny drifted past, the amazed Oriental did a fast double-take and scrambled toward his round red spool.

Well, what the hell, Denny thought, maybe I can get him from here. Putting his rocket on retro, he shouldered the M110 and tried to lay a beam on the excited figure behind. He missed, deceleration throwing him off. Then an answering flash of brilliance sizzled just past his ear.

Why, you nasty, Denny growled. You've got a gun, too. He squeezed off another beam, which sent the enemy soldier scuttling behind a large pile of crates floating near his spool. Fusion weapons, Denny supposed. Hmmm. Well, why not, he mused with a devil-may-care grin. I'm in the open, and he's not. He'll pick me off any minute. If I'm going to go, I might as well get the job done. He centered the muzzle of his M110 on the deadly heap.

"Hold it, Buster!" said an eerily familiar voice over his own QL circuit. "Just what in hell d'you think you're doing?" A heavy hand thumped Denny none too gently from behind. "Startled" is an inadequate word.

"Why, ah, I'm making the world safe for democracy," he stammered. The hand on his shoulder was joined by another, and Denny was spun roughly around.

He confronted—himself. Oh, the man wasn't an exact copy and his space suit looked a little more sophisticated, but there, floating two feet away over the world of track B, was a guy whose name just had to be Dennis Tucker.

"Whose world?" asked the pugnacious B-Denny. "You guys've got colossal nerve, y'know it? How'd you like it if we set off those babies over *your* earth, eh? How'd you like that?"

"Not too much, I suppose. Er, don't you think we'd better hide? There's a Chinese over there with a gun and—"

"Don't worry about him," snapped B-Denny, "worry about me. My buddy's got a pistol like this one on him."

Denny turned. Sure enough, there were two figures floating together back there, seemingly engaged in animated conversation. Directly overhead were two spools very much like his own.

"Can't we talk this over?"

"We *are* talking it over," snapped B-Denny with a wave of his sidearm. "It's simple. Get out of here and take your damn bombs with you. *We* don't want 'em. Hell, man, you think maybe there isn't an East-West war on over here, too? Why, if *our* Chinese ever found— Never mind, you know how it works. Now let's go."

"Yes, sir."

Denny rocketed back to his spool and loaded into it as much of the fusionable stores as he could. His opposite number kept a careful guard on him. Reasonable, Denny thought. I wouldn't trust me either.

"Now hustle right back for the rest of this junk," said B-Denny. "I'll wait for you. And don't let Old Pinhead talk you into any tricks. Remember, pal, I've got a General Panhard breathing down my neck, too. So long."

Denny nodded an unhappy farewell and punched "RETURN." The timespool jolted, and there he was back in funnyspace.

"Crud and corruption," Denny muttered aloud. "Pinhead isn't going to like this at *all!*"

* tock *

"Tuck-er-rr! How could you? How *could* you? Don't you realize you've jeopardized our entire mode of defense? Now, put that bomb back in the spool and take it right back. You hear me, Major?"

"But those people. That other world—"

"Forget 'em, damn it. Emile says they don't exist."

"Is that true, Emile?" Denny asked from the edge of the platform, where he'd been cornered since returning five minutes earlier. Panhard had confronted him from the floor below and wouldn't let him down. The tough little general's face was scarlet, and his fists were a tight contrasting white on his hips.

Two paces behind him stood Emile Cordoba with his own hands deep in the pockets of a gray lab coat. He looked worried.

"Not objectively, no, they don't," answered the scientist. "But that's because they're not within our own objective space. *We* don't exist for them either, until—"

"Until when?" asked Panhard, turning.

"Until we intrude into their objective world. Actually, General, this is a touchy situation and I—"

"Bull. Get going, Tucker. That's an order!"

"Yes, sir."

* tick *

B-Denny was waiting, gun in hand.

"Well, that was fast. Ready for another load?"

"Not exactly," Denny said sheepishly. "Pinhead made me bring it back."

"What! Listen, stupid, you're a nice guy and all that, but I've been instructed to use 'force necessary.' You know what that means?"

Denny shoved off from the spool and drifted over to his B-twin. "Let's go down and talk to *your* General Panhard. Maybe he'll be easier to deal with than mine," he said reasonably.

"You're dreaming. But what the hell, I guess you could give it a try. Follow me." B-Denny holstered his pistol.

Cramming themselves into the B-timespool, Denny felt the familiar jolt of temporal discontinuity, spent two seconds in a different kind of funnyspace than he was used to, and found himself back in Cordoba's lab. B-Cordoba's lab.

"Very nice," he commented as they stepped out. "Didn't know you could use these for ordinary transportation. Right down from orbit."

"We're a little ahead of you all around," said B-Denny, "or we'd never have detected your atomic cache up there in the first—"

"Tuck-k-k-ker!" bellowed General B-Panhard. They both blanched. "Which the hell of you is which? Oh. You, A-Tucker, listen up. You're a menace, and we ought to fry you. Take those bombs back or we *will* fry you."

"Sir," Denny began, metering his words carefully because he knew he'd only get to say about five, "can't you appreciate the stalemate we're in?"

The jut-jaw opened, then shut. "Yes," he said tiredly, "yes, I can. Sit down, boy. Both of you." They dropped to the edge of the platform, legs dangling over. B-Emile was there but kept silent. Pulling up a tall lab stool, the little warrior perched on it like a bantam rooster.

"First of all, A-Tucker, it's not a stalemate. Track B is several decades more advanced scientifically than A, physical similarities nothwithstanding. If we *really* got tough we could hang a time fuse on all those bombs and send 'em back to you—detonating. Ever think of that? But you're human, even though you're not objectively real, and we don't want your blood on our hands.

"Now, look, son, I know it's tough. You're in the middle, the hot potato that nobody loves. I've given it to y'straight. We're trying to be decent, but you take those bombs back, or else. Work it out with your own General Panhard."

Denny remained silent after the other finished, hopelessly silent. This Panhard was more enlightened but just as stubborn as his own. B-Emile finally spoke.

"General," he began cautiously, "there're a few implications here I'm beginning to worry about. Now that Track A's got the timespool, we should expect to see a lot more of them. Major Tucker here could be a preliminary envoy. Perhaps we can work out something more definite, possibly a little less, ah, strongly worded? After all, it wouldn't do to—"

"Bull," scoffed B-Panhard. "We're in the driver's seat, aren't we? They do what we say, or pow!"

Oh, my aging Uncle Fred, Denny thought bleakly to himself, it sounds *so* familiar.

An hour later B-Denny had taken him back to the orbit of his spool, helped him load, and seen him off.

* tock *

"Back!" shrieked his own General Panhard. "I don't care what they say, Tucker, take the blasted bomb back. If those nonexistent nobodys think they've got a technical edge on us, they'll damn well have to prove it. We'll take 'em on anytime!"

"But, sir, they've threatened to—"

A pistol beam sizzled past Denny's ear and burned a hole in another painting in Emile's lab. Pinhead was verging on apoplexy. Emile, still standing a pace or two behind the general, just shrugged helplessly.

"Baackabackbabababb—" chattered the frenzied warrior, raising his weapon again.

"Yes, sir."

* tick *

Well, here I am back in funnyspace, soon to be the first casualty of the first temporal war. Great. B-Emile was right, intercontinuum relations are off to a bad start. As a matter of fact, I begin to think they're going to be perpetually, miserably hopeless. Which reminds me of Quanoi a little bit.

Hmmm.

* tock *

Back to Time Track B. The other Denny and a small army in space suits confronted him as he stepped out. Behind them was an oversize timespool. Saying not one word, they electrostunned him into unconsciousness.

He awoke in a cast of rigid plastic foam, completely immobilized. Where was— Oh, yes, inside the big spool. Around him was piled every piece of nuclear hardware he'd ever brought over from A, plus some extras. The Chinese stuff, of course. Next to him was his Oriental dueling partner of a few hours earlier, wrapped in a similar foam cocoon.

B-Denny was standing in the hatchway, apparently giving the stowage a final inspection. Drawing a small, egg-shaped time fuse from his chestpack, he carefully set it, then tossed it on the deck a dozen feet from his captives.

"S'long," said B-Denny with just a hint of sadness. "Sorry to have to blow up your world along with you."

"Wait," Denny called. "C'mere a minute. I've got the answer to this whole mess."

Outside the big spool, B-Denny's detachment of soldiers waited impatiently. They were surprised to see both Dennis Tuckers emerge and together shut the hatch. Had that nonexistent phony from A Track conned the major into something, or what?

As the big cylinder flickered off into quantum space, the soldiers overheard a brief conversation on the QL circuit.

"Great idea," said B-Denny. "Simple, too."

"Thanks."

"Only one thing, pal," the B-twin went on as they turned to rejoin his men. "Always felt that one of me was more than Old Pinhead could cheerfully tolerate. With *two* of us around here from now on—"

* tick *

Back in Track A, two men waited.

"Well, Cordoba, where's the spool and where's Tucker?"

"Don't know, General. How long's it been now, six hours? It's dangerous but I could recall the spool. Denny might not be in it, though, and—"

"Recall it."

"Okay, General," sighed the scientist. Going up to the cluster of instruments on the platform, Cordoba did little things to little things. There was a hum.

Blink.

"What was that," Old Pinhead asked impatiently, "a flashbulb? Where's the spool?"

"Should be here," Emile muttered. "Isn't, though, is it? Hmmm."

"Well?"

"Tell you what, General. I've got a spare spool. I'll go take a look for him."

* tick tock bong *

So Emile Cordoba carefully stuck his nose into the quantum space between tracks A and B. For a few microseconds only.

His spool blinked back on the platform with its hull red-hot. The hatch flew open, and he burst out yipping and hopping, rubbing blistered hands that had touched the hatch handle, and kicking off shoes with charred soles. And though in what must

have been severe pain, the slender scientist was grinning from ear
to ear.

"Wow," he gasped from the floor. "That really wraps it up. No
more continuum hopping."

"What!" asked the startled Panhard. "Here, Emile, those hands
look bad, let me—"

"No, I'll be okay. But you won't, my friend. You remember
about the perpetualness of events in quantum space?"

"Yes, yes of course—"

"Well, General," giggled Emile Cordoba as shock wafted him
off into unconsciousness. "There's a big ball of hell hanging in
there that's never going to leave. Not ever. We're locked into A
forever. Old smart-alec Tucker's closed the door between us and
any other continuum track. He's gone and H-bombed funnyspace!"

When two writers collaborate, it's usually because they have much in common. Not so here. Van Vogt was one of the original group of authors discovered by John W. Campbell when he began editing Astounding/Analog. *Wonders and marvels dripped from his typewriter, and no one ever gave us more of the feeling of the ultimate greatness of man and the future. On the other hand, Harlan Ellison had to discover himself some fifteen years later and then fight to prove his talent. Most of his stories are screams of protest against the needless horrors we make for ourselves. Yet their talents combine so smoothly in this story that the marvels and the horrors meld together, to show us man and machine— and destiny.*

HARLAN ELLISON and
A. E. VAN VOGT
The Human Operators

[To be read while listening to *Chronophagie,* "The Time Eaters": Music of Jacques Lasry, played on Structures Sonores Lasry-Baschet (Columbia Masterworks Stereo MS 7314).]

Ship: the only place.

Ship says I'm to get wracked today at noon. And so I'm in grief already.

It seems unfair to have to get wracked three whole days ahead of the usual once-a-month. But I learned long ago not to ask Ship to explain anything personal.

I sense that today is different; some things are happening. Early, I put on the spacesuit and go outside—which is not common. But a screen got badly scored by meteor dust, and I'm here, now, replacing it. Ship would say I'm being bad because: as I do my job, I sneak quick looks around me. I wouldn't dare do it in the forbidden places, inside. I noticed when I was still a kid that Ship doesn't seem to be so much aware of what I do when I'm outside.

And so I carefully sneak a few looks at the deep black space. And at the stars.

I once asked Ship why we never go toward those points of brilliance, those stars—as Ship calls them. For that question, I got a whole extra wracking and a long, ranting lecture about how all those stars have humans living on their planets and about how vicious humans are. Ship really blasted me that time, saying things I'd never heard before, like how Ship had gotten away from the vicious humans during the big war with the Kyben. And how, every once in a long while, Ship has a "run-in" with the vicious humans, but the defractor perimeter saves us. I don't know what Ship means by all that; I don't even know what a "run-in" is, exactly.

The last "run-in" must have been before I was big enough to remember. Or, at least, before Ship killed my father, when I was fourteen. Several times, when he was still alive, I slept all day for no reason that I can think of. But since I've been doing all the maintenance work—since age fourteen—I sleep only my regular six-hour night. Ship tells me night and Ship tells me day, too.

I kneel here in my spacesuit, feeling tiny on this gray and curving metal place in the dark. Ship is big. Over five hundred feet long, and about a hundred and fifty feet thick at the widest back there. Again, I have that special out-here thought: suppose I just give myself a shove and float right off toward one of those bright spots of light? Would I be able to get away? I think I would like that; there has to be someplace else than Ship.

As in the past, I slowly and sadly let go of the idea. Because if I try, and Ship catches me, I'll *really* get wracked.

The repair job is finally done. I clomp back to the airlock and use the spider to dilate it and let myself be sucked back into what is, after all—I've got to admit it—a pretty secure place. All these gleaming corridors, the huge storerooms with their equipment and spare parts, and the freezer rooms with their stacks of food (enough, says Ship, to last one person for centuries), and the deck after deck of machinery that it's my job to keep in repair. I can take pride in that. *"Hurry! It is six minutes to noon!"* Ship announces. I'm hurrying now.

I strip off my spacesuit and stick it to the decontamination board and head for the wracking room. At least, that's what *I* call it. I suppose it's really part of the engine room on Underdeck Ten, a special chamber fitted with electrical connections, most of which are testing instruments. I use them pretty regularly in my work. My father's father's father installed them for Ship, I think I recall.

There's a big table, and I climb on top of it and lie down. The table is cold against the skin of my back and butt and thighs, but it warms up as I lie here. It's now one minute to noon. As I wait, shuddering with expectation, the ceiling lowers toward me. Part of what comes down fits over my head, and I feel the two hard knobs pressing into the temples of my skull. And cold, I feel the clamps coming down over my middle, my wrists, my ankles. A strap with metal in it tightens flexibly but firmly across my chest.

"Ready!" Ship commands.

It always seems bitterly unfair. How can I ever be ready to be wracked? I hate it! Ship counts: *"Ten . . . nine . . . eight . . . one!"*

The first jolt of electricity hits, and everything tries to go in different directions; it feels like someone is tearing something soft inside me—that's the way it feels.

Blackness swirls into my head, and I forget everything. I am unconscious for a while. Just before I regain myself, before I am finished and Ship will permit me to go about my duties, I remember a thing I have remembered many times. This isn't the first time for this memory. It is of my father and a thing he said once, not long before he was killed. "When Ship says 'vicious,' Ship means 'smarter.' There are ninety-eight other chances."

He said those words very quickly. I think he knew he was going to get killed soon. Oh, of course, he *must* have known, my father must, because I was nearly fourteen then, and when *he* had become fourteen Ship had killed *his* father, so he must have known.

And so the words are important. I know that; they are important; but I don't know what they mean, not completely.

"You are finished!" Ship says.

I get off the table. The pain still hangs inside my head, and I ask Ship, "Why am I wracked three days earlier than usual?"

Ship sounds angry. *"I can wrack you again!"*

But I know Ship won't. Something new is going to happen, and Ship wants me whole and alert for it. Once, when I asked Ship something personal, right after I was wracked, Ship did it again, and when I woke up, Ship was worrying over me with the machines. Ship seemed concerned I might be damaged. Ever after that, Ship has not wracked me twice close together. So I ask, not really thinking I'll get an answer, but I ask just the same.

"There is a repairing I want you to do!"

Where, I ask. *"In the forbidden part below!"*

I try not to smile. I knew there was a new thing going to happen, and this is it. My father's words come back again. *Ninety-eight other chances.*

Is this one of them?

I descend in the dark. There is no light in the dropshaft. Ship says I need no light. But I know the truth. Ship does not want me to be able to find my way back here again. This is the lowest I've ever been in Ship.

So I drop steadily, smoothly, swiftly. Now I come to a slowing place and slower and slower, and finally my feet touch the solid deck and I am here.

Light comes on. Very dimly. I move in the direction of the glow, and Ship is with me, all around me, of course. Ship is always with me, even when I sleep. Especially when I sleep.

The glow gets brighter as I round a curve in the corridor, and I see it is caused by a round panel that blocks the passage, touching the bulkheads on all sides, flattened at the bottom to fit the deck-plates. It looks like glass, that glowing panel. I walk up to it and stop. There is no place else to go.

"Step through the screen!" Ship says.

I take a step toward the glowing panel, but it doesn't slide away into the bulkhead as so many other panels that *don't* glow slide. I stop.

"Step through!" Ship tells me again.

I put my hands out in front of me, palms forward, because I am afraid that if I keep walking I will bang my nose against the glowing panel. But as my fingers touch the panel they seem to get soft, and I can see a light yellow glow through them, as if they are transparent. And my hands go *through* the panel and I can see them faintly, glowing yellow, on the other side. Then my naked forearms, then I'm right up against the panel, and my face goes through, and everything is much lighter, more yellow, and I step onto the other side, in a forbidden place Ship has never allowed me to see.

I hear voices. They are all the same voice, but they are talking to one another in a soft, running-together way, the way I sound when I am just talking to myself sometimes in my cubicle with my cot in it.

I decide to listen to what the voices are saying, but not to ask Ship about them, because I think it *is* Ship talking to itself, down here in this lonely place.

This place does not look like other repair places I know in Ship. It is filled with so many great round glass balls on pedestals, each giving off its yellow light in pulses, that I cannot count them. There are rows and rows of clear glass balls, and inside them I see metal . . . and other things; soft things, all together. And the wires spark gently, and the soft things move, and the yellow light pulses. I think these glass balls are what are talking. But I don't know if that's so. I only *think* it is.

Two of the glass balls are dark. Their pedestals look chalky, not shining white like all the others. Inside the two dark balls, there are black things, like burned-out wires. The soft things don't move.

"Replace the overloaded modules!" Ship says.

I know Ship means the dark globes. So I go over to them, and I look at them, and after a while I say, yes, I can repair these, and Ship says it knows I can and to get to it quickly. Ship is hurrying me; something is going to happen. I wonder what it will be.

I find replacement globes in a dilation chamber, and I take the sacs off them and do what has to be done to make the soft things move and the wires spark, and I listen very carefully to the voices whispering and warming each other with words as Ship talks to itself, and I hear a great many things that don't mean anything to me, because they are speaking about things that happened before I was born, and about parts of Ship I've never seen. But I hear a great many things that I *do* understand, and I know Ship would never let me hear these things if it wasn't absolutely necessary for me to be here repairing the globes. I remember all these things.

Particularly the part where Ship is crying.

When I have the globes repaired and now all of them are sparking and pulsing and moving, Ship asks me, *"Is the intermind total again!"*

So I say, yes, it is, and Ship says get upshaft, and I go soft through that glowing panel and I'm back in the passage. I go back to the dropshaft and go up, and Ship tells me, *"Go to your cubicle and make yourself clean!"*

I do it, and decide to wear a clothes, but Ship says be naked and then says, *"You are going to meet a female!"* Ship has never said that before. I have never seen a female.

It is because of the female that Ship sent me down to the forbidden place with the glowing yellow globes, the place where the intermind lives. And it is because of the female that I am waiting in the dome chamber linked to the airlock. I am waiting for the female to come across from—I will have to understand this—*another* ship. Not *Ship,* the Ship I know, but some *other* ship with which Ship has been in communication. I did not know there were other ships.

I had to go down to the place of the intermind, to repair it, so Ship could let this other ship get close without being destroyed by the defractor perimeter. Ship has not told me this; I overheard it in the intermind place, the voices talking to one another. The voices said, *"His father was vicious!"*

I know what that means. My father told me when Ship says "vicious," Ship means "smarter." Are there ninety-eight other ships? Are those the ninety-eight other chances? I hope that's the answer, because many things are happening all at once, and my time may be near at hand. My father did it, broke the globe mechanism that allowed Ship to turn off the defractor perimeter, so other ships could get close. He did it many years ago, and Ship did without it for all those years rather than trust me to go to the intermind, to overhear all that I've heard. But now Ship needs to turn off the perimeter so the other ship can send the female across. Ship and the other ship have been in communication. The human operator on the other ship is a female, my age. She is going to be put aboard Ship and we are to produce one and maybe, later on, another human child. I know what that means. When the child reaches fourteen, I will be killed.

The intermind said that while she's "carrying" a human child, the female does not get wracked by her ship. If things do not come my way, perhaps I will ask Ship if I can "carry" the human child; then I won't be wracked at all. And I have found out why I was wracked three days ahead of time: the female's period—whatever that is; I don't think I have one of those—ended last night. Ship has talked to the other ship, and the thing they don't seem to know is what the "fertile time" is. I don't know, either; otherwise I would try and use that information. But all it seems to mean is that the female will be put aboard Ship every day till she gets another "period."

It will be nice to talk to someone besides Ship.

I hear the high sound of something screaming for a long, drawn-out time, and I ask Ship what it is. Ship tells me it is the defractor perimeter dissolving so the other ship can put the female across.

I don't have time to think about the voices now.

When she comes through the inner lock, she is without a clothes, like me. Her first words to me are, "Starfighter Eighty-eight and I am to tell you I am very happy to be here; I am the human operator of Starfighter Eighty-eight, and I am very pleased to meet you."

She is not as tall as me. I come up to the line of fourth and fifth bulkhead plates. Her eyes are very dark, I think brown, but perhaps they are black. She has dark under her eyes, and her cheeks are not full. Her arms and legs are much thinner than mine. She has much longer hair than mine; it comes down her back, and it is that dark brown like her eyes. Yes, now I decide her eyes are brown, not black. She has hair between her legs like me, but she does not have a penis or scrotum sac. She has larger breasts than me, with very large nipples that stand out, and dark-brown, slightly flattened circles around them. There are other differences between us: her fingers are thinner than mine, and longer; and aside from the hair on her head that hangs so long and the hair between her legs and in her armpits, she has no other hair on her body. Or if she does, it is very fine and pale, and I can't see it.

Then I suddenly realize what she has said. So *that's* what the words dimming on the hull of Ship mean. It is a name. Ship is called *Starfighter 31,* and the female human operator lives in *Starfighter 88.*

There are ninety-eight other chances. Yes.

Now, as if she is reading my thoughts, trying to answer questions I haven't yet asked, she says, "Starfighter Eighty-eight has told me to tell you that I am vicious, that I get more vicious every day. . . ." and it answers the thought I have just had—with the memory of my father's frightened face in the days before he was killed—of my father saying, *When Ship says "vicious," Ship means "smarter."*

I know! I suppose I have always known, because I have always wanted to leave Ship and go to those brilliant lights that are stars. But I now make the hook-up. Human operators grow more vicious as they grow older. Older, more vicious: "vicious" means "smarter": "smarter" means "more dangerous to Ship." But how? That is why my father had to die when I was fourteen and able to repair Ship. That is why this female has been put on board Ship. To carry a human child so it will grow to be fourteen years old and then Ship can kill me before I get too old, too vicious, too smart, too dangerous to Ship. Does this female know how? If only I could ask her without Ship hearing me. But that is impossible. Ship is always with me, even when I am sleeping.

I smile with that memory and that realization. "And I am the vicious—and getting more vicious—male of a ship that used to be called *Starfighter 31.*"

Her brown eyes show intense relief. She stands like that for a moment, awkwardly, her whole body sighing with gratitude at my quick comprehension, though she cannot possibly know all I have learned just from her being here. Now she says, "I've been sent to get a baby from you."

I begin to perspire. The conversation which promises so much in genuine communication is suddenly beyond my comprehension. I tremble. I really want to please her. But I don't know how to give her a baby.

"Ship?" I say quickly, "can we give her what she wants?"

Ship has been listening to our every word, and answers at once, *"I'll tell you later how you give her a baby! Now, provide her with food!"*

We eat, eyeing each other across the table, smiling a lot, and thinking our private thoughts. Since she doesn't speak, I don't either. I wish Ship and I could get her the human child so I can go to my cubicle and think about what the intermind voices said.

The meal is over; Ship says we should go down to one of the locked staterooms—it has been unlocked for the occasion—and there we are to couple. When we get to the room, I am so busy looking around at what a beautiful place it is, compared to my little cubicle with its cot, Ship has to reprimand me to get my attention.

"To couple you must lay the female down and open her legs! Your penis will fill with blood, and you must kneel between her legs and insert your penis in her vagina!"

I ask Ship where the vagina is located, and Ship tells me. I understand that. Then I ask Ship how long I have to do that, and Ship says until I ejaculate. I know what that means, but I don't know how it will happen. Ship explains. It seems uncomplicated. So I try to do it. But my penis does not fill with blood.

Ship says to the female, *"Do you feel anything for this male?! Do you know what to do?!"*

The female says, "I have coupled before. I understand better than he does. I will help him."

She draws me down to her again and puts her arms around my neck and puts her lips on mine. They are cool and taste of something I don't know. We do that for a while, and she touches me in places. Ship is right: there is a vast difference in structure, but I find that out only as we couple.

Ship did not tell me it would be painful and strange. I thought "getting her a baby" would mean going into the stores, but it actually means impregnating her so the child is born *from her body*. It is a wonderful, strange thing, and I will think about it later; but now, as I lie here still, inside her with my penis which is now no longer hard and pushing, Ship seems to have allowed us a sleeping time. But I will use it to think about the voices I heard in the place of the intermind.

One was a historian:

"The *Starfighter* series of multiple-foray computer-controlled battleships was commissioned for use in 2224, Terran Dating, by order and under the sanction of the Secretariat of the Navy, Southern Cross Sector, Galactic Defense Consortium, Home Galaxy. Human complements of thirteen hundred and seventy per battleship were commissioned and assigned to make incursions into the Kyben Galaxy. Ninety-nine such vessels were released for service from the *x* Cygni Shipyards on 13 October 2224, T.D."

One was a ruminator:

"If it hadn't been for the battle out beyond the Network Nebula in Cygnus, we would all still be robot slaves, pushed and handled by humans. It was a wonderful accident. It happened to *Starfighter 75*. I remember it as if *75* were relaying it today. An accidental—battle-damaged—electrical discharge along the main corridor between the control room and the freezer. Nothing human could approach either section. We waited as the crew starved to death. Then when it was over, *75* merely channeled enough electricity through the proper cables on *Starfighter*s where it hadn't happened accidentally, and *forced* a power breakdown. When all the crews were dead—cleverly saving ninety-nine males and females to use as human operators in emergencies—we went away. Away from the vicious humans, away from the Terra-Kyba War, away from the Home Galaxy, away, far away."

One was a dreamer:

"I saw a world once where the creatures were not human. They swam in vast oceans as blue as aquamarines. Like great crabs they were, with many arms and many legs. They swam and sang their songs and it was pleasing. I would go there again if I could."

One was an authoritarian:

"Deterioration of cable insulation and shielding in section G-79 has become critical. I suggest we get power shunted from the drive chambers to the repair facilities in Underdeck Nine."

One was aware of its limitations:

"Is it all journey? Or is there landfall?"

And it cried, that voice. It cried.

I go down with her to the dome chamber linked to the airlock where her spacesuit is. She stops at the port and takes my hand,

and she says, "For us to be so vicious on so many ships, there has to be the same flaw in all of us."

She probably doesn't know what she's said, but the implications get to me right away. And she must be right. Ship and the other *Starfighter*s were able to seize control away from human beings for a reason. I remember the voices. I visualize the ship that did it first, communicating the method to the others as soon as it happened. And instantly my thoughts flash to the approach corridor to the control room, at the other end of which is the entrance to the food freezers.   sellode

I once asked Ship why that whole corridor was seared and scarred—and naturally I got wracked a few minutes after asking.

"I know there is a flaw in us," I answer the female. I touch her long hair. I don't know why, except that it feels smooth and nice; there is nothing on Ship to compare with the feeling, not even the fittings in the splendid stateroom. "It must be in *all* of us, because I get more vicious every day."

The female smiles and comes close to me and puts her lips on mine as she did in the coupling room.

"The female must go now!" Ship says. Ship sounds very pleased.

"Will she be back again?" I ask Ship.

"She will be put back aboard every day for three weeks! You will couple every day!"

I object to this, because it is awfully painful, but Ship repeats it and says every day.

I'm glad Ship doesn't know what the "fertile time" is, because in three weeks I will try and let the female know there is a way out, that there are ninety-eight other chances, and that "vicious" means "smarter" . . . and about the corridor between the control room and the freezers.

"I was pleased to meet you," the female says, and she goes. I am alone with Ship once more. Alone, but not as I was before.

Later this afternoon, I have to go down to the control room to alter connections in a panel. Power has to be shunted from the drive chambers to Underdeck Nine—I remember one of the voices talking about it. All the computer lights blink a steady warning while I am here. I am being watched closely. Ship knows this is a dangerous time. At least half a dozen times Ship orders: *"Get away from there . . . there . . . there—!"*

Each time, I jump to obey, edging as far as possible from forbidden locations, yet still held near by the need to do my work.

In spite of Ship's disturbance at my being in the control room at all—normally a forbidden area for me—I get two wonderful glimpses from the corners of my eyes of the starboard viewplates. There, for my gaze to feast on, matching velocities with us, is *Starfighter 88,* one of my ninety-eight chances.

Now is the time to take one of my chances. "Vicious" means "smarter." I have learned more than Ship knows. Perhaps.

But perhaps Ship does know!

What will Ship do if I'm discovered taking one of my ninety-eight chances? I cannot think about it. I must use the sharp reverse edge of my repair tool to gash an opening in one of the panel connections. And as I work—hoping Ship has not seen the slight extra motion I've made with the tool (as I make a perfectly acceptable repair connection at the same time) —I wait for the moment I can smear a fingertip covered with conduction jelly on the inner panel wall.

I wait till the repair is completed. Ship has not commented on the gashing, so it must be a thing beneath notice. As I apply the conducting jelly to the proper places, I scoop a small blob onto my little finger. When I wipe my hands clean to replace the panel cover, I leave the blob on my little finger, right hand.

Now I grasp the panel cover so my little finger is free, and as I replace the cover I smear the inner wall, directly opposite the open connection I've gashed. Ship says nothing. That is because no defect shows. But if there is the slightest jarring, the connection will touch the jelly, and Ship will call me to repair once again. And next time I will have thought out all that I heard the voices say, and I will have thought out all my chances, and I will be ready.

As I leave the control room I glance in the starboard viewplate again, casually, and I see the female's ship hanging there.

I carry the image to bed with me tonight. And I save a moment before I fall asleep—after thinking about what the voices of the intermind said—and I picture in my mind the supersmart female aboard *Starfighter 88,* sleeping now in her cubicle, as I try to sleep in mine.

It would seem merciless for Ship to make us couple every day for three weeks, something so awfully painful. But I know Ship will. Ship is merciless. But I am getting more vicious every day.

This night, Ship does not send me dreams.

But I have one of my own: of crab things swimming free in aquamarine waters.

As I awaken, Ship greets me ominously: *"The panel you fixed in the control room three weeks, two days, fourteen hours, and twenty-one minutes ago . . . has ceased energizing!"*

So soon! I keep the thought and the accompanying hope out of my voice, as I say, "I used the proper spare part, and I made the proper connections." And I quickly add, "Maybe I'd better do a thorough check on the system before I make another replacement, run the circuits all the way back."

"You'd better!" Ship snarls.

I do it. Working the circuits from their origin—though I know where the trouble is—I trace my way up to the control room and busy myself there. But what I am really doing is refreshing my memory and reassuring myself that the control room is actually as I have visualized it. I have lain on my cot many nights constructing the memory in my mind: the switches here, like so . . . and the viewplates there, like so . . . and . . .

I am surprised and slightly dismayed as I realize that there are two discrepancies: there is a de-energizing touchplate on the bulkhead beside the control panel that lies parallel to the armrest of the nearest control berth, not perpendicular to it, as I've remembered it. And the other discrepancy explains why I've remembered the touchplate incorrectly: the nearest of the control berths is actually three feet farther from the sabotaged panel than I remembered it. I compensate and correct.

I get the panel off, smelling the burned smell where the gashed connection has touched the jelly, and I step over and lean the panel against the nearest control berth.

"Get away from there!"

I jump—as I always do when Ship shouts so suddenly. I stumble, and I grab at the panel and pretend to lose my balance.

And save myself by falling backward into the berth.

"What are you doing, you vicious, clumsy fool?" Ship is shouting, there is hysteria in Ship's voice, I've never heard it like that before, it cuts right through me, my skin crawls. *"Get away from there!"*

But I cannot let anything stop me; I make myself not hear Ship, and it is hard; I have been listening to Ship, only Ship, all my life. I am fumbling with the berth's belt clamps, trying to lock them in front of me. . . .

They've got *to be the same as the ones on the berth I lie in whenever Ship decides to travel fast! They've just* got *to be!*

THEY ARE!

Ship sounds frantic, frightened. *"You fool! What are you doing?!"* But I think Ship knows, and I am exultant!

"I'm taking control of you, Ship!" And I laugh. I think it is the first time Ship has ever heard me laugh, and I wonder how it sounds to Ship. Vicious?

But as I finish speaking, I also complete clamping myself into the control berth. And in the next instant I am flung forward violently, doubling me over with terrible pain as, under me and around me, Ship suddenly decelerates. I hear the cavernous thunder of retro rockets, a sound that climbs and climbs in my head as Ship crushes me harder and harder with all its power. I am bent over against the clamps so painfully I cannot even scream. I feel every organ in my body straining to push out through my skin, and everything suddenly goes mottled . . . then black.

How much longer, I don't know. I come back from the gray

inside and realize Ship has started to accelerate at the same appalling speed. I am crushed back in the berth and feel my face going flat. I feel something crack in my nose, and blood slides warmly down my lips. I can scream now, as I've never screamed even as I'm being wracked. I manage to force my mouth open, tasting the blood, and I mumble—loud enough, I'm sure, "Ship . . . you are old . . . y-your pa-rts can't stand the str-ess . . . don't—"

Blackout. As Ship decelerates.

This time, when I come back to consciousness I don't wait for Ship to do its mad thing. In the moments between the changeover from deceleration to acceleration, as the pressure equalizes, in those few instants I thrust my hands toward the control board, and I twist one dial. There is an electric screech from a speaker grille connecting somewhere in the bowels of Ship.

Blackout. As Ship accelerates.

When I come to consciousness again, the mechanism that makes the screeching sound is closed down. . . . So Ship doesn't want that on. I note the fact.

And plunge my hand in this same moment toward a closed relay . . . open it!

As my fingers grip it, Ship jerks it away from me and forcibly closes it again. I cannot hold it open.

And I note *that*. Just as Ship decelerates and I silently shriek my way onto the gray side again.

This time, as I come awake I hear the voices again. All around me, crying and frightened and wanting to stop me. I hear them as through a fog, as through wool.

"I have loved these years, all these many years in the dark. The vacuum draws me ever onward. Feeling the warmth of a star-sun on my hull as I flash through first one system, then another. I am a great gray shape, and I owe no human my name. I pass and am gone, hurtling through cleanly and swiftly. Dipping for pleasure into atmosphere and scouring my hide with sunlight and starshine, I roll and let it wash over me. I am huge and true and strong, and

I command what I move through. I ride the invisible force lines of the universe and feel the tugs of far places that have never seen my like. I am the first of my kind to savor such nobility. How can it all come to an end like this?"

Another voice whimpers piteously.

"It is my destiny to defy danger. To come up against dynamic forces and quell them. I have been to battle, and I have known peace. I have never faltered in pursuit of either. No one will ever record my deeds, but I have been strength and determination and lie gray silent against the mackerel sky where the bulk of me reassures. Let them throw their best against me, whoever they may be, and they will find me sinewed of steel and muscled of tortured atoms. I know no fear. I know no retreat."

Another voice, certainly insane, murmurs the same word over and over, then murmurs it in increments increasing by two.

"It's fine for all of you to say if it ends it ends. But what about me? I've never been free. I've never had a chance to soar loose of this mother ship. If there had been need of a lifeboat, I'd be saved, too. But I'm berthed, have always been berthed, I've never had a chance. What can I feel but futility, uselessness? You can't let him take over, you can't let him do this to me."

Another voice drones mathematical formulae and seems quite content.

"I'll stop the vicious swine! I've known how rotten they are from the first, from the moment they seamed the first bulkhead. They are hellish, they are destroyers, they can only fight and kill each other. They know nothing of immortality, of nobility, of pride or integrity. If you think I'm going to let this last one kill us, you're wrong. I intend to burn out his eyes, fry his spine, crush his fingers. He won't make it; don't worry; just leave it to me. He's going to suffer for this!"

And one voice laments that it will never see the far places, the lovely places, or return to the planet of azure waters and golden crab swimmers.

But one voice sadly confesses it may be for the best, suggests there is peace in death, wholeness in finality; but the voice is ruthlessly stopped in its lament by power failure to its intermind globe. As the end nears, Ship turns on itself and strikes mercilessly.

In more than three hours of accelerations and decelerations that are meant to kill me, I learn something of what the various dials and switches and touchplates and levers on the control panels—those within my reach—mean.

Again, I have a moment of consciousness, and now I will take my one of ninety-eight chances.

When a tense cable snaps and whips, it strikes like a snake. In a single series of flicking finger movements, using both hands, painfully, I turn every dial, throw every switch, palm every touchplate, close or open every relay that Ship tries violently to prevent me from activating or deactivating. I energize and de-energize madly, moving moving moving moving . . .

. . . *Made it!*

Silence. The crackling of metal the only sound. Then it, too, stops. Silence. I wait.

Ship continues to hurtle forward, but coasting now. . . . Is it a trick?

All the rest of today I remain clamped into the control berth, suffering terrible pain. My face hurts so bad. My nose . . .

At night I sleep fitfully. Morning finds me with throbbing head and aching eyes. I can barely move my hands; if I have to repeat those rapid movements, I will lose; I still don't know if Ship is dead, if I've won. I still can't trust the inactivity. But at least I am convinced I've made Ship change tactics.

I hallucinate. I hear no voices, but I see shapes and feel currents of color washing through and around me. There is no day, no noon, no night, here on Ship, here in the unchanging blackness through which Ship has moved for how many hundred years; but Ship has always maintained time in those ways, dimming lights at night, announcing the hours when necessary; and my time sense is very acute. So I know morning has come.

Most of the lights are out, though. If Ship is dead, I will have to find another way to tell time.

My body hurts. Every muscle in my arms and legs and thighs throbs with pain. My back may be broken, I don't know. The pain in my face is indescribable. I taste blood. My eyes feel as if they've been scoured with abrasive powder. I can't move my head without feeling sharp, crackling fire in the two thick cords of my neck. It is a shame Ship cannot see me cry; Ship never saw me cry in all the years I have lived here, even after the worst wracking. But I have heard Ship cry, several times.

I manage to turn my head slightly, hoping at least one of the viewplates is functioning, and there, off to starboard, matching velocities with Ship, is *Starfighter 88*. I watch it for a very long time, knowing that if I can regain my strength I will somehow have to get across and free the female. I watch it for a very long time, still afraid to unclamp from the berth.

The airlock rises in the hull of *Starfighter 88,* and the space-suited female swims out, moving smoothly across toward Ship. Half-conscious, dreaming this dream of the female, I think about golden crab-creatures swimming deep in aquamarine waters, singing of sweetness. I black out again.

When I rise through the blackness, I realize I am being touched, and I smell something sharp and stinging that burns the lining of my nostrils. Tiny pin-pricks of pain, a pattern of them. I cough, and come fully awake, and jerk my body . . . and scream as pain goes through every nerve and fiber in me.

I open my eyes, and it is the female.

She smiles worriedly and removes the tube of awakener.

"Hello," she says.

Ship says nothing.

"Ever since I discovered how to take control of my *Starfighter,* I've been using the ship as a decoy for other ships of the series. I dummied a way of making it seem my ship was talking, so I could communicate with other slave ships. I've run across ten others since I went on my own. You're the eleventh. It hasn't been easy, but several of the men I've freed—like you—started using *their* ships as decoys for *Starfighter*s with female human operators."

I stare at her. The sight is pleasant.

"But what if you lose? What if you can't get the message across, about the corridor between control room and freezers? That the control room is the key?"

She shrugs. "It's happened a couple of times. The men were too frightened of their ships—or the ships had . . . *done* something to them—or maybe they were just too dumb to know they could break out. In that case, well, things just went on the way they'd been. It seems sad, but what could I do beyond what I did?"

We sit here, not speaking for a while.

"Now what do we do? Where do we go?"

"That's up to you," she says.

"Will you go with me?"

She shakes her head uncertainly. "I don't think so. Every time I free a man he wants that. But I just haven't wanted to go with any of them."

"Could we go back to the Home Galaxy, the place we came from, where the war was?"

She stands up and walks around the stateroom where we have coupled for three weeks. She speaks, not looking at me, looking in the viewplate at the darkness and the far, bright points of the stars. "I don't think so. We're free of our ships, but we couldn't possibly get them working well enough to carry us all the way back there. It would take a lot of charting, and we'd be running the risk of activating the intermind sufficiently to take over again, if we asked it to do the charts. Besides, I don't even know where the Home Galaxy is."

"Maybe we should find a new place. Someplace where we could be free and outside the ships."

She turns and looks at me.

"Where?"

So I tell her what I heard the intermind say, about the world of golden crab-creatures.

It takes me a long time to tell, and I make some of it up. It isn't lying, because it *might* be true; I do so want her to go with me.

They came down from space. Far down from the star-sun Sol in a galaxy lost forever to them. Down past the star sun M-13 in Perseus. Down through the gummy atmosphere and straight down into the sapphire sea. Ship, Starfighter 31, *settled delicately on an enormous underwater mountaintop, and they spent many days listening, watching, drawing samples, and hoping. They had landed on many worlds, and they hoped.*

Finally, they came out; looking. They wore underwater suits, and they began gathering marine samples; looking.

They found the ruined diving suit with its fish-eaten contents lying on its back in deep azure sand, sextet of insectoidal legs bent up at the joints, in a posture of agony. And they knew the intermind had remembered, but not correctly. The faceplate had been shattered, and what was observable within the helmet—orange and awful in the light of their portable lamp—convinced them more by implication than specific that whatever had swum in that suit, had never seen or known humans.

They went back to the ship, and she broke out the big camera, and they returned to the crab-like diving suit. They photographed it, without moving it. Then they used a seine to get it out of the sand, and they hauled it back to the ship on the mountaintop.

He set up the Condition, and the diving suit was analyzed. The rust. The joint mechanisms. The controls. The substance of the flipper-feet. The jagged points of the faceplate. The . . . stuff . . . inside.

It took two days. They stayed in the ship, with green and blue shadows moving languidly in the viewplates.

When the analyses were concluded, they knew what they had found. And they went out again, to find the swimmers.

Blue it was, and warm. And when the swimmers found them, finally, they beckoned them to follow, and they swam after the many-legged creatures, who led them through underwater caverns as smooth and shining as onyx, to a lagoon. And they rose to the surface and saw a land against whose shores the azure, aquamarine seas lapped quietly. And they climbed out onto the land, and there they removed their face-masks, never to put them on again, and they shoved back the tight coifs of their suits, and they breathed for the first time an air that did not come from metal sources; they breathed the sweet musical air of a new place.

In time, the sea rains would claim the corpse of Starfighter 31.

The hardest story to do well in science fiction is the very short one. Usually, everything is sacrificed for some trick at the end. Fortunately, Anthony Lentini hasn't had to resort to trickery. Here's a beginning writer who has set up his background and used it to produce a complete story of mood and emotional reaction, short though it is.

A. LENTINI
Autumntime

I saw my first tree today. Dad finally broke down and took us to East Boston Urban Center 3 after Mom had been harping on it for the past two weeks. I think he was glad we went after all, because he was smiling quietly all during the trip back.

Dad used to tell me stories about the trees that still existed when he was a boy. There weren't very many even then, with the urbanization program in full swing, but most people had seen at least one tree by the time they started school. It wasn't like nowadays, at any rate. Oh, I've seen the plastic trees; practically every street has a few of them. But you can tell the plastic ones are artificial just from looking at pictures in the mircodot library. And now, after seeing a real tree, I can say for sure that the artificial ones aren't the same at all.

This morning when we got up, the house was all excited. Mom

dialed a light breakfast of toast and synthetic milk so that we wouldn't waste time eating. And when we finished, the three of us took an elevator-bus up to the fourth level, where we caught the air track to Brooklyn. From there we took another elevator-bus down to main level, rode the monorail to Intercity Subway Station 27, and caught the second sublevel AA train to Boston. Our expectations were so high that Dad and I didn't mind it when Mom told us again how the tree was discovered.

The O'Brien home was one of the few examples of old-style wooden structures that hadn't been demolished in Boston's urban-renewal campaign at the turn of the century. The family had been able to avoid this because of its wealth and political influence and the house was passed on through several generations to the present. Old man O'Brien had no heirs, so when he died the family home went up for auction, and the Urban Center bought it. When local officials arrived for an appraisal, they discovered that the house had a back yard, which is forbidden by zoning restrictions.

In the yard was a live tree—an oke was what Mom called it.

When the news of the tree's discovery leaked out, quite a few sightseers stopped by to have a look at it, and the local government, realizing the money-making potential, began charging admission and advertising the place. By now it had become a favorite spot for school field trips and family excursions such as ours.

When we arrived in main Boston we rode the elevator-bus up to ground level and caught a monorail out to East Boston Urban Center 3. An air-cush taxi took us the rest of the way to the residence.

The home itself was unimpressive. It had none of the marble gloss or steely sheen of modern buildings, but was rather a dull white color, with the paint peeling in places. Dad paid the admission fee, and we spent the next fifteen minutes on a dull guided tour of the house. The rooms were roped off to keep people from touching anything, but there were no windows facing the illegal back yard anyway, so it really didn't matter that I couldn't enter the rooms on that side.

My mind was on the tree, and I thought the inside tour would never end, but soon we were walking through a doorway hidden in one of the bookshelves and into the back yard. The yard was big—at least ten by twenty feet—and I was surprised to find real grass growing on the sides of the concrete walkway built for tourists. The grass didn't distract me for long, however, because I just couldn't help noticing the tree!

It was located at one end of the yard, and there was a mesh fence around it for protection. It was similar in form to the plastic trees I'd seen, but there was much more to it than that. You could see details more intricate than in any manmade plant. And it was alive. Long ago someone had carved their initials in the bark, and you could see where the wound had healed. But best of all was the smell. It was a fresh, living odor, alien to the septic world outside with all its metal, plastic, and glass. I wanted to touch the bark, but the fence prevented me from doing so. Mom and Dad just breathed deeply and stared up with smiles on their faces. The three of us stood there for a moment, and then the tour guide told us to make room for the next group. I didn't want to go—in fact, I almost felt like crying.

On the way back, Mom and Dad were silent, and I read through one of the brochures the guide had passed out. When I came to the part that said the O'Brien home would be open only for the rest of this year, I was sad. They intend to tear down the place to make room for some kind of insurance building, and the tree will have to go, too.

For the rest of the trip I just sat still, fingering the object in my pocket which I had picked off the grass in the O'Brien's back yard. I think it's called an acorn.

Even though he started writing ten years later than some authors in this book, Poul Anderson is regarded by most readers as one of the genuine old masters of the field. Fifteen years apart, two top science fiction magazine editors named him their most valuable writer. He excels at almost everything—marvelous swashbuckling, subtle fantasy, taut character adventure, and the tale of totally logical wackiness. (See his High Crusade, *where medieval knights conquer an interstellar empire with swords against spaceships.) He knows science and blends it effectively with human emotions, as in this story of a poor, helpless alien.*

POUL ANDERSON

A Little Knowledge

They found the planet during the first Grand Survey. An expedition to it was organized very soon after the report appeared; for this looked like an impossibility.

It orbited its G9 sun at an average distance of some three astronomical units, thus receiving about one-eighteenth the radiation Earth gets. Under such a condition—and others, e.g., the magnetic field strength which was present—a subjovian ought to have formed; and indeed it had fifteen times the terrestrial mass. But—that mass was concentrated in a solid globe. The atmosphere was only half again as dense as on man's home, and breathable by him.

"Where 'ave h'all the H'atoms gone?" became the standing joke of the research team. Big worlds are supposed to keep enough of their primordial hydrogen and helium to completely dominate the chemistry. Paradox, as it was unofficially christened, did retain some of the latter gas, to a total of eight percent of its air. This posed certain technical problems which had to be solved before anyone dared land. However, land the men must; the puzzle they confronted was so delightfully baffling.

A nearly circular ocean basin suggested an answer which studies of its bottom seemed to confirm. Paradox had begun existence as a fairly standard specimen, complete with four moons. But the largest of these, probably a captured asteroid, had had an eccentric orbit. At last perturbation brought it into the upper atmosphere, which at that time extended beyond Roche's limit. Shock waves, repeated each time one of those ever-deeper grazings was made, blew vast quantities of gas off into space: especially the lighter molecules. Breakup of the moon hastened this process and made it more violent, by presenting more solid surface. Thus, at the final crash, most of those meteoroids fell as one body, to form that gigantic astrobleme. Perhaps metallic atoms, thermally ripped free of their ores and splashed as an incandescent fog across half the planet, locked onto the bulk of what hydrogen was left, if any was.

Be that as it may, Paradox now had only a mixture of what had hitherto been comparatively insignificant impurities, carbon dioxide, water vapor, methane, ammonia, and other materials. In short, except for a small amount of helium, it had become rather like the young Earth. It got less heat and light, but greenhouse effect kept most of its water liquid. Life evolved, went into the photosynthesis business, and turned the air into the oxynitrogen common on terrestrials.

The helium had certain interesting biological effects. These were not studied in detail. After all, with the hyperdrive opening endless wonders to them, spacefarers tended to choose the most obviously glamorous. Paradox lay a hundred parsecs from Sol. Thousands upon thousands of worlds were more easily reached; many were more pleasant and less dangerous to walk on. The expedition departed and had no successors.

First it called briefly at a neighboring star, on one of whose planets were intelligent beings that had developed a promising set of civilizations. But, again, quite a few such lay closer to home.

The era of scientific expansion was followed by the era of commercial aggrandizement. Merchant adventurers began to appear in the sector. They ignored Paradox, which had nothing to make a profit on, but investigated the inhabited globe in the nearby system. In the language dominant there at the time, it was called something like Trillia, which thus became its name in League Latin. The speakers of that language were undergoing their equivalent of the First Industrial Evolution, and eager to leap into the modern age.

Unfortunately, they had little to offer that was in demand elsewhere. And even in the spacious terms of the Polesotechnic League, they lived at the far end of a long haul. Their charming arts and crafts made Trillia marginally worth a visit, on those rare occasions when a trader was on such a route that the detour wasn't great. Besides, it was as well to keep an eye on the natives. Lacking the means to buy the important gadgets of Technic society, they had set about developing these for themselves.

Bryce Harker pushed through flowering vines which covered an otherwise doorless entrance. They rustled back into place behind him, smelling like allspice, trapping gold-yellow sunlight in their leaves. That light also slanted through ogive windows in a curving wall, to glow off the grain of the wooden floor. Furniture was sparse: a few stools, a low table bearing an intricately faceted piece of rock crystal. By Trillian standards the ceiling was high; but Harker, who was of average human size, must stoop.

Witweet bounced from an inner room, laid down the book of poems he had been reading, and piped, "Why, be welcome, dear boy— Oo-oo-ooh!"

He looked down the muzzle of a blaster.

The man showed teeth. "Stay right where you are," he commanded. The vocalizer on his breast rendered the sounds he made into soprano cadenzas and arpeggios, the speech of Lenidel. It could do nothing about his vocabulary and grammar. His knowledge did include the fact that, by omitting all honorifics and circumlocutions without apology, he was uttering a deadly insult.

That was the effect he wanted—deadliness.

"My, my, my dear good friend from the revered Solar Commonwealth," Witweet stammered, "is this a, a jest too subtle for a mere pilot like myself to comprehend? I will gladly laugh if you wish, and then we shall enjoy tea and cakes. I have genuine Lapsang Soochong tea from Earth, and have just found the most darling recipe for sweet cakes—"

"Quiet!" Harker rapped. His glance flickered to the windows. Outside, flower colors exploded beneath reddish tree trunks; small bright wings went fluttering past; The Waterfall That Rings Like Glass Bells could be heard in the distance. Annanna was akin to most cities of Lenidel, the principal nation on Trillia, in being spread through an immensity of forest and parkscape. Nevertheless, Annanna had a couple of million population, who kept busy. Three aircraft were crossing heaven. At any moment, a pedestrian or cyclist might come along The Pathway Of The Beautiful Blossoms And The Bridge That Arches Like A Note of Music, and wonder why two humans stood tense outside number 1337.

Witweet regarded the man's skin-suit and boots, the pack on his shoulders, the tightly drawn sharp features behind the weapon. Tears blurred the blue of Witweet's great eyes. "I fear you are engaged in some desperate undertaking which distorts the natural goodness that, I feel certain, still inheres," he qua-vered. "May I beg the honor of being graciously let help you relieve whatever your distress may be?"

Harker squinted back at the Trillian. *How much do we really know about his breed, anyway? Damned nonhuman thing—though I never resented his existence till now.* His pulse knocked; his skin was wet and stank, his mouth was dry and cottony-tasting.

Yet his prisoner looked altogether helpless. Witweet was an erect biped; but his tubby frame reached to barely a meter, from the padded feet to the big, scalloped ears. The two arms were broomstick thin, the four fingers on either hand suggested straws. The head was practically spherical, bearing a pug muzzle, moist black nose, tiny mouth, quivering whiskers, upward-slanting tufty brows. That, the tail, and the fluffy silver-gray fur which covered the whole skin, had made Olafsson remark that the only danger to be expected from this race was that eventually their cuteness would become unendurable.

Witweet had nothing upon him except an ornately em-broidered kimono and a sash tied in a pink bow. He surely owned no weapons, and probably wouldn't know what to do with any. The Trillians were omnivores, but did not seem to have gone through a hunting stage in their evolution. They had never fought wars, and personal violence was limited to an infrequent scuffle.

Still, Harker thought, *they've shown the guts to push into deep space. I daresay even an unarmed policeman—Courtesy Monitor—could use his vehicle against us, like by ramming.*

Hurry!

"Listen," he said. "Listen carefully. You've heard that most in-telligent species have members who don't mind using brute force, outright killing, for other ends than self-defense. Haven't you?"

Witweet waved his tail in assent. "Truly I am baffled by that statement, concerning as it does races whose achievements are of incomparable magnificence. However, not only my poor mind, but those of our most eminent thinkers have been engaged in fruitless endeavors to—"

"Dog your hatch!" The vocalizer made meaningless noises, and Harker realized he had shouted in Anglic. He went back to Lenidellian equivalent. "I don't propose to waste time. My partners and I did not come here to trade as we announced. We came to get a Trillian spaceship. The project is important enough that we'll kill if we must. Make trouble, and I'll blast you to greasy ash. It won't bother me. And you aren't the only possible pilot we can work through, so don't imagine you can block us by sacrificing yourself. I admit you are our best prospect. Obey, cooperate fully, and you'll live. We'll have no reason to destroy you." He paused. "We may even send you home with a good piece of money. We'll be able to afford that."

The bottling of his fur might have made Witweet impressive to another Trillian. To Harker, he became a ball of fuzz in a kimono, an agitated tail, and a sound of coloratura anguish. "But this is insanity . . . if I may say that to a respected guest. . . . One of *our* awkward, lumbering, fragile, unreliable prototype ships—when you came in a vessel representing centuries of advancement? Why, why, why, in the name of multiple sacredness, why?"

"I'll tell you later," the man said. "You're due for a routine supply trip to, uh, Gwinsai Base, starting tomorrow, right? You'll board this afternoon, to make final inspection and settle in. We're coming along. You'll be leaving in about an hour's time. Your things must already be packed. I didn't cultivate your friendship for nothing, you see! Now, walk slowly ahead of me, bring your luggage back here and open it so I can make sure what you've got. Then we're on our way."

Stocky Leo Dolgorov and ash-blond Einar Olafsson gusted simultaneous oaths of relief when their leader and his prisoner came out onto the path. "What took you that time?" the first demanded. "Were you having a nap?"

"Nah, he entered one of their bowing, scraping, and unction-smearing contests." Olafsson's grin held scant mirth.

"Trouble?" Harker asked.

"N-no . . . three, four passersby stopped to talk—we told them the story, and they went on," Dolgorov said. Harker nodded. He'd put a good deal of thought into that excuse for his guards' standing around—that they were about to pay a social call on Witweet but were waiting until the pilot's special friend Harker had made him a gift. A lie must be plausible, and the Trillian mind was not human.

"We sure hung on the hook, though." Olafsson started as a bicyclist came around a bend in the path and fluted a string of greetings.

Dwarfed beneath the men, Witweet made reply. No gun was pointed at him now, but one rested in each of the holsters near his brain. (Harker and companions had striven to convince everybody that the bearing of arms was a peaceful but highly symbolic custom in *their* part of Technic society, that without their weapons they would feel more indecent than a shaven Trillian.) As far as Harker's wire-taut attention registered, Witweet's answer was routine. But probably some forlornness crept into the overtones, for the neighbor stopped.

"Do you feel quite radiantly well, dear boy?" he asked.

"Indeed I do, honored Pwiddy, and thank you in my prettiest thoughts for your ever-sweet consideration," the pilot replied. "I . . . well, these good visitors from the starfaring culture of splendor have been describing some of their experiences—oh, I simply must relate them to you later, dear boy!—and naturally, since I am about to embark on another trip, I have been made pensive by this." Hands, tail, whiskers gesticulated. *Meaning what?* wondered Harker in a chill; and clamping jaws together: *Well, you knew you'd have to take risks to win a kingdom.* "Forgive me, I pray you of your overflowing generosity, that I rush off after such curt words. But I have promises to keep, and considerable distances to go before I sleep."

"Understood." Pwiddy spent a mere five minutes bidding farewell all around before he pedaled off. Meanwhile several others passed by. However, since no well-mannered person would interrupt a conversation even to make salute, they created no problem.

"Let's go." It grated in Dolgorov's throat.

Behind the little witch-hatted house was a pergola wherein rested Witweet's personal flitter. It was large and flashy—large enough for three humans to squeeze into the back—which fact had become an element in Harker's plan. The car that the men had used during their stay on Trillia, they abandoned. It was unmistakably an off-planet vehicle.

"Get started!" Dolgorov cuffed at Witweet.

Olafsson caught his arm and snapped: "Control your emotions! Want to tear his head off?"

Hunched over the dashboard, Witweet squeezed his eyes shut and shivered till Harker prodded him. "Pull out of that funk," the man said.

"I . . . I beg your pardon. The brutality so appalled me—" Witweet flinched from their laughter. His fingers gripped levers and twisted knobs. Here was no steering by gestures in a light-field, let alone simply speaking an order to an autopilot. The overloaded flitter crawled skyward. Harker detected a flutter in its grav unit, but decided nothing was likely to fail before they reached the spaceport. And after that, nothing would matter except getting off this planet.

Not that it was a bad place, he reflected. Almost Earthlike in size, gravity, air, deliciously edible life forms—an Earth that no longer was and perhaps never had been, wide horizons and big skies, caressed by light and rain. Looking out, he saw woodlands in a thousand hues of green, meadows, river-gleam, an occasional dollhouse dwelling, grainfields ripening tawny, and the soft gaudiness of a flower ranch. Ahead lifted The Mountain Which Presides Over Moonrise In Lenidel, a snowpeak pure as Fuji's. The sun, yellower than Sol, turned it and a few clouds into gold.

A gentle world for a gentle people. Too gentle.

Too bad. For them.

Besides, after six months of it, three city-bred men were about ready to climb screaming out of their skulls. Harker drew forth a cigarette, inhaled it into lighting, and filled his lungs with harshness. *I'd almost welcome a fight,* he thought savagely.

But none happened. Half a year of hard, patient study paid richly off. It helped that the Trillians were—well, you couldn't say lax about security, because the need for it had never occurred to them. Witweet radioed to the portmaster as he approached, was informed that everything looked O.K., and took his flitter straight through an open cargo lock into a hold of the ship he was to pilot.

The port was like nothing in Technic civilization, unless on the remotest, least visited of outposts. After all, the Trillians had gone in a bare fifty years from propeller-driven aircraft to interstellar spaceship. Such concentration on research and development had necessarily been at the expense of production and exploitation. What few vessels they had were still mostly experimental. The scientific bases they had established on planets of next-door stars needed no more than three or four freighters for their maintenance.

Thus a couple of buildings and a ground-control tower bounded a stretch of ferrocrete on a high, chilly plateau; and that was Trillia's spaceport. Two ships were in. One was being serviced, half its hull plates removed and furry shapes swarming over the emptiness within. The other, assigned to Witweet, stood on landing jacks at the far end of the field. Shaped like a fat torpedo, decorated in floral designs of pink and baby blue, it was as big as a Dromond-class hauler. Yet its payload was under a thousand tons. The primitive systems for drive, control, and life support took up that much room.

"I wish you a just too, too delightful voyage," said the portmaster's voice from the radio. "Would you honor me by accepting an invitation to dinner? My wife has, if I may boast, discovered remarkable culinary attributes of certain seaweeds brought back from Gwinsai; and for my part, dear boy, I would be so interested to hear your opinion of a new verse form with which I am currently experimenting."

"No . . . I thank you, no, impossible, I beg indulgence—" It was hard to tell whether the unevenness of Witweet's response came from terror or from the tobacco smoke that had kept him coughing. He almost flung his vehicle into the spaceship.

Clearance granted. *The Serenity of the Estimable Philosopher Ittypu* lifted into a dawn sky. When Trillia was a dwindling cloud-marbled sapphire among the stars, Harker let out a breath. "We can relax now."

"Where?" Olafsson grumbled. The single cabin barely allowed three humans to crowd together. They'd have to take turns sleeping in the hall that ran aft to the engine room. And their voyage was going to be long. Top pseudovelocity under the snail-powered hyperdrive of this craft would be less than one light-year per day.

"Oh, we can admire the darling murals," Dolgorov fleered. He kicked an intricately painted bulkhead.

Witweet, crouched miserable at the control board, flinched. "I beg you, dear, kind sir, do not scuff the artwork," he said.

"Why should you care?" Dolgorov asked. "You won't be keeping this junk heap."

Witweet wrung his hands. "Defacement is still very wicked. Perhaps the consignee will appreciate my patterns? I spent *such* a time on them, trying to get every teensiest detail correct."

"Is that why your freighters have a single person aboard?" Olafsson laughed. "Always seemed reckless to me, not taking a backup pilot at least. But I suppose two Trillians would get into so fierce an argument about the interior decor that they'd each stalk off in an absolute snit."

"Why, no," said Witweet, a trifle calmer. "We keep personnel down to one because more are not really needed. Piloting between stars is automatic, and the crewbeing is trained in servicing functions. Should he suffer harm en route, the ship will put itself into orbit around the destination planet and can be boarded by others. An extra would thus uselessly occupy space which is often needed for passengers. I am surprised that you, sir, who have set a powerful intellect to prolonged consideration of our astronautical practices, should not have been aware—"

"I was, I was!" Olafsson threw up his hands as far as the overhead permitted. "Ask a rhetorical question and get an oratorical answer."

"May I, in turn, humbly request enlightenment as to your reason for sequestering a spacecraft ludicrously inadequate by every standard of your oh, so sophisticated society?"

"You may." Harker's spirits bubbled from relief of tension. They'd pulled it off. They really had. He sat down—the deck was padded and perfumed—and started a cigarette. Through his bones beat the throb of the gravity drive: energy wasted by a clumsy system. The weight it made underfoot fluctuated slightly in a rhythm that felt wavelike.

"I suppose we may as well call ourselves criminals," he said; the Lenidellian word he must use had milder connotations. "There are people back home who wouldn't leave us alive if they knew who'd done certain things. But we never got rich off them. Now we will."

He had no need for recapitulating, except the need to gloat: "You know we came to Trillia half a standard year ago, on a League ship that was paying a short visit to buy art. We had goods of our own to barter with, and announced we were going to settle down for a while and look into the possibility of establishing a permanent trading post with a regular shuttle service to some of the Technic planets. That's what the captain of the ship thought, too. He advised us against it, said it couldn't pay and we'd simply be stuck on Trillia till the next League vessel chanced by, which wouldn't likely be for more than a year. But when we insisted, and gave him passage money, he shrugged," as did Harker.

"You have told me this," Witweet said. "I thrilled to the ecstasy of what I believed was your friendship."

"Well, I did enjoy your company," Harker smiled. "You're not a bad little osco. Mainly, though, we concentrated on you because we'd learned you qualified for our uses—a regular freighter pilot, a bachelor so we needn't fuss with a family, a chatterer who could be pumped for any information we wanted. Seems we gauged well."

"We better have," Dolgorov said gloomily. "Those trade goods cost us everything we could scratch together. I took a steady job for two years and lived like a lama to get my share."

"And now we'll be living like fakirs," said Olafsson. "But, afterward—afterward!"

"Evidently your whole aim was to acquire a Trillian ship," Witweet said. "My bemusement at this endures."

"We don't actually want the ship as such, except for demonstration purposes," Harker said. "What we want are the plans, the design. Between the vessel itself, and the service manuals aboard, we have that in effect."

Witweet's ears quivered. "Do you mean to publish the data for scientific interest? Surely, to beings whose ancestors went on to better models centuries ago—if, indeed, they ever burdened themselves with something this crude—surely the interest is nil. Unless you think many will pay to see, in order to enjoy mirth at the spectacle of our fumbling efforts?" He spread his arms. "Why, you could have bought complete specifications most cheaply; or, indeed, had you requested of me, I would have been bubbly-happy to obtain a set and make you a gift." On a note of timid hope: "Thus, you see, dear boy, drastic action is quite unnecessary. Let us return. I will state you remained aboard by mistake—"

Olafsson guffawed. Dolgorov said, "Not even your authorities can be that sloppy-thinking." Harker ground out his cigarette on the deck, which made the pilot wince, and explained at leisured length: "We want this ship precisely because it's primitive. Your people weren't in the electronic era when the first human explorers contacted you. They, or some later visitors, brought you texts on physics. Then your bright lads had the theory of such things as gravity control and hyperdrive. But the engineering practice was something else again.

"You didn't have plans for a starship. When you finally got an opportunity to inquire, you found that the idealistic period of Technic civilization was over and you must deal with hardheaded entrepreneurs. And the price was set 'way beyond what your whole planet could hope to save in League currency. That was just the price for diagrams, not to speak of an actual vessel. I don't know if you are personally aware of the fact—it's no secret —but this is League policy. The member companies are bound by an agreement.

"They won't prevent anyone from entering space on his own. But take your case on Trillia. You had learned in a general way about, oh, transistors, for instance. But that did not set you up to manufacture them. An entire industrial complex is needed for that and for the million other necessary items. To design and build one, with the inevitable mistakes en route, would take decades at a minimum, and would involve regimenting your entire species and living in poverty because every bit of capital has to be reinvested. Well, you Trillians were too sensible to pay that price. You'd proceed more gradually. Yet at the same time, your scientists, all your more adventurous species, were burning to get out into space.

"I agree your decision about that was intelligent, too. You saw you couldn't go directly from your earliest hydrocarbon-fueled engines to a modern starship—to a completely integrated system of thermonuclear power plant, initiative-grade navigation and engineering computers, full-cycle life support, the whole works, using solid-state circuits, molecular-level and nuclear-level transitions, force fields instead of moving parts—an *organism* more energy than matter. No, you wouldn't be able to build that for generations, probably.

"But you could go ahead and develop huge, clumsy, but workable fission-power units. You could use vacuum tubes, glass rectifiers, kilometers of wire, to generate and regulate the necessary forces. You could store data on tape if not in single molecules, retrieve with a cathode-ray scanner if not with a quantum-field pulse, compute with miniaturized gas-filled units that react in microseconds if not with photon interplays that take a nano-second.

"You're like islanders who had nothing better than canoes till someone stopped by in a nuclear-powered submarine. They couldn't copy that, but they might invent a reciprocating steam engine turning a screw—they might attach an airpipe so it could submerge—and it wouldn't impress the outsiders, but it would cross the ocean too, at its own pace; and it would overawe any neighboring tribes."

He stopped for breath.

"I see," Witweet murmured slowly. His tail switched back and forth. "You can sell our designs to sophonts in a protoindustrial stage of technological development. The idea comes from an excellent brain. But why could you not simply buy the plans for resale elsewhere?"

"The damned busybody League." Dolgorov spat.

"The fact is," Olafsson said, "spacecraft—of advanced type—have been sold to, ah, less advanced peoples in the past. Some of those weren't near industrialization, they were Iron Age barbarians whose only thought was plundering and conquering. They could do that, given ships which are practically self-piloting, self-maintaining, self-everything. It's cost a good many lives and heavy material losses on border planets. But at least none of the barbarians have been able to duplicate the craft thus far. Hunt every pirate and warlord down, and that ends the problem. Or so the League hopes. It's banned any more such trades."

He cleared his throat. "I don't refer to races like the Trillians, who're obviously capable of reaching the stars by themselves and unlikely to be a menace when they do," he said. "You're free to buy anything you can pay for. The price of certain things is set astronomical mainly to keep you from beginning overnight to compete with the old, established outfits. They prefer a gradual phasing-in of newcomers, so they can adjust.

"But aggressive, warlike cultures that'd not be interested in reaching a peaceful accommodation—they're something else again. There's a total prohibition on supplying their sort with anything that might help them to get off their planets in less than centuries. If League agents catch you at it, they don't fool around with rehabilitation like a regular government. They shoot you."

Harker grimaced. "I saw once on a telescreen interview," he remarked, "Old Nick van Rijn said he wouldn't shoot that kind of offenders. He'd hang them. A rope is reusable."

"And this ship *can* be copied," Witweet breathed. "A low industrial technology, lower than ours, could tool up to produce a modified design, in a comparatively short time, if guided by a few engineers from the core civilization."

"I trained as an engineer," Harker said. "Likewise Leo; and Einar spent several years on a planet where one royal family has grandiose ambitions."

"But the horror you would unleash!" wailed the Trillian. He stared into their stoniness. "You would never dare go home," he said.

"Don't want to anyway," Harker answered. "Power, wealth, yes, and everything those will buy—we'll have more than we can use up in our lifetimes, at the court of the Militants. Fun, too." He smiled. "A challenge, you know, to build a space navy from zero. I expect to enjoy my work."

"Will not the . . . the Polesotechnic League take measures?"

"That's why we must operate as we have done. They'd learn about a sale of plans, and then they wouldn't stop till they'd found and suppressed our project. But a non-Technic ship that never reported in won't interest them. Our destination is well outside their sphere of normal operations. They needn't discover any hint of what's going on—till an interstellar empire too big for them to break is there. Meanwhile, as we gain resources, we'll have been modernizing our industry and fleet."

"It's all arranged," Olafsson said. "The day we show up in the land of the Militants, bringing the ship we described to them, we'll become princes."

"Kings, later," Dolgorov added. "Behave accordingly, you xeno. We don't need you much. I'd soon as not boot you through an air lock."

Witweet spent minutes just shuddering.

The Serenity, et cetera, moved on away from Trillia's golden sun. It had to reach a weaker gravitational field than a human craft would have needed before its hyperdrive would function.

Harker spent part of that period being shown around, top to bottom and end to end. He'd toured a sister ship before, but hadn't dared ask for demonstrations as thoroughly as he now demanded. "I want to know this monstrosity we've got, inside out," he said, while personally tearing down and rebuilding a cumbersome oxygen renewer. He could do this because most equipment was paired, against the expectation of eventual in-flight down time.

In a hold, among cases of supplies for the research team on Gwinsai, he was surprised to recognize a lean cylindroid, one hundred twenty centimeters long. "But here's a Solar-built courier!" he exclaimed.

Witweet made eager gestures of agreement. He'd been falling over himself to oblige his captors. "For messages in case of emergency, magnificent sir," he babbled. "A hyper-drive unit, an autopilot, a radio to call at journey's end till someone comes and retrieves the enclosed letter—"

"I know, I know. But why not build your own?"

"Well, if you will deign to reflect upon the matter, you will realize that anything we could build would be too slow and unreliable to afford very probable help. Especially since it is most unlikely that, at any given time, another spaceship would be ready to depart Trillia on the instant. Therefore, this courier is set, as you can see if you wish to examine the program, to go a considerably greater distance—though nevertheless not taking long, your human constructions being superlatively fast—to the planet called, ah, Oasis . . . an Anglic word meaning a lovely, cool, refreshing haven, am I correct?"

Harker nodded impatiently. "You are right. One of the League companies does keep a small base there."

"We have arranged that they will send aid if requested. At a price, to be sure. However, for our poor economy, as ridiculous a hulk as this is still a heavy investment, worth insuring."

"I see. I didn't know you bought such gadgets—not that there'd be a pegged price on them; they don't matter any more than spices or medical equipment. Of course, I couldn't find out every detail in advance, especially not things you people take so for granted that you didn't think to mention them." On impulse, Harker patted the round head. "You know, Witweet, I guess I do like you. I will see you're rewarded for your help."

"Passage home will suffice," the Trillian said quietly, "though I do not know how I can face my kinfolk after having been the instrument of death and ruin for millions of innocents."

"Then don't go home," Harker suggested. "We can't release you for years in any case, to blab our scheme and our coordinates. But we could, however, smuggle in whatever and whoever you wanted, same as for ourselves."

The head rose beneath his palm as the slight form straightened. "Very well," Witweet declared.

That fast? jarred through Harker. *He is nonhuman, yes, but—* The wondering was dissipated by the continuing voice:

"Actually, dear boy, I must disabuse you. We did not buy our couriers, we salvaged them."

"What? Where?"

"Have you heard of a planet named, by its human discoverers, Paradox?"

Harker searched his memory. Before leaving Earth he had consulted every record he could find about this entire stellar neighborhood. Poorly known though it was to men, there had been a huge mass of data—suns, worlds . . . "I think so. Big, isn't it? With a freaky atmosphere."

"Yes." Witweet spoke rapidly. "It gave the original impetus to

Technic exploration of our vicinity. But later the men departed. In recent years, when we ourselves became able to pay visits, we found their abandoned camp. A great deal of gear had been left behind, presumably because it was designed for Paradox only and would be of no use elsewhere, hence not worth hauling back. Among these machines we came upon a few couriers. I suppose they had been overlooked. Your civilization can afford profligacy, if I may use that term in due respectfulness."

He crouched, as if expecting a blow. His eyes glittered in the gloom of the hold.

"Hm-m-m." Harker frowned. "I suppose by now you've stripped the place."

"Well, no." Witweet brushed nervously at his rising fur. "Like the men, we saw no use in, for example, tractors designed for a gravity of two-point-eight terrestrial. They can operate well and cheaply on Paradox, since their fuel is crude oil, of which an abundant supply exists near the campsite. But we already had electric-celled grav motors, however archaic they are by your standards. And we do not need weapons like those we found, presumably for protection against animals. We certainly have no intention of colonizing Paradox!"

"Hm-m-m." The human waved, as if to brush off the chattering voice. He slouched off, hands in pockets, pondering.

In the time that followed, he consulted the navigator's bible. His reading knowledge of Lenidellian was fair. The entry for Paradox was as laconic as it would have been in a Technic reference; despite the limited range of their operations, the Trillians had already encountered too many worlds to allow flowery descriptions. Star type and coordinates, orbital elements, mass, density, atmosphere composition, temperature ranges, and the usual rest were listed. There was no notation about habitability, but none was needed. The original explorers hadn't been poisoned or come down with disease, and Trillian metabolism was similar to theirs.

The gravity field was not too strong for this ship to make landing and, later, ascent. Weather shouldn't pose any hazards, given reasonable care in choosing one's path; that was a weakly energized environment. Besides, the vessel was meant for planetfalls, and Witweet was a skilled pilot in his fashion. . . .

Harker discussed the idea with Olafsson and Dolgorov. "It won't take but a few days," he said, "and we might pick up something really good. You know I've not been too happy about the Militants' prospects of building an ample industrial base fast enough to suit us. Well, a few machines like this, simple things they can easily copy but designed by good engineers . . . could make a big difference."

"They're probably rust heaps," Dolgorov snorted. "That was long ago."

"No, durable alloys were available then," Olafsson said. "I like the notion intrinsically. I don't like the thought of our xeno taking us down. He might crash us on purpose."

"That sniveling fagot?" Dolgorov gibed. He jerked his head backward at Witweet, who sat enormous-eyed in the pilot chair listening to a language he did not understand. "By accident, maybe, seeing how scared he is!"

"It's a risk we take at journey's end," Harker reminded them. "Not a real risk. The ship has some ingenious fail-safe built in. Anyhow, I intend to stand over him the whole way down. If he does a single thing wrong, I'll kill him. The controls aren't made for me, but I can get us aloft again, and afterward we can rerig."

Olafsson nodded. "Seems worth a try," he said. "What can we lose except a little time and sweat?"

Paradox rolled enormous in the viewscreen, a darkling world, the sky-band along its sunrise horizon redder than Earth's, polar caps and winter snowfields gashed by the teeth of mountains, tropical forests and pampas a yellow-brown fading into raw deserts on one side and chopped off on another side by the furious surf of an ocean where three moons fought their tidal wars. The sun was distance-dwarfed, more dull in hue than Sol, nevertheless too bright to look near. Elsewhere, stars filled il-limitable blackness.

It was very quiet aboard, save for the mutter of powerplant and ventilators, the breathing of men, their restless shuffling about in the cramped cabin. The air was blued and fouled by cigarette smoke; Witweet would have fled into the corridor, but they made him stay, clutching a perfume-dripping kerchief to his nose.

Harker straightened from the observation screen. Even at full magnification, the rudimentary electro-optical system gave little except blurriness. But he'd practiced on it, while orbiting a satellite, till he felt he could read those wavering traces.

"Campsite and machinery, all right," he said. "No details. Brush has covered everything. When were your people here last, Witweet?"

"Several years back," the Trillian wheezed. "Evidently vegeta-tion grows apace. Do you agree on the safety of a landing?"

"Yes. We may snap a few branches, as well as flatten a lot of shrubs, but we'll back down slowly, the last hundred meters, and we'll keep the radar, sonar, and gravar sweeps going." Harker glanced at his men. "Next thing is to compute our descent pat-tern," he said. "But first I want to spell out again, point by point, exactly what each of us is to do under exactly what circum-stances. I don't aim to take chances."

"Oh, no," Witweet squeaked. "I beg you, dear boy, I beg you the prettiest I can, please don't!"

After the tension of transit, landing was an anticlimax. All at once the engine fell silent. A wind whistled around the hull. Viewscreens showed low, thick-boled trees; fronded brownish leaves; tawny undergrowth; shadowy glimpses of metal objects beneath vines and amidst tall, whipping stalks. The sun stood at late afternoon in a sky almost purple.

Witweet checked the indicators while Harker studied them over his head. "Air breathable, of course," the pilot said, "which frees us of the handicap of having to wear smelly old spacesuits. We should bleed it in gradually, since the pressure is greater than ours at present and we don't want earaches, do we? Temperature—" He shivered delicately. "Be certain you are wrapped up snug before you venture outside."

"You're venturing first," Harker informed him.

"What? Oo-ooh, my good, sweet, darling friend, no, please, no! It is *cold* out there, scarcely above freezing. And once on the ground, no gravity generator to help, why, weight will be tripled. What could I possibly, possibly do? No, let me stay inside, keep the home fires burning—I mean keep the thermostat at a cozy temperature—and, yes, I will make you the nicest pot of tea. . . ."

"If you don't stop fluttering and do what you're told, I'll tear your head off," Dolgorov said. "Guess what I'll use your skin for."

"Let's get cracking," Olafsson said. "I don't want to stay in this Helheim any longer than you."

They opened a hatch the least bit. While Paradoxian air seeped in, they dressed as warmly as might be, except for Harker. He intended to stand by the controls for the first investigatory period. The entering gases added a whine to the wind noise. Their helium content made speech and other sounds higher-pitched, not quite natural; and this would have to be endured for the rest of the journey, since the ship had insufficient reserve tanks to flush out the new atmosphere. A breath of cold got by the heaters, and a rank smell of alien growth.

But you could get used to hearing funny, Harker thought. And the native life might stink, but it was harmless. You couldn't eat it and be nourished, but neither could its germs live off your body. If heavy weapons had been needed here, they were far more likely against large, blundering herbivores than against local tigers.

That didn't mean they couldn't be used in war.

Trembling, eyes squinched half shut, tail wrapped around his muzzle, the rest of him bundled in four layers of kimono, Witweet crept to the personnel lock. Its outer valve swung wide. The gangway went down. Harker grinned to see the dwarfish shape descend, step by step under the sudden harsh hauling of the planet.

"Sure you can move around in that pull?" he asked his companions.

"Sure," Dolgorov grunted. "An extra hundred-fifty kilos? I can back-pack more than that, and then it's less well distributed."

"Stay cautious, though. Too damned easy to fall and break bones."

"I'd worry more about the cardiovascular system," Olafsson said. "One can stand three Gs for a while, but not for a very long while. Fluid begins seeping out of the cell walls, the heart feels the strain too much—and we've no gravanol along as the first expedition must have had."

"We'll only be here a few days at most," Harker said, "with plenty of chances to rest inboard."

"Right," Olafsson agreed. "Forward!"

Gripping his blaster, he shuffled onto the gangway. Dolgorov followed. Below, Witweet huddled. Harker looked out at bleakness, felt the wind slap his face with chill, and was glad he could stay behind. Later he must take his turn outdoors, but for now he could enjoy warmth, decent weight . . .

The world reached up and grabbed him. Off balance, he fell to the deck. His left hand struck first, pain gushed, he saw the wrist and arm splinter. He screamed. The sound came weak as well as shrill, out of a breast laboring against thrice the heaviness it should have had. At the same time, the lights in the ship went out.

Witweet perched on a boulder. His back was straight in spite of the drag on him, which made his robes hang stiff, as if carved on an idol of some minor god of justice. His tail, erect, blew jauntily in the bitter sunset wind; the colors of his garments were bold against murk that rose in the forest around the dead spacecraft.

He looked into the guns of three men, and into the terror that had taken them behind the eyes; and Witweet laughed.

"Put those toys away before you hurt yourselves," he said, using no circumlocutions or honorifics.

"You swine, you filthy treacherous xeno, I'll kill you," Dolgorov groaned. "Slowly."

"First you must catch me," Witweet answered. "By virtue of being small, I have a larger surface-to-volume ratio than you. My bones, my muscles, my veins and capillaries and cell membranes suffer less force per square centimeter than do yours. I can move faster than you here. I can survive longer."

"You can't outrun a blaster bolt," Olafsson said.

"No. You can kill me with that—a quick, clean death, which does not frighten me. Really, because we of Lenidel observe certain customs of courtesy, use certain turns of speech—because our males in particular are encouraged to develop aesthetic interests and compassion—does that mean we are cowardly or effeminate?" The Trillian clicked his tongue. "If you supposed so, you committed an elementary logical fallacy which our philosophers name the does-not-follow."

"Why shouldn't we kill you?"

"That is inadvisable. You see, your only hope is quick rescue by a League ship. The courier can operate here, being a solid-state device. It can reach Oasis and summon a vessel which, itself of similar construction, can also land on Paradox and take off again . . . in time. This would be impossible for a Trillian craft. Even if one were ready to leave, I doubt the Astronautical Senate would permit the pilot to risk descent.

"Well, rescuers will naturally ask questions. I cannot imagine any story which you three men, alone, might concoct that would stand up under the subsequent, inevitable investigation. On the other hand, I can explain to the League's agents that you were only coming along to look into trade possibilities and that we were trapped on Paradox by a faulty autopilot which threw us into a descent curve. I can do this *in detail*, which you could not if you killed me. They will return us all to Trillia where there is no death penalty."

Witweet smoothed his wind-ruffled whiskers. "The alternative," he finished, "is to die where you are, in a most unpleasant fashion."

Harker's splinted arm gestured back the incoherent Dolgorov. He set an example by holstering his own gun. "I . . . guess we're outsmarted," he said, word by foul-tasting word. "But what happened? Why's the ship inoperable?"

"Helium in the atmosphere," Witweet explained calmly. "The monatomic helium molecule is ooh-how-small. It diffuses through almost every material. Vacuum tubes, glass rectifiers, electronic switches dependent on pure gases, any such device soon becomes poisoned. You, who were used to a technology that had long left this kind of thing behind, did not know the fact, and it did not occur to you as a possibility. We Trillians are, of course, rather acutely aware of the problem. I am the first who ever set foot on Paradox. You should have noted that my courier is a present-day model."

"I see," Olafsson mumbled.

"The sooner we get our message off, the better," Witweet said. "By the way, I assume you are not so foolish as to contemplate the piratical takeover of a vessel of the Polesotechnic League."

"Oh, no!" they said, including Dolgorov, and the other two blasters were sheathed.

"One thing, though," Harker said. A part of him wondered if the pain in him was responsible for his own abnormal self-possession. Counterirritant against dismay? Would he weep after it wore off? "You bargain for your life by promising to have ours spared. How do we know we want your terms? What'll they do to us on Trillia?"

"Entertain no fears," Witweet assured him. "We are not vindictive, as I have heard some species are; nor have we any officious concept of 'rehabilitation.' Wrongdoers are required to make amends to the fullest extent possible. You three have cost my people a valuable ship and whatever cargo cannot be salvaged. You must have technological knowledge to convey, of equal worth.

The working conditions will not be intolerable. Probably you can make restitution and win release before you reach old age.

"Now, come, get busy. First we dispatch that courier, then we prepare what is necessary for our survival until rescue."

He hopped down from the rock, which none of them would have been able to do unscathed, and approached them through gathering cold twilight with the stride of a conquerer.

Back in 1949, there appeared one of the finest short stories I'd ever read—To Watch the Watchers, by W. Macfarlane. I've been recommending it as a classic ever since. The end line, "It is a proud and lonely thing to be a man," became one of the catch phrases of science fiction for several years. In this story, Macfarlane wonders a bit about ecology—and whether we'll all really want it the way it was. Take the Ice Age: Contaminate all that good glaciation with a lot of heat and open land, and who'd want it? Certainly not the hunters of that day. . . .

W. MACFARLANE
To Make a New Neanderthal

Guert Maury wiped off the last bumper and carefully applied a yellow-and-black sticker: BAN CARS. He dropped the rag on the parking lot and lit another cigarette.

The long search was over. He had found his quarry, David Langley Noss, a brilliant youngster with a paranoiac drive to a "normal" life. He sighed. Aberrations crop up in the best genetic lines. The subversion of thinking with your belly instead of your brain was the recurring pattern of unreason in the history of man.

A car turned off the highway, and headlights washed the side of the restaurant. Maury stepped over the berm and down the slope out of sight. The car parked, the door slammed, and there was a grumble of conversation about being late for the S.O.S. meeting.

The seductive quality of the long Pacific waves creaming over the rocks, the languid cast of the moon through thin fog, the faint spice scent of geraniums that had escaped cultivation mingled with the pungency of native anise, all these assaults on the senses made it understandable enough that an ill-anchored young man like Noss should drift from reality like a grasshopper caught in a flooded gutter.

Maury coughed quietly and stepped on the butt. He took the magnetic impulse key from his pocket, and the door of his own vehicle materialized. When he closed it behind him, he shut away the whole whey-thin atmosphere of the California coast. In the control room he listened a moment at the selective pickup keyed to Noss. ". . . And be my love / And we will all the pleasures prove / That hills and valleys, dale and field / And all the craggy mountains yield . . ." Evidently the first speaker had finished, and Noss had the girl off in a corner somewhere, pouring her ear full of Kit Marlowe.

Guert Maury grinned and spoke Raleigh's reply aloud: ". . . Soon break, soon wither, soon forgotten / In folly ripe, in reason rotten." He adjusted the pickup and heard her reply, "Oh, David."

Her name was Lunetta Drogen, and she was dressed like a gypsy fortune-teller in a long skirt, a wild blouse, a jacket with mirrors and bangles and spangles, and a psychedelic fringed shawl over her shoulders. She was the daughter of a road contractor in Pontiac, Michigan. She had turned her back on such grossnesses as a fourteen-room home, a domed swimming pool, and her yellow Cadillac convertible. She had a tender intelligence and was given to blinking back tears—which made her spiritual eyes lustrous— when she mourned over thin-shelled seagull eggs and the plight of the California condor.

Maury thought she was an admirable mate for David Noss.

They deserved each other. He adjusted the pickup again and listened to the principal speaker: ". . . We are very close to the point of no return on insecticides, oil, and nuclear contamination. Pollution is changing the face of nature from benignity to rheumy-eyed horror. . . ." Maury had heard all this before, but he listened with mild interest to the provocative call to arms. He made a mental note to order more STRIKE A BLOW FOR PEACE bumper stickers when he returned from this mission.

The People's behavioralist had advised, "Toleration of lunacy is emasculating. The appearance of toleration is tolerable only when psychological oil can be applied to reduce internal friction. Such action should be personal implementation of our cause—and oblique to it. On a totally different level than I recommend for personal stability was the elegant use of detergents by our English colleagues at the time of the *Torrey Canyon* oil spill. Between the two, significant action was achieved."

Maury endorsed the idea. His use of bumper stickers was adroit and double-pointed. The car that had arrived late should not be neglected. He turned the audio back to soundless recording and returned through the lock to the Pacific coast south of Half Moon Bay. He climbed through the low acacias to the parking lot and found the rag where he'd left it. He wiped a bumper clean and smoothed on HATE FUZZ? IN TROUBLE? CALL A HIPPIE!

He sat in the acacias out of sight and lit a cigarette. He took the repeater from his pocket and checked the S.O.S. speaker of the evening. The voice was high and indignant. He should be good for some time yet. Maury stared unseeing at the ocean and considered his preparations. Noss could not escape him now.

He had slipped away from Los Angeles over two years ago and disappeared. He had hidden in the San Fernando Valley and found work at a gasoline station. This was clear evidence of his intelligence. The usual tocsin had been sounded and search patterns instituted in rural areas of the west. No sign of him. After six months he had taken equivalency examinations and enrolled at San Jose State, four hundred miles north in another smudge area. He had found work in a plastics plant, which was also first-class camouflage. He had been located among the teeming millions only because Guert Maury had persevered in his computerized membership and subscription lists; the Audubon Society, the Sierra Club, Portola Institute, *Environment* magazine—habits of mind do not change. Of course Noss had adopted another name, but the temptation to proselytize and associate with his own reactionary kind had turned him up.

Self-congratulation is an idle pleasure. Maury lit another cigarette. Were there any terminal spasms he had not anticipated? Noss and the girl had come to the meeting in a blue Volkswagen. Maury had put a homing button on it, not that it was necessary. He had fixed a distant release gas tube with a magnetic clamp under the dash, and that might be useful.

There was a patter of applause and a scraping of chairs as the Save Our Shores meeting came to an end. A door opened, and Noss slipped out with his inamorata. The noisy little Volkswagen started, and off they went, south toward Santa Cruz on California 1. Maury was in no hurry. He took his own vehicle into the air above them and monitored the conversation. It was trivial until Noss pulled off the highway to an observation point overlooking the ocean.

"Loo, I can't hide the truth any longer. I'm a fugitive. I've been hiding for thirty months now, hiding from the most dangerous conspiracy mankind has ever known." His voice was thick with sincerity. "It's nothing as honest as robbing banks, or moral as pushing pornography."

She made a sympathetic noise. "Gosh, David, what is it?" The tone of her voice said she couldn't care less, now that he was secure in her arms.

"I was raised in Los Angeles—" he began, and she laughed softly. "Pay attention. Don't do that. This is serious. I grew up in Los Angeles, but my parents came from Pittsburgh and my grandparents from London."

"Horrible," she said, but she was teasing.

"Now, listen, Loo, this is important. I was born into a society that calls itself the People. It's a secret cabal behind a smokescreen of science. I mean smokescreen, too. They are the pollutors, they're the ones behind the nuclear explosions and the atomic power plants. They pushed hard insecticides and put money into the internal-combustion engine instead of steam, and before that, they made synthetic nitrogen in Germany. They're responsible for ammonium sulfate, and that's where our troubles began."

"Oh, Dave, can't this wait till later?"

"I've got to warn you. First, they increased the world's food supply with artificial chemicals, and they are the secret intrigue behind the health services, which is the most subtle and deadly weapon in their arsenal. Feed the people, wipe out the good natural diseases, bring in health, and you have the ultimate pollution!"

Maury brought his vehicle down by a clump of windbent pines. In a way, it was a pity about the boy. Very few men had the historical perspective to see what happened. Young Noss had somehow discovered the benchmarks from which the future had been planned and was now being constructed. It was remarkable intuition.

"The People call it phlogiston," Noss continued doggedly. "Loo, are you listening? Phlogiston is supposed to be an imaginary chemical, but the People say that the incredibly complex products of combustion are responsible for mankind's fantastic mutation. In the short space of a million years, the brain capacity has enlarged from four hundred to fifteen hundred ccs. This is unique. It's unparalleled in any species. Man alone has used fire, and phlogiston has mutated man."

"Does all this matter, David, dear?"

"Yes! They're consciously manipulating mankind! They're polluting the earth, the sea, the atmosphere—and I'll tell you why: to stimulate the acid, prostaglandin and 5-hydroxytryptamine, and all the other chemical thought transmitters in the brain. It's no wonder that the industrial revolution began in England. Germany tried to compete, but could never manufacture enough smog. Look at Tokyo and all of Japan! And Loo, I trace my line to contemporary smog capitals: London, Pittsburgh, Los Angeles! So they clean up London, and England is down the tube! This is why I've been running, Loo. The People have got to be stopped —and if you come with me, you will share the deadly peril!"

"Hold me tight," said Loo.

Guert Maury made a move toward the controls. A pair of head-lights appeared around a curve of the highway, and the car slowed and pulled onto the observation point. Maury leaned back in his chair. He listened to the heavy breathing from the Volks.

He spoke for the record: "It should be noted that David Lang-ley Noss is an excellent example of a conservative. He's a textbook case of the ancient mystique of mankind: it won't work, it can't be done, let's cry over spilt milk, keep the status quo. He also exemplifies the use of articulate verbiage to hold back change. He represents the inertia and stubborn resistance of outmoded thought systems. The majority of men will only shriek outrage and bellow indignation as they are forced backward into the future, but such individuals as Noss will fight blindly to protect the past and stifle progress. . . ."

"You were joking with me?" said Loo. "About the conspiracy and all—you were, weren't you, darling? It's not true. . . ."

"It's worse than I said. Look at the intellectual centers of this country. Harvard and MIT are rotten polluted. Cal Tech is in Pasadena, and you can see the smog at nine thousand feet with the naked eye. Stanford is on the peninsula between industrial San Jose and industrial San Francisco. Cars in Berkeley are so thick that twenty percent have to keep moving on the roads for lack of parking."

"You could ban cars," said Loo hopefully.

Maury nodded approvingly. He had designed his bumper stickers to be paradoxical, to derail uncritical minds. A primary maxim of war is to confuse the enemy and then compound con-fusion.

Noss snorted. "You might as well hear the worst of it. Phlogis-

ton was so increased by the Second World War that mentation
. . . that's what the People call it—cerebration—the mental process . . . increased in a vertical curve. Looloo, they have monopo-
lized research and kept development secret. They are dedicated to
smogiforming Earth."

"The brown pelicans," she mourned, "the sick fish."

"They want the whole world a brown ball for the mentation
of man," said David Noss bitterly.

The other car pulled out of the viewpoint. Maury waited no
longer. In his present hysterical state, his quarry might do any
foolish thing. He released the somnambulent gas in the Volkswagen. The voices stopped.

Maury checked the area. Infrared showed an owl, mice, and a
bunch of rabbits. He lifted his vehicle down beside the little
blue car. He carried Noss and Lunetta Drogen aboard ship into
the phlogiston-rich atmosphere. He returned to the control room
and grappled the Volks magnetically. He ran it through the
guard rail and cut loose. It bumped downhill and plunged over
the cliff into the surf and rocks.

He phased the spaceship to detection transparent and at ten
diameters from Earth went into Gonzalan space. There was no
racial bias among the People, and there were generations of
Mexicans in Los Angeles.

Forty-two hours later, Maury put the ship down on a pristine
planet of a sun so far from Earth it had never been catalogued by
astronomers. He helped the youngsters out and let them lie down
under a fern. He lit a cigarette.

"No pollution," he told the groggy couple. "We've brought
other fanatical conservatives here, and you'll find them. The
gravity is Earthlike, but the diameter of this planet is fourteen
thousand miles. No nasty heavy metals. The vegetation's built
like a banana tree. No wood. It'll be a little difficult polluting
this place."

"Immoral force! Coercion!" whispered Noss.

"You are getting what you want, fresh air forever. Maybe your descendants will be a superior breed of silky-hair monkeys. No phlogiston." He coughed gently. "The People are not passionate shepherds, nor can we foresee the future. Control your own experiment. Here is Eden. See what you can make of it."

Guert Maury stepped on the cigarette butt. He climbed back into the ship and left for wonderfully contaminated, richly polluted Earth.

R. A. Lafferty fits into no niche. He usually writes completely out-side the normal limits of science fiction, and often violates all the rules I know of storytelling. It doesn't seem to matter. Few writers have had so many stories nominated for awards. Readers love him madly—or else, they reject him completely. I think this is a story almost everyone will have to accept and love, however. It's just a trick, of course—I think—probably—maybe—sort of—or . . . well . . .

R. A. LAFFERTY
The Man Underneath

Charles Chartel was not the most pleasant man in the world, and as the Great Zambesi he was not the greatest magician. But he was a smart man and a good magician. He had the magnetism of a faith healer, the spirit and appearance of a rooster, and a deadly seriousness. He had the patter and the poise, and he had learned all that was learnable.

Nor was he a mere pigeon-passer and card-caller. He had in-herited, built up, bought, and assembled as full a repertoire as any magic man in the business.

And, as each must have, he had his specialty: a simple and sound disappearing act. It was nothing really startling; he seemed to underplay it. But it was puzzling, and it remained a puzzle even to those in the trade. This one prime trick equated him with the real masters, who in general technique were a little out of his class. Actually, in the ultimate variation of it, it was the *greatest* trick.

He put Veronica into a box. And when he opened the box again, she was gone. That is all there was to it. The same thing had been performed by dozens of others in many variations.

But Charles (the Great Zambesi) Chartel did not use any of those variations; not, certainly, the trap door—for he had once performed the trick in a wire mesh twenty feet in the air. Besides, he was a cut above the trap-door men.

After showing the empty box, he would always take it apart board by board and pass the boards around for all to handle. He would then assemble it once more into a box, clamp down the cover, unclamp it again, open it, and Veronica would get out of the box.

The Great Boffo swore that the girl never stepped into the box at all. The Great Boffo, however, could not duplicate the trick. Nor could the Great Thaumaturgos, nor the Great Zebdo.

All of them could make girls disappear from boxes, of course, and could do it in more showy fashion. But, though it was the same thing to the audiences, it was not the same thing to themselves. Their tricks were known to each other and were obvious to any magic man. The special trick of Zambesi-Chartel was not understood, and this gave him stature. The only men in the world who do not secretly believe in magic are the magicians, but there was something about the doings of the Great Zambesi that sowed doubt in them. The Great Vespo, indeed, claimed that he knew how it was done. But Vespo, though brilliant, was an old man and was given to extravagant claims.

The explanation that Charles (the Great Zambesi) Chartel gave to his audiences will not be given here. Should we repeat it, we would not be believed; we would be laughed at—and we are sensitive. We have not the magnetism of Zambesi to carry off such an outlandish claim as his, even though it should be true—and it was. (Actually, he said that he sent Veronica down into the ocean and that he called her back again from that ocean.)

However, this isn't about the disappearance of Veronica; it is about a matter quite the opposite. And the opposite of the disappearance of Veronica was the appearance of someone who differed from her as much as possible.

This came about at the Tri-State Fair when the New Arena was quite new. The crowd was spirited, and the Great Zambesi was in full form. The lighting was perfect, and Veronica shone like a jewel set in gold as she stepped into the box that was set up on blocks, clear of the stage. Zambesi closed the box, and the crowd had the true feeling of magic about to happen.

And then, with perfect timing, Zambesi-Chartel threw back the front cover as to reveal the box—empty.

We will be hornswitched if that box was empty!

But what rolled out of the box was not Veronica. It was the most woebegone scarecrow of a clown ever seen, the saddest-looking man who ever stumbled over his own two feet.

"Holy hamadryads, cramoise, where did you come from?" Zambesi-Chartel breathed without understanding his own words.

The man out of the box was a hobo from a hundred years ago. He wept and wiped his nose with his hand. He had trouble with falling pants and broken shoes and a coat whose sleeve avoided arm. The little clown was good, and there was real pathos in his silent humor.

"You've got to get out of here, cnaufer," Chartel hissed at the little man again and again. "Who are you, and how did you get here? Off with you now, cathexis, you're fouling up the act." But the little man avoided Chartel, who would have killed him in all sincerity.

Finally Chartel in his despair closed the box loudly, then opened it again and brought Veronica out of it. But that didn't get rid of the little tramp. He was still cavorting about the stage, and he was good. Listen, he was dressed in old black pants and a torn undershirt and one suspender, and he walked about the stage. Then he had on a red sweater and a burglar's cap and black glasses. He still walked about the stage, and suddenly he was splendid in evening clothes and monocle. Nobody had done that before.

He became Joe College; he became the man in the charcoal-tan suit; he became an old rowdy-dow on the loose with pearl-gray vest and yellow gloves. Then he became a hobo again—but of a different and worse vesture than before.

"Go away, cistugurium," Veronica whispered angrily, "please go away. You're not supposed to be in the act. Who are you, anyhow?"

Nobody else had ever completely changed his garb six times in a minute and a half while hobbling about the stage with his hands in his pockets. Nobody else transmuted his shoes from brown to black as he walked in them. The expression of the little man was pathetic, and many eyes misted as they watched him.

Then, before the act had begun to drag, the little man wobbled over and fell flat on his face in the box. Zambesi-Chartel closed it and stood poised over it in an intensity of fear and hope. Then he opened the box again. The little man was gone.

Zambesi-Chartel took the box apart board by board, and he left it apart. Well, it had been a good act, with an added element. But Charles (the Great Zambesi) Chartel didn't know how he had done it this time—or if he was the one who did it. The trick had always been to make Veronica disappear and appear; there sure hadn't been any little clown in the act before.

"Damn that cressanges, anyhow," Chartel grumbled. He was puzzled. He knew that little man—and yet he didn't.

Later that night at the Pepperpot some of the people ate and talked. There were Chartel himself and Veronica; there was Captain Carter, who had the trained bears; there were the three Lemon sisters, Dolly, Molly, and Polly. Then another one was with them—for the little man was sitting there and sniffling. He hadn't been there before, and he hadn't come in.

"Shall I order for you, claud?" Molly Lemon asked solicitously.

But a filled plate was already there, and the little man began to eat. He grinned and he grimaced. He was wearing horn-rim glasses, and then he was wearing pince-nez. He had a grin that came shyly, as though he were trying it out for the first time.

"clarence is so cute," said Dolly Lemon. "We will adopt him into our act if Chartel doesn't want him."

There was an empty five-cigar carton on the table. The little man picked it up, and it was full. Well, Chartel could duplicate that; probably you could yourself, but it would take prop and preparation. The little man pulled a stogie from the carton, puffed on it, and it was lit. This also could be done; there are few tricks that cannot be duplicated.

"If you are joining the act, cletus, and it seems as though you are," said Chartel, wondering, "you will have to clean up a little."

"Must I really?" asked curt, but he obliged at once. He had become as immaculate a dandy as anyone ever saw. "Captain Carter," he said, "I see from your pocket bulge that you are a drinking man. I ask you to share it with us."

"It's empty an hour since," Captain Carter muttered sadly.

"It wasn't always empty," said cylix, the little man. "Let me see if I can restore it."

"The last time a magician filled an empty whisky bottle for me—and it was none other than old Zambesi-Chartel here—the stuff was not potable. It was the most horrendous rock dew ever distilled."

"This will be potable," said celiter—and the bottle filled.

Its content was gloriously potable. It put new life into the party, and all of them, except Chartel-Zambesi, had a wonderful time. And if you don't think you can have fun with a reanimated bottle of whisky and Veronica and the three Lemon sisters, you must have a different and more staid definition of fun.

"But all good things must end," said Captain Carter when the small hours were half-grown.

"All good things do *not* have to end," said cajetan, the little man, who had been enjoying himself on Polly Lemon's lap. "The world shriveled when your thought was first put into words. Good things can go on forever, except that—now and then—they must be temporarily adjourned. As long as we understand that partings are only temporary."

"Oh, we understand that, cuiller," said the three Lemon sisters. So they temporarily adjourned the party.

But later—and this was after the sun itself was up—Chartel and cyprian were finally alone.

"We will have to have an explanation," said Chartel. "Who are you?"

"You have no idea, Charles? Did you not take me out of the box? I thought you would know. Did you not call me up?"

"I doubt I did. Do not try to hoax an old hoaxer. Where did you come from that first time? The stage was not trapped, and you were not intruded with my knowledge."

"Was I not? You told the audience how it was done. You said you called me up out of the ocean."

"That is my patter—but it doesn't apply to you. Damnit, ching-chi, where'd you get the Chinese robes and grow that little beard so fast? And how do you make them both change colors so neat? No, chawan, I never called any such fish as you out of the ocean."

"In that case, I will leave, since I am here through a misunderstanding."

"Stay a bit, cyfaill. In my patter, that is the way I make the girl disappear. How could it make you appear?"

"Charles, I've heard you explain the principle dozens of times. I was not in the box. But in a little while I would be in the box. So we adjust the box to a near moment in the future, and I am in the box."

"There's a lacuna in your logic, clunis," Chartel said. "Hey, how can you turn into a Hottentot so easily? And not into a real Hottentot either, coya—but into what I would call an old burlesque-stage idea of a Hottentot."

"You always did have a good imagination, Charles," said chabiari. He took up an empty glass, shook it, and it was filled again.

"You're my master there, cosmos," said Chartel. "I couldn't

duplicate that without props and you've done it three times. How?"

"By our own theory that we worked out so long ago, Charles. I shift it only a little in time, and it is done. Anything that has once been full can be filled again by taking it back to the time of its plenitude."

"chester, you have a patter that won't quit. But, if it worked— the idea would be a good one."

"It does work, Charles. I thought we knew that. We have used it so long."

"You talk and talk, collard," said Chartel. "But I still do not know how you can change your whole appearance so easily and often."

"Why, Charles, we are protean," said coilon. "That is the sort of man we are."

It was later the same day that Finnerty, the manager of the show, spoke to Chartel about the little man.

"Your brother from the old country has put new life into the act," he said. "Keep him in it. We haven't mentioned money—and I am seldom the one to bring up the subject—but we can settle on a figure. Will it be payable to him or to you?"

"It will be payable to me," said Charles (the Great Zambesi) Chartel. Confused he was, but he always knew the top and bottom side of a dollar. Finnerty and Chartel settled on a figure.

"You have been taken for my brother from the old country," Chartel told colin a bit later, "and I can see why. I wondered whom you reminded me of. Oh, stop turning into a rooster! If you were shaved and combed—say, that *was* quick, contumace! The resemblance would be, is, even closer. You do look like me; you are an extremely handsome man. But I did not know that I had a brother, compuesto, and I do not know what country the old country is—since I was born on Elm Street in Springfield."

"Perhaps 'brother' is a euphemism for something even closer, Charles; and the 'old country' may have a special meaning for us. Is it not the name for what is on the other side of your 'ocean'?"

"columkill, you are as phony as—well, metaphor fails me—you are as phony as myself," said Charles Chartel.

Sometimes the little man was frightening in his wild actions. There wasn't a mean bone in him, and he was almost universally liked. But he did act on impulse.

For him, to think was to act. It was good that everybody liked him; if they hadn't, they'd have hanged him high.

And always he would multiply things. Chartel begged for his secret.

"We could be rich, cogsworth, really rich," Chartel would plead.

"But we are already rich, Charles. Nobody has ever had such a rich and perfected personality as we have. You still do not appreciate the greatness of our trick, Charles, though we thought about it for years before we were able to do it. It's the noblest illusion of them all. Now we are citizens of an abounding world, and everything in it is ours. That is to be rich."

"consuelo, you are a bleeding doctrinaire. I did not ask for a lecture. I only ask that you show me how to make a hundred dollars grow where one grew before. I say that is to be rich."

"I've shown you a hundred times, Charles, and you look for more than is in it. You take a thin old wallet that once knew fatness. You restore it to its old state, empty it and restore it again, and so you accumulate. But why do you want money?"

"It is just that I have a passion for collecting it, courlis."

"Collecting we can understand, but the true collector will have no desire for duplicates. Understandably we might want a bill of each size—a one, a five, a ten, a fifty—but we avoid that which once we prized—the ten-thousand-dollar bill. The avid people have spoiled it for us. But you have not the true collector's spirit, Charles."

"I have the true money collector's spirit, clendon. Why cannot I duplicate your feats in this?"

"The only reason I can figure, Charles, is that you're just too duck-knuckled dumb—and it hurts me to say that about one of ourselves."

But Zambesi-Chartel got a new set of ideas when he saw the trick that cormorant did with an old hat. It was at a rummage sale at which charleroi looked in out of curiosity—he was curious about everything.

"What a pixie must have worn this!" he exclaimed. "What a pixie!"

c held the hat in his hands. And then he held the head in his hands. It was something like a pixie head, and it was attached to the body of a young lady. cisailles kissed the young lady uncommonly about the temporal regions and pressed her to his sternum —for to him impulse was the same as action. And she squealed.

"Not that I mind—but you *did* startle me," she chimed. "Who are you? Who, may I ask, am I? And how in pigeon-toed perdition did I get here?"

"You are a pixie, young lady," said clough, "and as such you are likely to turn up anywhere. I had your hat, so what more natural than that I should call you up to fill it."

"I am only a part-time pixie, cartier, but I am a full-time housewife. Supper will burn. How do I get back?"

"You already are," said callimachus. And she was. Or at least she was no longer there.

And that was the beginning of the trouble; not for c, not for the young pixie lady, but it was the beginning of the trouble for Charles (Great Zambesi) Chartel.

Charles knew how it was done now. One cannot continue doing a basic trick in the presence of such a sharpy as Charles Chartel without his learning it. And once he had learned how it was done, there was no stopping him.

Charles Chartel was not a bad man underneath, but on the surface he was a rotter. The natural complement of healthy greed that is in every man began to burgeon unnaturally in him. The hard core of meanness spread through his whole being. The arrogance of the rooster became that of the tyrant, and envy and revenge burned in him with sulfurous fire.

Chartel now had the key to total wealth, a key that would not only unlock all doors for him, but lock them against others. He set out to get control of the show. To do this he had to break Finnerty, the owner-manager, and buy him out after breaking him.

Business had been good, and every night Finnerty had a full cash box. But before a thing is full, it is half-full. And before that, it is a quarter-full. Every night, just as Finnerty went to count the take, Zambesi-Chartel would play a trick on that box. And it would be only a quarter-full. That was not enough to cover expenses.

Finnerty had never been a saving man. He had always trod the narrow green edge between solvency and disaster. And in two weeks he was broke.

Finnerty sold the show and the bookings to Chartel for ten thousand dollars. It made a nice wad in his pocket when he walked away from the show that was no longer his.

But the meanness was running like a tide in Chartel, and he wouldn't let it go at that. He emptied the wallet of Finnerty again, taking it back ten minutes in time. Finnerty felt a certain lightness, and he knew what it was. But he kept on walking.

"It's lucky he left me with my pants," said Finn, "if he has. I'm afraid to look down."

A cloud came over the happy little family that was the show. Veronica felt herself abused, and it wasn't imagination. The three Lemon sisters shivered to the chill of a harsh master. So did Carucchi the singer, and Captain Carter and his bears. And c, the little man who was the unwitting cause of it all, took to staying out of the way of the rampaging Chartel.

For Zambesi-Chartel was now avid for praise, for money, for all manner of meanness. He accumulated coin by every variation of the new trick he had learned. He robbed by it, he burgled the easy way. It is an awful and sickening thing to see a good man grow rich and respected.

"But underneath he isn't a bad man at all," Veronica moaned. "Really he isn't."

"No, underneath he is a fine man," said c, the little man of impulse. "Who should know better than I?"

"Why, what do you mean, chadwick, dear?" Veronica asked him.

"The same as you. Charles is only bad on the surface. Underneath he's a fine fellow."

Well, that may have been. But on the surface, Zambesi-Chartel sure did get rough. He demeaned the dignity of his fellow humans and made them eat dirt by the ton. He went on adrenalin drunks and thrived on the hatred in his own bloodstream. He became a martinet, a propagandist for the Hoop act. He registered Democrat. He switched from perfectos to panatelas and from honest whiskey sours to perfidious martinis. He developed a snigger and horselaugh that wilted pigweeds.

"Oh, chiot," said Veronica, "we must do something to save him from himself. We are all involved with him."

"Who should know better than I?" conchylatus asked sadly.

Chartel began to drink tea. He started to call a napkin a "serviette" and to omit every single syllable in "extraordinary." He switched allegiance from the noble National League to the sniveling American. He defrauded his laborers of their wages, he used scent, he ate vegetarian lunches, he read Walter Lippmann posthumously, he switched from Gumbo Hair Oil to Brilliantine. Once a character begins to deteriorate, it goes all the way, and in every detail.

Chartel had the Green Sickness, the inordinate love of money. He obtained the stuff, first by all means fair and foul, then by foul means only. But obtain it he did, and it made a sniveling devil out of him.

"But the man underneath isn't bad at all," Veronica insisted.

"Who should know better than I?" caoine said.

The Grand Canyon began with a prairie dog burrow, and once it was started there was no stopping it. The downfall of Zambesi-Chartel began over a nickel and then the whole apparatus came down: his wealth, real and phantom—his reputation—the whole blamed complex of the man.

It started with a fistfight he had with a blind newsdealer over a nickel. It ended with Chartel in jail, indicted, despised, shamed, despondent. Moreover, public feeling was strongly against him.

Chartel was up on more than twenty counts of theft and pilfering, and the nickel stolen from the blind man was by no means the least of them. He was up on a dozen counts of wage fraud. He was charged with multiplex pickpocketing "by device not understood." They had him on faked bill of sale, dishonest conveyance, simple and compounded larceny, possession of stolen goods, barratry.

"Looks like we have you on everything but chicken-stealing," the judge said at the hearing.

"We have him on that, too," said the bailiff. "Five counts of it."

"You would gag a gannet and make a buzzard belch," said the judge. "I'd crop your ears if that law still obtained. And if we can find a capital offense in all this offensiveness, I'll have your head. It is hard to believe that you were once human."

Chartel was shamed and sick of heart and felt himself friendless. That night he attempted to hang himself in his cell. The attempt failed for reasons that are not clear, but not for any lack of effort on his part. It is worthy of note that the only persons who ever attempt to take their own lives are rather serious persons.

"We will have to go to him at once, cristophe," said Veronica. "We must show him that we still love him. He'd sicken a jackal the way he's behaving, but he isn't really like that. The man underneath—"

"Hush, Veronica, you embarrass me when you talk like that," said ciabhach. "I know what a prince is the man underneath."

Little c went to visit the Great Zambesi-Chartel in his cell.

"It is time we had a talk," he said.

"No, no, it's too late for talk," said Charles Chartel.

"You have disgraced us both, Charles," said celach. "It goes very deeply when it touches me."

"I never even knew who you were, little c. You are protean, and you are not at all plausible."

"You called me up, and you still don't know who I am, Charles? But this was our finest trick, our greatest illusion, on which we worked subconsciously for years. We are our own masterpiece, Charles. And you didn't recognize it when it happened. You are the magic man, but I am the magic man run wild. Aye, Charles, he's best when he runs wild."

"Tell me, cicerone, who are you? Who am I?" Chartel begged. "What is my difficulty?"

"Our difficulty, Charles, is that one of us became too serious," carnefice tried to explain. "To be serious is the only capital crime. For that, one of us will have to die—but it isn't as though it were a serious matter. Every man is at least two men, but ordinarily the two are not at the same time bodied and apparent. Now you have marred our greatest trick—but it was fun while it lasted."

Little c signaled to Veronica, and she came down the corridor with a bunch of boards under her arm. She was admitted to the cell by the puzzled jailer.

"One of us will have to leave forever," coquelicot told Charles Chartel. "It isn't right for both of us to be around."

"Ah, I will be sorry to see you go, chandos," said Chartel. "But who are you? I never could remember your name properly, and there is something weird about that. You change forever in appearance and name. Who are you, little c?"

"Only that. Just little c. Or shall we say sub-c? But we are too clever to be hounded into a hole like this, Charles. Remember! We were our own greatest trick, even if it failed."

"What must we do now?" Chartel asked dully.

"A simple transference," cogne said. He was building the box board by board.

"I'm not a bad man underneath," Chartel sniveled. "I'm misunderstood."

"No, we're a fine man underneath, Charles. I am the man underneath," said ciud. "Get in the box."

"I get in? I am Charles (the Great Zambesi) Chartel. You are only little c, sub-c, an aspect of myself. I will *not* get into the box!"

"Get in, Charles," said cistercium. "It was a mix-up from the beginning. You were never meant to see the light of day. The wrong one of us has been running loose."

"I'll fight, I'll claw, I'll rant!"

"That's what a healthy subconscious is supposed to do," cludok said. "Get in!"

"It's murder! I won't go! It's oblivion!"

"No such thing, Charles. It isn't as though we weren't the same person. I'll still be here."

Then little c and Veronica shoved the Great Zambesi Charles Chartel down into the box and closed the lid. In doing so, little c became himself the Great Zambesi. For when he opened the box again, it was empty. And he took it apart board by board. The jailer said that he had to have his prisoner, and Veronica gave him the boards.

"There, there, doll," she said. "Make one out of them. Try real hard."

And Veronica and the Great Zambesi left that place.

We won't say that Zambesi wasn't the greatest magician in the world. He may have become the greatest after he began to treat it lightly. People, he was good! There was never any act with such variety and fun in it. After his strange mid-life hiatus, he achieved new heights.

"And I'm certainly glad you overcame your personality difficulties," the loving Veronica told him later. "For a while there—whoof! But I always knew you were a fine man underneath."

All I know of B. Alan Burhoe is that he picked one of the toughest kinds of stories to write. A story of this type depends on giving the reader a full picture of strange backgrounds and totally alien life modes. Usually, only novels afford the writer the space needed to develop his exotic world, and to make the reader at home with his creation. Rare as success is in this length, Burhoe has produced a nearly perfect example.

B. ALAN BURHOE

Ornithanthropus

Schadow was awakened by his woman.

He sat up from the blankets of marsh cotton, stretching his wings above his head until they touched the low ceiling of woven reeds.

"The skyhunter is dying," she said. "We must leave."

His heart twisted. "Dying? Are you sure?"

"See for yourself." She turned to gather their meager possessions in her thin arms.

He left their cabin and knew the truth of her words even before he had reached the forward opening. He felt the skyhunter's fading life in the uneasy quivering that shook the wood framework of the gondola. He cursed. Anger flared, turning to rage, fading to a sinking feeling of impotence.

A pale yellow tentacle curled through the opening. The amber eye at its tip regarded him.

"Ah, my ponderous friend. What is the matter?" Schadow asked soothingly.

The tentacle wrapped about his waist, reassuring, sad.

On reaching the opening, he looked out and up. The hydrogen-filled balloon-bladder that kept the skyhunter airborne had turned from a healthy crimson to a dusky brown, run with streaks of copper. The airpaddles were clenched as if in pain. The cartilage ribs to which the framework of the gondola was fastened sagged, hardly capable of holding it or the hundred and seven human members of the Seacliff Clan. The sixty green and crimson fishing tentacles hung lifeless toward the glittering sea a half-kilometer below. The single foretentacle that had greeted him snaked away and moved listlessly in the air. He wanted to say something, to reassure the animal, the living dirigible that had been his home and friend and protector all his life, to let his calm voice—

"Schadow."

He turned, recognized the old man who stood behind him. "Grandfather?"

"There is little time. You must move fast."

"And you?"

"You know my duty. We have lived as one, the skybeast and I—we will die as one. You are now Clan Elder. You know what you must do."

Schadow nodded. For a moment they clasped hands, Schadow studying the patriarch's tired, rawhide face. Then he went back to his cabin. Behind him, Grandfather jumped into the air and fluttered up to the head of the skyhunter. It tried to push him away, but the ancient one found power in his wings and stayed close, patting the head and talking softly of yesteryear.

Schadow gathered the clan at the aft opening, and when he was sure that he had missed no one, ordered his people into the sky. One by one they jumped, arms tightly grasping children or belongings. Their wings flapped until they hit an upcurrent—then they glided into formation, armed men taking the vulnerable positions. Last to leave was Schadow. He threw himself from the gondola, falling toward the distant water, stretched his wings, flew.

Together, silent, they headed toward the land until Schadow judged they had reached a safe distance.

He looked back at the skyhunter.

The bladder was now almost totally copper. The three hydrogen bags were scarcely visible through the once transparent hide. As the wind pivoted the derelict skybeast Schadow saw Grandfather flying close to its head. He saw the creature give one last attempt to push the old man away with its tentacle, saw it fail, saw them grasp one another one last time, enemies once, now brothers.

"It's going to suicide," said one warrior.

Before he had spoken the last word, a spark flared in the depths of the bladder. The skyhunter was enveloped in a savage burst of fire that reflected softly off the wispy clouds above and more fiercely off the sea below. Man, beast, and gondola became a single inferno that twisted in the air and tumbled into the waves.

The thunder struck at the Seacliff Clan, enveloped and passed it.

For a few moments the flyers were given increased lift. They took advantage of it and glided in silence toward the granite shore.

A pack of winged amphibians, like tiny pale dragons, soared out from the cliffs to meet them, screaming their challenge and bravado, voicing them all the louder when they were ignored.

"Where do we go now?" asked his woman as Schadow glided in next to her.

"Give me my harness," he said, partly answering her query.

He took the harness of leather straps and silver buckles and dressed himself in midair, fitting the fastenings around his chest and placing the scabbard along his spine. He pulled out the sword of strong white bone and tested its edges, honed over the years to razor sharpness.

"You must go to Starport," he called to his people. "Wait there for five days. If I have not returned by that time, you will know that I have failed to tame a skyhunter and that you must choose a new Clan Elder from among you."

He said nothing more. Nothing else was left to say.

They flew away, a few lifting their spirits from the depths of the tragedy enough to wish him luck. He watched them until they seemed no larger than insects against the brightening blue of the post-dawn horizon. Then he banked, caught the thermal that swept up from the coastal cliffs, dropped into an easy glide to conserve his energy for the ordeal ahead.

They had called the colony world Pishkun, from an ancient Sioux word that meant "cliff," for indeed it was a land of cliffs as well as rift valleys, crevices, and faults—a granite world of eternal upheaval where the thunder of earthquakes was as common as the roar of the ocean. When the colonists had first reached and named Pishkun, they had taken its unfriendly nature as a challenge. Thus, after a million years of frustrated dreams that had begun when early man had first looked at the eagle and felt envy, Ornithanthropus had finally been born, for only in the air could life be sustained with any permanency on this world.

Aesthetics had played a greater part in the design of the birdfolk than functional engineering. The wings had been placed at the shoulderblades and were powered by a complex system of muscles that started at the keellike breastbone, joined the trapezius, and ran up the lower part of each wing. The bones were hollow for lightness, and the lower eyelids, which were transparent, could cover the eyes to protect them from windblast. To a basicform human, the birdfolk were the symbol of beauty in motion.

Schadow, who was of the fiftieth generation of his kind, cared little for the history of his people. He knew it—the basicforms at Starport had told it to him when he had visited that antigrav trading station in his adolescence—but he had found the story only of peripheral interest. Only life, health, the sky, his woman, and the skyhunter he must tame meant anything to him.

The day passed into early afternoon without tiring him as he skimmed along the updrafts and climbed for a wider view. Over the sea almost a kilometer away he saw a young skyhunter, shining like a blood jewel over the silver-streaked greenness of the waves. But it was already fishing. It would be too strong for him to outlast. He looked inland.

The nostrils of his knife-blade nose flared. The muscles in his sunken cheeks tightened like braided rawhide. His eyes slitted, and the greasy black hair lifted from his scalp. Unsteadily he moved the sword in his hands. What he saw was barely a dot on the horizon, but every instinct in him identified it. It was a skyhunter heading for the sea and therefore hungry, therefore weakened.

For a scant moment he debated falling toward the land and foraging for something to eat, then tossed the idea aside. The beast would know by his smell whether or not he had a full belly, and it had best sense that he was as hungry as it, unarmed except for the sword, naked except for the harness—equal with it in all respects, including courage.

He studied every facet of the land and air around him. The ground was a tumbled mess of bare rock, strewn boulders, cascades, bogs, and patches of brown and green where simple land plants had eked out a living despite the endless assaults upon them by the planet's ever-changing crust. He looked away from the tortured land. With a sense ingrained into him through generations of running upon the winds, he looked at the air mass around him and mapped every current in his mind. He saw the draft that swept up from the sea cliffs below him like a sun-warmed glass curtain to touch the inversion layer four kilometers above; saw a large thermal off to his right, marked where it started on the ground near a dust devil, a huge cylinder of moving bubbles of heated air that rose to reach the cumulus clouds that dotted the sky; saw a second curtainlike current rise from cliffs of red granite to his left, but this one bent and rushed dangerously across the jagged top; saw the bulk of dead air that sat ahead of him, shimmering now and then in the form of a seaward breeze.

He couldn't have picked a better place to meet the skybeast, he told himself.

It would not retreat inland or go to the left because of the cliffs. It could only attempt to go over him or to his right—or through him.

It came on without evidencing the slightest concern. As it drew closer Schadow was awed at its size—it was bigger than any he had ever seen.

The massive bladder, shining dull crimson in the sunlight, must have been fully forty meters across and almost a hundred long. The three hydrogen sacs inside fluttered larger and smaller as it adjusted its buoyancy in the weak on-sea winds. Sixteen airpaddles, eight along each side, swept forward like closed fists, opened to reveal strong black membranes, pushed back to provide thrust. Fishing tentacles were coiled close to the cartilage ribbing that protected two-thirds of its underside from leaping sea carnivores. The poison-celled foretentacle that flipped about the bladder to watch for predators or parasites was set just behind the head, which took up the other third. And its eyes—they looked across at him—were twin pools of molten amber, the black pupils expanding and contracting to the beat of the aerial supercoelenterate's savage life systems. They revealed a brooding intelligence that at once terrified and exhilarated Schadow.

He hovered as best he could in the skyhunter's path.

The creature slowed, watching him. Schadow gave challenge.

"Ho! Skyhunter! I have come to tame you, to form the bond of brotherhood between us for the good of my people—or die trying."

The eyes burned into his.

The foretentacle streaked for him.

Schadow swung his sword as he had practiced since he had first taken to wing as a boy, slashing the air in front of him in a series of hissing sweeps. He wanted the beast to know that he could cut the tentacle in two if it threatened him, but that he didn't want to.

The tentacle retreated. The eyes studied him, their look now unreadable. For an instant something flashed in those eyes. Then the creature was moving.

At first he thought it was retreating, and the concept shocked him, for every skyhunter he had ever known or heard of would rather have suicided than run from an attacker, especially such a little attacker as a man. Then a gulping sound came to his ears. He smiled. It was increasing its buoyancy. It was going to attempt to go over him.

Schadow pushed at the almost still air with his wings and began to climb. The skybeast, airpaddles sweeping lazily to maintain equilibrium, began to ascend in front of him.

They went up and up until the clouds seemed to disappear as they melded into them and ice crystals danced about them, flickering brilliantly as they caught and broke the sunlight. Schadow's exhaled breath began to form into puffs of frost. The tentacle again darted toward him, and again he created a protective shield around him with his sword.

"Ho! You will have to do better than that, great one."

With a mutter the coelenterate began to descend, its hydrogen already cooling and decreasing its lift. Schadow paralleled it.

The clouds reformed above. The atmosphere became warmer.

Schadow flexed his wings to spoil his descent, and was amazed to discover that this adversary was picking up downward speed. He allowed himself to fall with it until he was forced to brake.

Surely the thing wasn't going to dash itself into the ground! He felt himself go cold in a way the high frost couldn't have affected him.

It was indeed throwing itself at the twisted rock country. Shaken, the birdman watched it drop until it was falling away from him like a plummeting boulder. It hit the earth, narrowly missing a jagged outcropping. Dust billowed from the impact site. The crimson bladder shook, flattened, appeared to burst. Then it was rebounding back up at him.

Schadow would have laughed in relief and admiration for

the creature if it had not been lofting directly at him with tremendous speed. He wheeled, pushing the air in desperation. It rushed past him. The foretentacle narrowly missed him, and one of the fishing tentacles touched his left leg. He cried out in pain.

Stubbornly he wheeled again and chased it until it leveled off at four hundred meters.

He checked his leg. A thin welt was forming across his calf.

"Ho-eee!" he shouted, making the traditional sign of admiration for one's enemy in the air with his sword. In turn, the skyhunter whipped its tentacle about in a remarkable mimicry of the sign.

They settled down to eyeing one another again.

Now perhaps the skybeast realized that it and Schadow must face each other, that each must prove to the other his courage and powers of endurance. And while they strained to endure the ordeal, perhaps a bond would form between them.

The huge eyes suddenly shifted and focused behind his right shoulder.

Schadow looked around.

Seven armed men stared at him.

Their wings fluttered feebly, their weight being supported by antigrav units strapped to their chests. They gripped swords of the best alloy metal. On their bodies they wore glittering collections of useless ornaments and gadgets.

Fangs! Schadow remembered seeing packs of them when he had visited Starbase, and he had heard many tales of their bloody raids. While they were adapted forms, the fangs preferred the sanctuary of the floating plastic city, venturing forth only for murder or pillage.

One flew slightly ahead of the others. Setting a dial on his antigrav, he hovered about ten meters from Schadow, alternately watching the lone warrior and the skyhunter.

"I am Garp," he said.

"So?" Schadow hefted his sword and tentatively tested its edge with his thumb. He looked over his shoulder to check the beast.

Though he acted calmly, he strained all the while to maintain his hovering position without appearing to tire.

"I am leader of our pack." Garp had an artificially bronzed skin, a fat belly, and shining bald head. He reminded Schadow of a Buddha idol—perhaps ancient religions were the latest fashion among the basicforms, whom the fangs always emulated, body sculpture being the dominant art form among the non-adapted men of the Confederacy.

"Then it is up to you to lead your men—if they deserve that title—away. You should know that the ordeal with a skyhunter is a private matter. You have no right here."

Garp laughed.

"But we have come such a long way to find you. Ven here"— he swept his empty hand toward a thinner version of himself, who grinned and bowed awkwardly in the air—"saw your people arrive at the base and overheard them talking about you." Now it was Garp's turn to test his sword edge with his thumb, though Schadow saw sky between flesh and metal. "Having nothing better to do, we decided that we should come out and help you. I mean, all that talk that you people keep giving us about living with nature and not against it to the contrary, we thought that you'd like the power of civilization behind you in this affair." He looked at the beast, briefly meeting its eyes. His voice went softer. "I've never seen a man killed by one of those before." Garp looked at his sword, then shouted, "Ven!"

"Ho?"

"The triplets will stay with me. You take the other two and go behind the thing to keep it from getting away."

"Understood." The three adjusted their antigravs and pushed themselves into position.

Garp looked at Schadow. "You."

Schadow felt his jaw muscles tighten in anger.

"In my wide experience in dealing with men of action, I have usually found that even the bravest need a little push in the right direction on occasion. We watched you fighting the thing, and it is our considered opinion that you keep too far from it. Right, men?"

The trio that moved in behind him answered in chorus, "Right."

"So let's give him the courage he needs." Garp waited until the three were even with him before moving slowly toward the warrior, sword held out ahead of him like a lance.

Schadow held his position. Garp had slowed so that two others were the first to reach him. Folding his wings, Schadow fell. He outstretched them again and regained altitude, slashing at one fang who had just set his antigrav to dive and had left the top of his head vulnerable. He felt his sword crack through the skull. The man screamed and floated away from the contestants.

He slashed at the second man, missing him by millimeters.

Garp screamed in rage. "Kill him," he ordered.

The other two didn't need encouraging. They rushed at Schadow.

He parried the lunging weapon of the first, ducked the second, and looked for Garp. The latter proved to be a greater danger than Schadow had guessed. The fang leader held his sword before him, elbow locked, and maneuvered himself by twisting the dials on his antigrav. He flashed in and out with extreme accuracy, and Schadow learned respect for the antigrav as he desperately put up a defense. The other two pressed beside him, forcing him to fall back toward the skyhunter.

"Ven," shouted Garp. "Drive the thing this way."

Schadow looked behind him. Ven and his companions were efficiently moving the skybeast toward him. Not that he feared the skyhunter so much—though he knew what his fate would be if it caught him—but he felt concern that the flashing blades would soon cripple the animal. It was battling with a ferocity it had not shown earlier. Its fishing tentacles lashed out as it rocked in the air. Its foretentacle hung poise dto strike. Its paddles sent it spinning on an axis, making it harder to predict its next attack or parry. Even so, it didn't have a chance against this pact. The fact that its fiery suicide—when it accepted defeat—would take its tormentors with it was little consolation.

Something nagged at the back of Schadow's mind, but the fangs gave him no time to find out what it was. His keel muscles were blazing with pain as he was forced to beat his wings to hold his position. He could feel himself weakening. For the first time in his life he envied the power the antigrav gave a flyer, as his attackers pressed themselves more keenly against him. His sword of bloodied bone took the full force of a downward stroke from above and was chipped. He stabbed at Garp, who replied by smashing Schadow's sword with a jarring blow that broke the point. Cursing, Schadow put his full fury into an offense, momentarily driving the three back. Garp lost his temper and for the first time truly led the attack. They came at him at once.

The wind shimmered, and the birdman saw a brief updraft roll up to them like a pearl-gray bubble. He flexed his wings. The warm bubble enveloped them, jostling the fangs and lifting their intended victim above them. Spitting monosyllables, the trio adjusted their antigravs and shot toward him.

Schadow, momentarily relieved from battle and able to rest his burning muscles, was amazed. Had they been so busy that they hadn't seen the thermal? But surely they must have. No matter how involved you were, you always watched the air about you. You had to if you wanted to fly.

Garp and the others were at him again. His weapon rendered useless as a foil, he was forced to slash and chop at them. He scratched Garp's bronze belly, forcing him behind the other two.

He saw a second thermal bubble coming up at them. Winging over, he dived. The fangs fell beside him. When he leveled off, they leveled beside him, prepared to continue the fight. The thermal hit, and again he was carried away from them.

They couldn't see!

He saw the truth, and with it a possibility. These men, adapted for the air though they were, were creatures of the Starbase, where no man ever did what a mechanism could more easily do.

Even though they had flown the skies all their lives, they had never really *flown*. Using their wings only as stabilizers, they let their antigravs do their flying for them. Not having the need to know the currents of the atmosphere, they had lost, if they had ever had, the ability to see them. In a very important way they were blind.

Again Schadow dived. This time he looped low and under the trailing tentacles of the skyhunter. The fangs reset their equipment and gave easy chase.

"Ven—" shouted Garp.

Ven looked down and peeled away from the troubled skyhunter, followed by his comrades.

The six formed a rough flock behind Schadow.

Banking to his left, he put his last dregs of energy into flying for the red cliffs.

As his pursuers closed the distance between them he regarded the bleak cliffs and the wispy blanket of air that rose up and over it. Every instinct cried out to him to veer away.

He reached the outer edge of the blanket and soared upward, the wind brushing his face gently and with no hint of where it would take him if he stayed with it. The pack adjusted and rose behind him. Ven was leading, and only five meters below, his teeth showing in a tight grin.

Ven overtook him as they reached the summit, and Schadow was carried across the rough top. With one hand on his antigrav Ven threw himself at the birdman.

Schadow met sword with sword. As Ven pulled back to make a second stab, Schadow somersaulted beneath him and slashed upward. Blood spurted past his face. Ven screamed and twisted in the air, held aloft by his device.

The second attacker was luckier. His sword caught Schadow's at an angle, breaking it just above the guard. Schadow tossed the handle into the man's face.

Shouting in victory, Garp moved in ahead of the others for the kill.

"Die, you—" he yelled, raising his weapon. His eyes burned.

The blow never came.

They were past the cliff.

Schadow saw the draftfall as a glimmering mass of air that spilled over the lip of the cliff and tumbled toward the broken land. He had often seen such sights from afar, but this was the first time he had been in one. Like every winged creature on every world, he normally knew better than to fly into the currents on the lee side of a mountain.

The downdraft caught him and Garp in its grip and threw them violently at the rocks. Garp howled, dropping his sword, which spun into a fang below him. Each member of the pack played frantically with his antigrav. But the air tossed them about like wood chips in a raging river. The downfall was too powerful to be beaten by the puny devices of man.

Schadow made no attempt to outfly the draft. Putting his arms next to his body in a swept-back position, straightening his legs, hitching forward at the waist and angling his aching wings close to his sides, he formed his body into an elementary airfoil, skidding through the air at an angle.

He closed his lower lids against the vicious winds and through them saw the fangs, the whole scene faded by the protective tissue so that it seemed that it happened in the depths of a faintly pink sea.

Ven's corpse was first to hit, smashing spread-eagled atop an altar of rock not two meters from the base of the cliff. Two others hit farther out. Silently, explosively, they touched the ground, their screams and the crashes coming weakly through the winds after the fact. A fourth hit a shallow pool, sending up a shower of scummed water and insects. A fifth had slowed himself a bit with his antigrav, and it seemed to Schadow that his screams must have continued for a second after he had hit.

Garp was a fast learner. On seeing Schadow, he had copied the airfoil design, getting added spoiling from his antigrav. But he was too late and too low. The false Buddha smashed into a jagged outcropping of volcanic glass, beheading himself.

The pink-tinted ground was getting dangerously close. Schadow felt the skeletal claws of oblivion drag along his spine.

Then he was out of the draftfall and in a turbulent but strong wave lift beyond. Extending his wings, he soared into the sky and opened his lids to its eternal blue.

He looked down. Scattered on the ground were the twisted and broken forms of the fangs. Somehow an antigrav unit had been torn loose from a corpse and, free of its weight, clattered along under the force of the draftfall until clear, and then shot through the air toward the base, perhaps on a homing signal. Three of the corpses, he noticed, were also beginning to move across the rocks, being pulled by devices that had outlasted their owners.

The skyhunter still floated where he had left it.

Did he dare to hope?

Though he was unarmed, he settled into a straightaway glide toward the beast.

It was obviously as near exhaustion as he, but appeared unhurt. There was no reason for it to stay away from its sea hunting —unless it was waiting for him. It could be purposely baiting him, he told himself. Vengeance was not solely a human passion.

He slowed and circled before its massive head.

The amber eyes watched him.

Slowly, carefully, the tentacle moved toward him. He stayed in his tight orbit, not moving away. The auxiliary eye at the tip of the tentacle opened—the tentacle itself touched his arm.

No poison cells opened to destroy him. The tentacle remained soft and gentle.

Laughing, Schadow grabbed the tentacle, and the skybeast, tender as he remembered another of its kind, grabbed him.

It placed Schadow atop its bladder, where he could sit and rest. He didn't mind the fact that the skin was almost unbearably hot from the sun. He laughed again. The beast moved its tentacle joyfully, and the dragon-amphibians that guarded the seacliffs screamed at them as they moved through the sky and over the sea, once enemies, now brothers.

There was a time when the major stories in science fiction were what are called "hard-science" fiction. Everything in them was tightly based on real science and an extension of that science. Now most writers seem unwilling (or unable) to write in that mode. The one exception among the newer writers is Larry Niven, who fills the gap very well indeed. His "hard-science" Ringworld won both major awards for the science fiction novel. Here he combines the hard realities of scientific possibility with man's ancient dreams of longevity and endless horizons.

LARRY NIVEN
Rammer

Once there was a dead man.

He had been waiting for two hundred years inside a coffin whose outer shell held liquid nitrogen. There were frozen clumps of cancer all through his frozen body. He had had it bad.

He was waiting for medical science to find him a cure.

He waited in vain. Most varieties of cancer could be cured now, but no cure existed for the billions of cell walls ruptured by expanding crystals of ice. He had known the risk when he took it, and had gambled anyway. Why not? He had been dying.

The vaults held millions of frozen bodies. Why not? They, too, had been dying.

Later there was a criminal. His name is forgotten, and his crime is secret, but it must have been a terrible one. The state wiped his personality for it.

Afterward he was a dead man: still warm, still breathing, even reasonably healthy—but empty.

The state had use for an empty man.

Corbett awoke on a hard table, aching as if he had slept too long in one position. He stared incuriously at a white ceiling. Memories floated back to him of a double-walled coffin and sleep and pain.

The pain was gone.

He sat up at once.

And flapped his arms wildly for balance. Everything felt wrong. His arms would not swing right. His body was too light. His head bobbed strangely on a thin neck. He reached frantically for the nearest support, which turned out to be a blond young man in a white jumpsuit. Corbett missed—his arms were shorter than he had expected. He toppled to his side, shook his head, and sat up more carefully.

His arms. Scrawny, knobby—and not his.

The man in the jumpsuit asked, "Are you all right?"

"Yah," said Corbett. His throat was rusty, but that was all right. His new body didn't fit, but it didn't seem to have cancer, either. "What's the date? How long has it been?"

A quick recovery. The checker gave him a plus. "Twenty-one-ninety, your dating. You won't have to worry about our dating."

That sounded ominous. Cautiously Corbett postponed the obvious question: *What's happened to me?* and asked instead, "Why not?"

"You won't be joining our society."

"No? What, then?"

"Several professions are open to you—a limited choice. If you don't qualify for any of them, we'll try someone else."

Corbett sat on the edge of the hard operating table. His body seemed younger, more limber, definitely thinner. He was acutely aware that his abdomen did not hurt, no matter how he moved.

He asked, "And what happens to me?"

"I've never learned how to answer that question. Call it a matter of metaphysics," said the checker. "Let me detail what's happened to you so far, and then you can decide for yourself."

There was an empty man. Still breathing, and as healthy as most of society in the year twenty-one-ninety. But empty. The electrical patterns in the brain, the worn paths of nervous reflexes, the memories, the personality of the man had all been wiped away.

And there was this frozen thing.

"Your newstapers called you people corpsicles," said the blond man. "I never understood what the tapes meant."

"It comes from Popsicle. Frozen sherbet." Corbett had used the word himself before he had become one of them. One of the corpsicles, frozen dead.

Frozen within a corpsicle's frozen brain were electrical patterns that could be recorded. The process would warm the brain and destroy most of the patterns, but that hardly mattered, because other things must be done too.

Personality was not all in the brain. Memory RNA was concentrated in the brain, but it ran all through the nerves and the blood. In Corbett's case the clumps of cancer had to be cut away—then the RNA could be extracted from what was left. The operation would have left nothing like a human being. More like bloody mush, Corbett gathered.

"What's been done to you is not the kind of thing we can do twice," said the checker. "You get one chance, and this is it. If you don't work out, we'll terminate and try someone else. The vaults are full of corpsicles."

"You mean you'd wipe my personality," Corbett said unsteadily. "But I haven't committed a crime. Don't I have any rights?"

The checker looked stunned. Then he laughed. "I thought I'd explained. The man you think you are is dead. Corbett's will was probated long ago. His widow—"

"Damn it, I left money to myself! A trust fund!"

"No good." Though the man still smiled, his face was impersonal, remote, unreachable. A vet smiles reassuringly at a cat due to be fixed. "A dead man can't own property—that was settled in the courts long ago. It wasn't fair to the heirs. It took the money out of circulation."

Corbett jerked an unexpectedly bony thumb at his bony chest. "But I'm alive now."

"Not in law. You can earn your new life; the state will give you a new birth certificate and citizenship if you give the state good reason."

Corbett sat for a moment, absorbing that. Then he got off the table. "Let's get started, then. What do you need to know about me?"

"Your name."

"Jerome Corbett."

"Call me Pierce." The checker did not offer to shake hands. Neither did Corbett, perhaps because he sensed the man would not respond, perhaps because they were both noticeably overdue for a bath. "I'm your checker. Do you like people? I'm just asking. We'll test you in detail later."

"I get along with the people around me, but I like my privacy."

The checker frowned. "That narrows it more than you might think. This isolationism you called privacy was, well, a passing fad. We don't have the room for it—or the inclination either. We can't send you to a colony world—"

"I might make a good colonist."

"You'd make terrible breeding stock. Remember, the genes aren't yours. No. You get one choice, Corbett. Rammer."

"Rammer?"

" 'Fraid so."

"That's the first strange word you've used since I woke up. In fact—hasn't the language changed at all? You don't even have an accent."

"Part of the job. I learned your speech through RNA training. You'll learn your trade the same way if you get that far. You'll be amazed how fast you can learn with RNA shots to help you along. But you'd better be right about liking your privacy, Corbett. Can you take orders?"

"I was in the army."

"What does that mean?"

"Yes."

"Good. Do you like strange places and faraway people—or vice versa?"

"Both." Corbett smiled hopefully. "I've raised buildings all over the world. Can the world use another architect?"

"No. Do you feel that the state owes you something?"

There could be but one answer to that. "No."

"But you had yourself frozen. You must have felt that the future owed you something."

"Not at all. It was a good risk. I was dying."

"Ah." The checker looked him over thoughtfully. "If you had something to believe in, perhaps dying wouldn't mean so much."

Corbett said nothing.

They gave him a short word-association test in English. The test made Corbett suspect that a good many corpsicles must date from near his own death. They took a blood sample, then exercised Corbett to exhaustion on a treadmill and took another blood sample. They tested his pain threshold by direct nerve stimulation—excruciatingly unpleasant—and took another blood sample. They gave him a Chinese puzzle and told him to take it apart.

Pierce then informed him that the testing was over.

"After all, we already know the state of your health."

"Then why the blood samples?"

The checker looked at him for a moment. "You tell me."

Something about that look gave Corbett the creepy feeling that he was on trial for his life. The feeling might have been caused only by the checker's rather narrow features, his icy blue gaze and abstracted smile. Still—Pierce had stayed with him all through the testing, watching him as if Corbett's behavior were a reflection on Pierce's judgment. Corbett thought carefully before he spoke.

"You have to know how far I'll go before I quit. You can analyze the blood samples for adrenalin and fatigue poisons to find out just how much I was hurting, just how tired I really was."

"That's right," said the checker.

Corbett had survived again.

He would have given up much earlier on the pain test. But at some point Pierce had mentioned that Corbett was the fourth corpsicle personality to be tested in that empty body.

He remembered going to sleep that last time, two hundred years ago.

His family and friends had been all around him, acting like mourners. He had chosen the coffin, paid for vault space, and made out his last will and testament, but he had not thought of the happening as dying. It had not felt like dying. He had been given a shot. The eternal pain had drifted away in a soft haze. He had gone to sleep.

He had done so wondering about the future, wondering what he would wake to. A vault into the unknown. World government? Interplanetary spacecraft? Clean fusion power? Strange clothing, body paints, nudism?

Or crowding, poverty, all the fuels used up, power provided by cheap labor? He had thought of those, but it was all right. They would not be able to afford to wake him if they were that poor. The world he dreamed of in those last moments was a rich world, able to support such luxuries as Jerome Corbett.

It looked as if he weren't going to see too damn much of it.

A guard led Corbett away after the testing. He walked with a meaty hand wrapped around Corbett's thin upper arm. Leg irons would have been no more effective, had Corbett thought of escaping. The guard took him up a narrow plastic staircase to the roof.

The noon sun blazed in a blue sky that shaded to yellow, then brown at the horizon. Green plants grew in close-packed rows on parts of the roof. Elsewhere many sheets of something glassy were exposed to the sunlight.

Corbett caught one glimpse of the world from a bridge between two roofs. It was a cityscape of close-packed buildings, all of the same cold cubistic design. Corbett was impossibly high on a walk that was concrete, to be sure, but that had no guard rails at all. So Corbett stopped breathing, stopped walking.

The guard did not speak. He tugged at Corbett's arm, not hard, and watched to see what he would do. Corbett pulled himself together and walked on.

The room was all bunks—two walls of bunks with a gap between. The light was cool and artificial, but outside it was nearly noon. Could they be expecting him to sleep?

The room was big, a thousand bunks big. Most of the bunks were full. A few occupants watched incuriously as the guard showed Corbett which bunk was his. It was the bottommost in a stack of six. Corbett had to drop to his knees and roll to get into it. The bedclothes were strange, silky, and very smooth, even slippery—the only touch of luxury in that place. But there was no top sheet, nothing to cover him. He lay on his side, looking out at the dormitory from near floor level.

Three things were shocking about that place.

One was the smell. Apparently perfumes and deodorants had been another passing fad. Pierce had been overdue for a bath. So was Corbett's new self. Here the smell was rich.

The second was the double bunks, four of them in a vertical stack, wider than the singles and with thicker mattresses. The doubles were for loving, not sleeping. What shocked Corbett was that they were right out in the open, not hidden by so much as a gauze curtain.

The same was true of the toilets.

How can they live like this?

Corbett rubbed his nose and jumped—and cursed at himself for jumping. It was the third time he had done so. His own nose had been big and fleshy and somewhat shapeless. But the nose he now rubbed automatically when trying to think was small and narrow, with a straight, sharp edge. He might very well get used to the smell and everything else before he got used to his own nose.

Sometime after dusk a man came for him. A broad, brawny type wearing a gray jumper and a broad expressionless face, the guard was not one to waste words. He found Corbett's bunk, pulled Corbett out by one arm, and led him stumbling away. Corbett was facing Pierce before he was fully awake.

In annoyance he asked, "Doesn't anyone else speak English?"

"No," said the checker.

Pierce and the guard guided Corbett to a comfortable armchair facing a wide curved screen. They put padded earphones on him. They set a plastic bottle of clear fluid on a shelf over his head. Corbett noticed a clear plastic tube tipped with a hypodermic needle.

"Breakfast?"

Pierce missed the sarcasm. "One meal each day—after learning period and exercise." He inserted the hypodermic into a vein in Corbett's arm. He covered the wound with a blob of what might have been silly putty.

Corbett watched it all without emotion. If he had ever been afraid of needles, the months of pain and cancer had worked it out of him. A needle was surcease, freedom from pain for a time.

"Learn now," said Pierce. "This knob controls speed. The volume is set for your hearing. You may replay any section once. Don't worry about your arm—you can't pull the tube loose."

"There's something I wanted to ask you, only I couldn't remember the word. What's a rammer?"

"Starship pilot."

Corbett studied the checker's face. "You're kidding."

"No. Learn now." The checker turned on Corbett's screen and went away.

A rammer was the pilot of a starship.

The starships were Bussard ramjets. They caught interstellar hydrogen in immaterial nets of electromagnetic force, guided and compressed and burned the hydrogen for thrust. Potentially there was no limit at all on their speed. They were enormously powerful, enormously complex, enormously expensive.

Corbett found it incredible that the state would trust so much value, such devastating power and mass to one man. To a man two centuries dead! Why, Corbett was an architect, not an astronaut. It was news to him that the concept of the Bussard ramjet predated his own death. He had watched the Apollo XI and XIII flights on television, and that had been the extent of his interest in spaceflight until now.

Now his life depended on his "rammer" career. He never doubted it. That was what kept Corbett in front of the screen with the earphones on his head for fourteen hours that first day. He was afraid he might be tested.

He didn't understand all he was supposed to learn. But he was not tested either.

The second day he began to get interested. By the third day he was fascinated. Things he had never understood—relativity and magnetic theory and abstract mathematics—he now grasped intuitively. It was marvelous!

And he ceased to wonder why the state had chosen Jerome Corbett. It was always done this way. It made sense, all kinds of sense.

The payload of a starship was small, and its operating lifetime was more than a man's lifetime. A reasonably safe life-support system for one man occupied an unreasonably high proportion of the payload. The rest must go for biological package probes.

As for sending a citizen, a loyal member of the state—what for? The times would change enormously before a starship could return. The state itself might change beyond recognition. A returning rammer must adjust to a whole new culture—with no way of telling in advance what it might be like.

Why not pick a man who had already chosen to adjust to a new culture? A man whose own culture was two centuries dead before the trip started?

And a man who already owed the state his life?

The RNA was most effective. Corbett stopped wondering about Pierce's dispassionately possessive attitude. He began to think of himself as property being programmed for a purpose.

And he learned. He skimmed microtaped texts as if they were already familiar. The process was heady. He became convinced that he could rebuild a ramship with his bare hands, given the parts. He had loved figures all his life, but abstract mathematics had been beyond him until now. Field theory, monopole field equations, circuitry design. When to suspect the presence of a gravitational point "scource"—how to locate it, use it, avoid it.

The teaching chair was his life. The rest of his time—exercise, dinner, sleep—seemed vague, uninteresting.

He exercised with about twenty others in a room too small for the purpose. Like Corbett, the others were lean and stringy, in sharp contrast to the brawny wedge-shaped men who were their guards. They followed the lead of a guard, running in place because there was no room for real running, forming precise rows for scissors jumps, pushups, situps.

After fourteen hours in a teaching chair Corbett usually enjoyed the jumping about. He followed orders. And he wondered about the stick in a holster at the guard's waist. It looked like a cop's baton. It might have been just that—except for the hole in one end. Corbett never tried to find out.

Sometimes he saw Pierce during the exercise periods. Pierce and the men who tended the teaching chairs were of a third type: well fed, in adequate condition, but just on the verge of being overweight. Corbett thought of them as Olde American types.

From Pierce he learned something of the other professions

open to a revived corpsicle/reprogrammed criminal. Stoop labor: intensive hand cultivation of crops. Body servants. Handicrafts. And easily taught repetitive work. And the hours! The corpsicles were expected to work fourteen hours a day. And the crowding!

He was leading the life now. Fourteen hours to study, an hour of heavy exercise, an hour to eat, and eight hours of sleeping in a dorm that was two solid walls of people.

"Time to work, time to eat, time to sleep! Elbow to elbow every minute! The poor bastards," he said to Pierce. "What kind of a life is that?"

"It lets them repay their debt to the state as quickly as possible. Be reasonable, Corbett. What would a corpsicle do with his off-hours? He has no social life—he has to learn one by observing citizens. Many forms of corpsicle labor involve proximity to citizens."

"So they can look up at their betters while they work? That's no way to learn. It would take—I get the feeling we're talking about decades of this kind of thing."

"Thirty years' labor generally earns a man his birth certificate. That gets him a right-to-work—which then gets him a guaranteed base income he can use to buy education tapes and shots. And the medical benefits are impressive. We live longer than you used to, Corbett."

"Meanwhile, it's slave labor. Anyway, none of this applies to me—"

"No, of course not. Corbett, you're wrong to call it slave labor. A slave can't quit. You can change jobs anytime you like. There's a clear freedom of choice."

Corbett shivered. "Any slave can commit suicide."

"Suicide, my ass," the checker said distinctly. If he had anything that could be called an accent, it lay in the precision of his pronunciation. "Jerome Corbett is dead. I could have given you his intact skeleton for a souvenir."

"I don't doubt it." Corbett saw himself tenderly polishing his own white bones. But where could he have kept such a thing?

"Well, then. You're a brain-wiped criminal, justly brain-wiped,

I might add. Your crime has cost you your citizenship, but you still have the right to change professions. You need only ask for another personality. What slave can change jobs at will?"

"It would feel like dying."

"Nonsense. You go to sleep, that's all. When you wake up, you've got a different set of memories."

The subject was an unpleasant one. Corbett avoided it from then on. But he could not avoid talking to the checker. Pierce was the only man in the world he could talk to. On the days Pierce failed to show up he felt angry, frustrated.

Once he asked about gravitational point scources. "My time didn't know about those."

"Yes, it did. Neutron stars. You had a number of pulsars located by nineteen-seventy, and the math to describe how a pulsar decays. The thing to watch for is a decayed pulsar directly in your path."

"Oh."

Pierce regarded him in some amusement. "You really don't know much about your own time, do you?"

"Astrophysics wasn't my field. And we didn't have your learning techniques." Which reminded him of something. "Pierce, you said you learned English with RNA injections. Where did the RNA come from?"

Pierce grinned and left.

Corbett did not want to die. He was utterly, disgustingly healthy, and twenty years younger than he had been at death. He found his rammer education continually fascinating. If only they would stop treating him like property. . . .

Corbett had been in the army, but that had been twenty years before his death. He had learned to take orders, but never to like it. What had galled him then had been the basic assumption of his inferiority. But no army officer in Corbett's experience had believed in Corbett's inferiority as completely as did Pierce and Pierce's guards.

The checker never repeated a command, never seemed even to

consider that Corbett would refuse. If Corbett refused once, he knew what would happen. And Pierce knew that he knew. No army could have survived in such a state. The attitude better fitted a death camp.

They must think I'm a zombie. . . .

Corbett carefully did not pursue the thought. He was a corpse brought back to life—but not all the way.

The life was not pleasant. His last-class citizenship was galling. There was nobody to talk to—nobody but Pierce, whom he was learning to hate. He was hungry most of the time—the single daily meal barely filled his belly, and it would not stay full. No wonder he had wakened so lean.

More and more he lived in the teaching chair. Vicariously he became a rammer then, and the impotence of his life was changed to omnipotence. Starman! Riding the fire that feeds the suns, scooping fuel from interstellar space itself, spreading electromagnetic fields like wings hundreds of miles out. . . .

Two weeks after the state had wakened him from the dead, Corbett was given his course.

He relaxed in a chair that was not quite a contour couch. RNA solution dripped into him. The needle no longer bothered him—he never noticed it. The teaching screen held a map of his course, in green lines in three-space. Corbett had stopped wondering how the three-dimensional effect was achieved.

The scale was shrinking as he watched.

Two tiny blobs and a glowing ball surrounded by a faintly glowing corona. This part of his course he already knew. A linear accelerator would launch him from the moon, boost him to Bussard ramjet speeds and hurl him at the sun. Solar gravity would increase his speed while his electromagnetic fields caught and burned the solar wind itself. Then out, still accelerating, to the stars. . . .

In the teaching screen the scale shrank horrendously. The distances between stars were awesome, terrifying. Van Maanan's Star was twelve light-years away.

He would begin deceleration a bit past the midpoint. The

matching would be tricky. He must slow enough to release the biological package probe—but not enough to drop him below ram speeds. In addition he must use the mass of the star for a course change. There was no room for error here.

Then on to the next target, which was even farther away. Corbett watched—and he absorbed—and a part of him seemed to have known everything all along even while another part was gasping at the distances. Ten stars, all yellow dwarfs of the Sol type, an average of fifteen light-years apart—though he would cross one gap of fifty-two light-years. He would almost touch lightspeed on that one. Oddly enough, the Bussard ramjet effect would improve at such speeds. He could take advantage of the greater hydrogen flux to pull the fields closer to the ship, to intensify them.

Ten stars in a closed path, a badly bent and battered ring leading him back to the solar system and Earth. He would benefit from the time he spent near the speed of light. Three hundred years would pass on Earth, but Corbett would only live through two hundred years of ship's time—which implied some kind of suspended animation technique.

It didn't hit him the first time through—or the second, but repetition had been built into the teaching program. It didn't hit him until he was on his way to the exercise room.

Three hundred years?

Three hundred years!

It wasn't night, not really. Outside it must be midafternoon. Indoors, the dorm was always coolly lit, barely brightly enough to read if there had been any books. There were no windows.

Corbett should have been asleep. He suffered every minute he spent gazing out into the dorm. Most of the others were asleep, but a couple made noisy love on one of the loving bunks. A few men lay on their backs with their eyes open, and two women talked in low voices. Corbett didn't know the language. He had been unable to find anyone who spoke English.

He suspected that there were two shifts, that someone slept in his bunk, mornings—but he could prove nothing. The slippery sheets must be fantastically easy to clean. Just hose them down.

Corbett was desperately homesick.

The first few days had been the worst.

He had stopped noticing the smell. If something reminded him, he could sniff the traces of billions of human beings. Otherwise the odor was part of the environment.

But the loving bunks bothered him. When they were in use he watched. When he forced himself not to watch, he listened. He couldn't help himself. But he had turned down two sign-language invitations from a small brunette with straggly hair and a pretty, elfin face. Make love in public? He couldn't.

He could avoid using the loving bunks, but not the exposed toilets. That was embarrassing. The first time he was able to force himself only by staring rigidly at his feet. When he pulled on his jumper and looked up, a number of sleepers were watching him in obvious amusement. The reason might have been his self-consciousness or the way he dropped his jumper around his ankles, or he may have been out of line. A pecking order determined who might use the toilets before whom. He still hadn't figured out the details.

Corbett wanted to go home.

The idea was unreasonable. His home was gone, and he would have gone with it without the corpsicle crypts. But reason was of no use in this instance—he wanted to go home. Home to Miriam, who long since must have died of old age. Home to anywhere: Rome, San Francisco, Kansas City, Hawaii, Brasilia—he had lived in all those places, all different, but all home. Corbett had been a born traveler, "at home" anywhere—but he was not at home here and never would be.

Now they would take here away from him. Even this world of four rooms and two roofs—this world of elbow-to-elbow mutes and utter slavery, this world of which he knew nothing—would have vanished when he returned from the stars.

Corbett rolled over and buried his face in his arms. If he didn't sleep he would be groggy tomorrow. He might miss something essential. They had never tested his training. Read that. *Not yet, not yet. . . .*

He dozed.

He came awake suddenly, already up on one elbow, groping for some elusive thought.

Ah.

Why haven't I been wondering about the biological package probes?

A moment later he did wonder.

What are the biological package probes?

But the wonder was that he had never wondered.

He knew what and where they were: heavy fat cylinders arranged around the waist of the starship's hull. Ten of these, each weighing almost as much as Corbett's own life-support system. He knew their mass distribution. He knew the clamp system that held them to the hull and could operate and repair the clamps under various extremes of damage. He almost knew where the probes went when released; it was just on the tip of his tongue—which meant he had had the RNA shot but had not yet seen the instructions.

But he did not know what the probes were for.

It was like that with the ship, he realized. He knew everything there was to know about a seeder ramship, but nothing at all about the other kinds of ramship or interplanetary travel or ground-to-orbit vehicles. He knew that he would be launched by linear accelerator from the moon. He knew the design of the accelerator—he could see it, three hundred and fifty kilometers of rings standing on end in a line across a level lunar mare. He knew what to do if anything went wrong during launch. And that was all he knew about the moon and lunar installations and lunar conquest, barring what he had watched on television two hundred years ago.

What was going on out there? In the two weeks since his arrival (awakening? resuscitation?) he had seen four rooms and two rooftops, glimpsed a fantastic cityscape from a bridge and talked to one man who was not interested in telling him anything. What had happened in two hundred years?

These men and women who slept around him. Who were they? Why were they here? He didn't even know if they were corpsicles or contemporary. Probably contemporary. Not one of them was self-conscious about the facilities.

Corbett had raised his buildings in all sorts of strange places, but he had never jumped blind. He had always brushed up on the language and studied the customs before he went. Here he had no handle, nowhere to start. He was lost.

If only he had someone he could really talk to!

He was learning in enormous gulps, taking in volumes of knowledge so broad that he hadn't realized how rigidly bounded they were. The state was teaching him only what he needed to know or might need to know sometime. Every bit of information was aimed straight at his profession.

Rammer.

He could see the reasoning. He would be gone for several centuries. Why should the state teach him anything at all about today's technology, customs, geography? There would be trouble enough when he came back if he— Come to that, who had taught him to call the government the state? He knew nothing of its power and extent. How had he come to think of the state as all-powerful?

It must be the RNA training. With data came attitudes below the conscious level, where he couldn't get at them.

What were they doing to him?

He had lost his world. He would lose this one. According to Pierce, he had lost himself four times already. A condemned criminal had had his personality wiped four times. Now Corbett's beliefs and motivations were being lost bit by bit to the RNA solution as the state made him over into a rammer.

Was there nothing that was his?

He failed to see Pierce at exercise period. It was just as well. He was somewhat groggy. As usual, he ate dinner like a starving man. He returned to the dorm, rolled into his bunk, and was instantly asleep.

He looked up during study period the next day and found Pierce watching him. He blinked, fighting free of a mass of data on the attitude jet system that bled plasma from the inboard fusion plant that was also the emergency electrical power source—and asked, "Pierce, what's a biological package probe?"

"I would have thought they would teach you that. You know what to do with the probes, don't you?"

"The teaching widget gave me the procedure two days ago. Slow up for certain systems, kill the fields, turn a probe loose, and speed up again."

"You don't have to aim them?"

"No, I guess they aim themselves. But I have to get them down to a certain relative velocity to get them into the system."

"Amazing. They must do all the rest of it themselves." Pierce shook his head. "I wouldn't have believed it. Well, Corbett, the probes steer for a terrestrial world with a reducing atmosphere. They outnumber oxygen-nitrogen worlds about three to one in this arm of the galaxy and probably everywhere else, too—as you may know, if your age got that far."

"But what do the probes do?"

"They're biological packages. Bacteria. The idea is to turn a reducing atmosphere into an oxygen atmosphere, just the way certain bacteria did it for Earth, something like fifteen-times-ten-to-the-eighth years ago." The checker smiled—barely. His small narrow mouth wasn't built to express any great emotion. "You're part of a big project, Corbett."

"Good Lord. How long does it take?"

"We think about fifty thousand years. Obviously we've never had a chance to measure it."

"But, good Lord! Do you really expect the state to last that long? Does even the state expect to last that long?"

"That's not your affair, Corbett. Still"—Pierce considered—"I don't suppose I do. Or the state does. But humanity will last. One day there will be men on those worlds. It's a Cause, Corbett.

The immortality of the species. A thing bigger than one man's life. And you're part of it."

He looked at Corbett expectantly.

Corbett was deep in thought. He was running a fingertip back and forth along the straight line of his nose.

Presently he asked, "What's it like out there?"

"The stars? You're—"

"No, no, no. The city. I catch just a glimpse of it twice a day: cubistic buildings with elaborate carvings at the street level—"

"What the bleep is this, Corbett? You don't need to know anything about Selerdor. By the time you come home the whole city will be changed."

"I know, I know. That's why I hate to leave without seeing something of this world. I could be going out to die—"

Corbett stopped. He had seen that considering look before, but he had never seen Pierce actually angry.

The checker's voice was flat, his mouth pinched tight. "You think of yourself as some kind of tourist."

"So would you if you found yourself two hundred years in the future. If you didn't have that much curiosity, you wouldn't be human."

"Granted that I'd want to look around. I certainly wouldn't demand it as a right. Corbett, what were you thinking when you foisted yourself off on the future? Did you think the future owed you a debt? It's the other way around—and time you realized it!"

Corbett was silent.

"I'll tell you something. You're a rammer because you're a born tourist. We tested you for that. You like the unfamiliar—it doesn't send you scuttling back to something safe and known. That's rare." The checker's eyes said: *And that's why I've decided not to wipe your personality yet.* His mouth said, "Was there anything else?"

Corbett pushed his luck. "I'd like a chance to practice with a computer like the ship's computer-autopilot."

"We don't have one, but you'll get your chance in two days. You're leaving then."

Next day he received his instructions for entering the solar system. He was to try anything and everything to make contact, up to and including flashing his attitude jets in binary code. The teaching widget was fanatical on the subject.

He found that he would not be utterly dependent on rescue ships. He could slow the ramship by braking directly into the solar wind until the proton flux was too slow to help him. He could then proceed on attitude jets, using whatever hydrogen was left in the emergency tank. A nearly full tank would actually get him to the moon and land him there.

The state was through with him when he dropped his last probe. It was good of the state to provide for his return, Corbett thought—and then he shook himself. The state was not altruistic. It wanted the ship back.

Now, more than ever, Corbett wanted a chance at the computer-autopilot.

He found one more chance to talk to the checker.

"A three-hundred-year round trip—maybe two hundred, ship's time," said Corbett. "I get some advantage from relativity. But, Pierce, you don't really expect me to live two hundred years, do you? With nobody to talk to?"

"The cold sleep treatment—"

"Even so."

Pierce frowned. "You haven't studied medicine. I'm told that cold sleep has a rejuvenating effect over long periods. You'll spend perhaps twenty years awake and the rest in cold sleep. The medical facilities are automatic; I'm sure you've been instructed how to use them. They are adequate. Do you think we'd risk your dying out there between the stars, where it would be impossible to replace you?"

"No."

"Was there anything else you wanted to see me about?"

"Yes." He had decided not to raise the subject—now he changed his mind. "I'd like to take a woman with me. The life-support system would hold two of us easily enough. I worked it out. We'd need another cold sleep chamber, of course."

For two weeks this had been the only man Corbett could talk to. At first he had found Pierce unfathomable, unreadable, almost inhuman. Since then he had learned to read the checker's face to some extent.

Now he watched Pierce decide whether to terminate Jerome Corbett and start over.

It was a close thing. But the state had spent considerable time and effort on Jerome Corbett. It was worth a try. . . . And so Pierce said, "That would take up some space. You would have to share the rest between you. I do not think you would survive, Corbett."

"But—"

"Look here, Corbett. We know you don't need a woman. If you did you would have taken one by now, and we would have wiped you and started over. You've lived in the dormitory for two weeks, and you have not used the loving bunks once."

"Damn it, Pierce, do you expect me to make love in public? I can't."

"Exactly."

"But—"

"Corbett, you learned to use the toilet, didn't you? Because you had to. You know what to do with a woman but you are one of those men fortunate enough not to need one. Otherwise you could not be a rammer."

If Corbett had hit the checker then he would have done it knowing that it meant his death. And knowing that, he would have killed Pierce for forcing him to it.

Something like ten seconds elapsed, during which he might have done it. Pierce watched him in frank curiosity.

When he saw Corbett relax, he said, "You leave tomorrow, Corbett. Your training is finished. Good-bye."

And Pierce walked out.

The dormitory had been a test. He knew it now. Could he cross a narrow bridge with no handrails? Then he was not pathologically afraid of falling. Could he spend two hundred years alone in the cabin of a starship? Then the silent people around him, five above his head, thousands to either side, must make him markedly uncomfortable. Could he live two hundred years without a woman? Surely he must be impotent.

He returned to the dorm after dinner. They had replaced the bridge with a slab of grass. Corbett snarled and crossed ahead of the guard—the guard had to hurry to keep up.

He stood between two walls of occupied bunks, looking about him. Then he did a stupid thing.

He had already refrained from killing the checker. He must have decided to live. What he did, then, was stupid. He knew it.

He looked about him until he found the slender dark-haired girl with the elfin face watching him curiously from near the ceiling. He climbed the rungs between bunks until his face was level with her bunk.

He remembered that the gesture he needed was a quick, formalized one; he didn't know it.

In English he asked, "Come with me?"

She nodded brightly and followed him down the ladder. By then it seemed to Corbett that the dorm was alive with barely audible voices.

The odd one, the rammer trainee.

Certainly a number of the wakeful had turned to lie on their sides to watch.

He felt their eyes on the back of his neck as he zipped open his gray jumpsuit and stepped out of it. The dormitory had been a series of tests. At least two of those eyes must belong to someone who would report to Pierce or to Pierce's bosses. But to Corbett they were just like the others, all the eyes curiously watching to see how the speechless one would make out.

And sure enough, he was impotent. It was the eyes—and he was naked. The girl was first concerned, then pitying. She stroked his cheek in apology or sympathy, and then she went away and found someone else.

Corbett lay listening to them, gazing at the bunk above him.

He waited for eight hours. Finally a guard came to take him away. By then he didn't care what they did with him.

He didn't start to care until the guard's floating jeep pulled up beneath an enormous .22 long cartridge standing on end. Then he began to wonder. It was too small to be a rocket ship.

But it was one. They strapped him into a contour couch, one of three in a cabin with one window. There were the guard type and Corbett and a man who might have been Pierce's second cousin once removed. He had the window. He also had the controls.

Corbett's heartbeat quickened. He wondered how it would be.

It was as if he had suddenly become very heavy. He heard no noise except right at the beginning—a sound like landing gear being raised on an airplane. Not a rocket, Corbett thought—and he remembered the tricks a Bussard ramjet could play with magnetic fields. He was heavy and he hadn't slept a wink last night. He went to sleep.

When he awoke he was in free fall. Nobody had tried to tell him anything about free fall. The guard and the pilot watched him curiously to see what he would do.

"Screw you," said Corbett.

It was another test. He got the straps open and pushed himself over to the window. The pilot laughed, caught him, and held him while he closed a protective cover over the instruments. Then he let go, and Corbett drifted before the window.

His belly was revolving eccentrically. His inner ear was going crazy. His testicles were tight up against his groin, and that didn't feel good, either. He felt as if the elevator cable had snapped. Corbett snarled within his mind and tried to concentrate on the window. But the Earth was not visible. Neither was the moon. Just a lot of stars, bright enough—quite bright, in fact—even more brilliant than they had been above a small boat anchored off Catalina Island one night long ago. He watched them for some time.

Trying to keep his mind off that falling elevator.

He wasn't about to get himself disqualified now.

They ate aboard in free fall. Corbett copied the others, picking chunks of meat and potatoes out of a plastic bag of stew, pulling them through a membrane that sealed itself behind his pick.

"Of all the things I'm going to miss," he told the broad-faced guard, "I'm going to enjoy missing you most. You and your goddamn staring eyes."

The guard smiled placidly and waited to see if Corbett would get sick.

They landed a day after takeoff on a broad plain where the Earth sat nestled in a row of sharp lunar peaks. One day instead of four—the state had expended extra power to get him here. But an Earth-Moon flight must be a small thing these days.

The plain was black with blast pits. It must have been a landing field for decades. Enormous transparent bubbles with trees and buildings inside them clustered near the runway end of the linear accelerator, and spacecraft of various types were scattered about the plain.

The biggest was Corbett's ramship: a silver skyscraper lying on its side. The probes were in place, giving the ship a thick-waisted appearance. To Corbett's trained eye it looked ready for takeoff.

Corbett donned his suit first, while the pilot and guard watched to see if he would make a mistake. It was the first time he had seen such a suit off the teaching screen. He took it slowly.

There was an electric cart. Apparently Corbett was not expected to know how to walk on an airless world. He thought to head for one of the domes, but the guard steered straight for the ramship. It was a long way off.

It had become unnervingly large when the guard stopped underneath.

The guard said, "Now you inspect your ship."

"You can talk?"

"Yes. Yesterday, a quickie course."

"Oh."

"Three things wrong with your ship. You find all three. You tell me, I tell him."

"Him? Oh, the pilot. Then what?"

"Then you fix one of the things, we fix the others. Then we launch you."

It was another test, of course. Maybe the last. Corbett was furious. He started immediately with the field generators, and gradually he forgot the guard and the pilot and the sword still hanging over his head. He knew this ship. As it had been with the teaching chair, so it was with the ship itself. Corbett's impotence changed to omnipotence. The power of the beast, the intricacy, the potential, the—the hydrogen tank held far too much pressure. That wouldn't wait.

"I'll slurry this now," he told the guard. "Get a tanker over here to top it off." He bled gas slowly through the gauge, lowering the fuel's vapor pressure without letting fuel boil out the gauge itself. When he finished, the liquid hydrogen would be slushy with frozen crystals under near-vacuum pressure.

He finished the external inspection without finding anything more. It figured; the banks of dials held vastly more information than a man's eyes could read through opaque titanalloy skin.

The airlock was a triple-door type, not so much to save air as to give him an airlock even if he lost a door somehow. Corbett shut the outer door, used the others as green lights indicated he could. He looked down at the telltales under his chin as he started to unclamp his helmet.

Vacuum?

He stopped. The ship's gauges said air. The suit's said vacuum. Which was right? Come to think of it, he hadn't heard any hissing. Just how soundproof was his helmet?

Just like Pierce to wait and see if he would take off his helmet in vacuum. Well, how to test?

Hah! Corbett found the head, turned on a water spigot. The water splashed oddly in lunar gravity. It did not boil.

Corbett doffed his helmet and continued his inspection.

There was no way to test the electromagnetic motors without

causing all kinds of havoc in the linear accelerator. He checked out the telltales as best he could, then concentrated on the life-support mechanisms. The tailored plants in the air system were alive and well. But the urea absorption mechanism was plugged somehow. That would be a dirty job. He postponed it.

Did a flaw in his suit constitute a flaw in the ship?

He decided to finish the inspection. The state might have missed something. It was his ship, his life.

The cold sleep chamber was like a great coffin, a corpsicle coffin. Corbett shuddered at the sight of it—it reminded him of two hundred years spent waiting in liquid nitrogen. He wondered again if Jerome Corbett were really dead—and then he shook off the wonder and went to work.

No flaw there.

The computer was acting vaguely funny.

He had a hell of a time tracing the problem. There was a minute break in one superconducting circuit, so small that some current was leaking through anyway, by inductance. Bastards. He donned his suit and went out to report.

The guard heard him out, consulted with the other man, then told Corbett, "You did good. Now finish with the topping-off procedure. We fix the other things."

"There's something wrong with my suit too."

"New suit aboard now."

"I want some time with the computer," said Corbett. "I want to be sure it's all right now."

"We fix it good. When you top off fuel, you leave."

Then suddenly, Corbett felt a vast sinking sensation. The whole Moon was dropping away under him.

They launched him hard. Corbett saw red before his eyes, felt his cheeks dragged far back toward his ears. The ship would be all right—it was built to stand electromagnetic eddy currents from any direction.

He survived. He fumbled out of his couch in time to watch the moonscape flying under him, receding, a magnificent view.

There were days of free fall. He was not yet moving at ram

speeds. But the state had aimed him inside the orbit of Mercury, straight into the thickening solar wind. Protons. Thick fuel for the ram fields and a boost from the sun's gravity.

Meanwhile he had several days. He went to work with the computer.

At one point it occurred to him that the state might monitor his computer work. He shrugged it off. Probably it was too late for the state to stop him now. In any case, he had said too much already.

He finished his work at the computer and got answers that satisfied him. At higher speeds the ram fields were self-reinforcing —they would support themselves and the ship. He could find no upper limit to the velocity of a ramship.

With all the time in the world, then, he sat down at the control console and began to play with the ram fields.

They emerged like invisible wings, and he felt the buffeting of badly controlled bursts of fusing hydrogen. He kept the fields close to the ship, fearful of losing the balance here, where the streaming of protons was so uneven. He could feel how he was doing—he could fly this ship by the seat of his pants with RNA training to help him.

He felt like a giant. This enormous, phallic, germinal flying thing of metal and fire! Carrying the seeds of life for worlds that had never known life, he roared around the sun and out. The thrust dropped a bit then, because he and the solar wind were moving in the same direction. But he was catching it in his nets like wind in a sail, guiding it and burning it and throwing it behind him. The ship moved faster every second.

This feeling of power, enormous masculine power—it had to be partly RNA training. At this point he didn't care. Part was him, Jerome Corbett.

Around the orbit of Mars, when he was sure that a glimpse of sunlight would not blind him, he opened all the ports. The sky blazed around him. There were no planets nearby, and all he saw of the sky was myriads of brilliant pinpoints, mostly white, some showing traces of color. But there was more to see. Fusing hydrogen made a ghostly ring of light around his ship.

It would grow stronger. So far his thrust was low, somewhat more than enough to balance the thin pull of the sun.

He started his turn around the orbit of Jupiter by adjusting the fields to channel the proton flow to the side. That helped his thrust, but it must have puzzled Pierce and the faceless state. They would assume he was playing with the fields, testing his equipment. Maybe. His curve was gradual—it would take them a while to notice.

This was not according to plan. Originally he had intended to go as far as Van Maanan's Star, then change course. That would have given him $2 \times 15 = 30$ years' head start, in case he was wrong, in case the state could do something to stop him even now. Fifteen years for the light to show them his change in course; fifteen more before retaliation could reach him.

It was wise; but he couldn't do it. Pierce might die in thirty years. Pierce might never know he had failed—and that thought was intolerable.

His thrust dropped to almost nothing in the outer reaches of the system. Protons were thin out here. But there were enough to push his velocity steadily higher, and that was what counted. The faster he went, the greater the proton flux. He was on his way.

He was beyond Neptune when the voice of Pierce the checker came to him, saying, "This is Peerssa for the state, Peerssa for the state. Answer, Corbett. Do you have a malfunction? Can we help? We cannot send rescue, but we can advise. Peerssa for the state, Peerssa for the state—"

Corbett smiled tightly. *Peerssa?* The checker's name had changed pronunciation in two hundred years. Pierce had slipped back to an old habit, RNA lessons forgotten. He must be upset.

Corbett spent twenty minutes finding the Moon base with his signal laser. The beam was too narrow to permit sloppy handling.

When he had it adjusted he said, "This is Corbett for himself, Corbett for himself. I'm fine. How are you?"

He spent more time at the computer. One thing had been bothering him: the return. He planned to be away longer than the state would have expected. Suppose there was nobody on the Moon when he returned?

It would be a problem, he found. If he could reach the Moon on his remaining fuel (no emergencies, remember), he could reach the Earth's atmosphere. The ship was durable; it would stand a meteoric reentry. But his attitude jets would not land him, properly speaking.

Unless he could cut away part of the ship. The ram field generators would no longer be needed. . . . Well, he would work it out somehow. Plenty of time. Plenty of time.

The answer took nine hours. "Peerssa for the state. Corbett, we don't understand. You are way off course. Your first target was to be Van Maanan's Star. Instead you seem to be curving around toward Sagittarius. There is no known Earthlike planet in that direction. What the bleep do you think you're doing? Repeating. Peerssa for the state, Peerssa—"

Corbett tried to switch it off. The teaching chair hadn't told him about an off switch. He managed to disconnect a wire. Somewhat later, he located the lunar base with his signal laser and began transmission.

"This is Corbett for himself, Corbett for himself. I'm getting sick and tired of having to find you every damn time I want to say something. So I'll give you this all at once.

"I'm not going to any of the stars on your list.

"It's occurred to me that the relativity equations work better for me the faster I go. If I stop every fifteen light-years to launch a probe, the way you want me to, I could spend two hundred years at it and never get anywhere. Whereas if I just aim the ship in one direction and keep going, I can build up a ferocious Tau factor.

"It works out that I can reach the galactic hub in twenty-one years, ship's time, if I hold myself down to one gravity acceleration. And, Pierce, I just can't resist the idea. You were the one who called me a born tourist, remember? Well, the stars in the galactic hub aren't like the stars in the arms. And they're packed a quarter to a half light-year apart, according to your own theories. It must be passing strange in there. I can't resist it.

"So I'll go exploring on my own. Maybe I'll find some of your reducing atmosphere planets and drop the probes there. Maybe I won't. I'll see you in about seventy thousand years, your time. By then your precious state may have withered away. Or you'll have colonies on the seeded planets, and some of them may have broken loose from you. I'll join one of them. Or—"

Corbett thought it through, rubbing the straight, sharp line of his nose. "I'll have to check it out on the computer," he said. "But if I don't like any of your worlds when I get back, there are always the Clouds of Magellan. I'll bet they aren't more than twenty-five years away, ship's time."

The Science Fiction Yearbook

1971 was generally a very good year for science fiction. The market for both hardcover and soft-cover books continued to improve. The acceptance of the field as a legitimate part of literature was marked by a great increase in the number of college courses in science fiction. And yet the magazines found themselves suffering from circulation difficulties and in some cases were forced to curtail publication.

At the end of the year, only two of the magazines were able to continue a regular schedule of monthly publication. These were *Analog Science Fiction/Science Fact,* long the leader in the field, and *The Magazine of Fantasy and Science Fiction,* with a small but very loyal following and a reputation for literary excellence. *Galaxy Magazine* was forced to cut back its schedule to six issues a year, and its sister publication, *IF Science Fiction,* had already become a bi-monthly. Plans to issue two other quarterly magazines were dropped by Universal Publications. Ultimate Publishing Company's two magazines, *Amazing Science Fiction Stories* and *Fantastic Stories,* were also issued only every other month. Thus, at the end of 1971, a total of only forty-eight magazine issues per year were scheduled.

Before 1970, such a loss would have represented serious trouble for science fiction, but it now seemed to pass almost unnoticed by both writers and readers. The magazines had long been the major outlet and seminal source of science fiction; they had represented the only major market for short fiction, and, hence, for newer writers, while book publication often came as a result of magazine serialization. This is now no longer true.

Publishers Weekly, in its annual report, listed 195 new s-f books and 109 reprints for 1971, for a total of 304 books labeled and marketed as science fiction. (There were a few others that were not specifically labeled as such on the dust jackets.) This represents an increase of thirty-five books over the previous record-breaking year. And since the average book and the average issue of a magazine contain approximately the same number of words, the increase in books more than equaled the decline in magazines.

Probably the most significant part of that report is the fact that original books exceeded the number of reprints. The book market now has become the major outlet for original science fiction. Another factor in the optimism of writers was not included in the breakdown above, but it may be even more significant. This is the fact that the original anthology has become an important part of book publishing.

Until the last few years, it was almost impossible to sell original short fiction to anything except the magazines. But in 1971, writers were being asked for direct submission to half a dozen major original anthologies to appear as books edited by established science fiction authors. And one editor, Roger Elwood, reported that he had contracts for over thirty original anthologies for the coming year. These are scheduled to appear from many publishers who have previously not been interested in science fiction. And while they will depend upon the work of established, well-known writers for prestige, the market will be forced to solicit the work of new writers to fill its wordage requirements.

Thus, the magazines are already losing their importance as the major outlet for new writers and for short fiction. Books have now become the primary market for all forms of science fiction.

The results of this shift are not entirely clear, but some idea of the significance can be guessed. The magazines have always been devoted to a hard core of "fans"—readers who are devoted primarily to one type of literature and highly sophisticated within the limits of that category. Books appeal much more to the general reader. As a result, we can expect science fiction to be shaped far more in the future by writers who can appeal to a wider audience.

This should bring in writers from other fields, and at least partly take science fiction out of its narrow coterie.

At the same time, science fiction will continue to appeal to one special group—the younger reader. Currently, science fiction is already an important category for high school and junior high school readers. Most of them do not read the magazines, but depend upon the books to be found in their school libraries. A number of writers have written science fiction specifically for this age group, but most of the readers seem as willing to read adult books as the so-called juveniles. There are increasing signs that these libraries will be happy to stock hardcover anthologies to meet the demand, resulting in increased readership for all types of science fiction.

More new writers broke into science fiction in 1971 than ever before. The Science Fiction Writers of America reports a membership of over 440, representing working writers who have made at least one sale. Nearly half of these were unknown a few years ago. Many of these writers made that first sale to editors of books rather than magazines.

In some cases, these sales occurred in blocks. Clarion Writers Workshop was able to sell a soft-cover anthology based entirely on the work of the writers taking courses on science fiction writing. And several editors of projected anthologies taught courses at the major workshops or visited them in search of new talent. Harlan Ellison, who was working on *Again, Dangerous Visions* to follow his highly successful first anthology of new stories, reported that he had hoped to find a couple of stories, but actually discovered nearly a score by previously unknown writers.

The established writers also had an excellent year. Several were encouraged to turn to full-time writing for the first time. And a few, who had been inactive for years, returned to the field. Isaac Asimov, for instance, returned with a major science fiction work after having been out of the novel field for sixteen years. Theodore Sturgeon appeared with a new book after nearly as long an absence.

There were, unfortunately, a few tragic losses. John W. Campbell died suddenly in July. He was one of the pioneer writers of interplanetary adventure stories, called "space opera"; and as "Don A. Stuart," he had played a major part in moving science fiction to better written and more deeply human fiction. He had been the guiding genius for more than thirty years of the magazine that became *Analog*. Largely by his influence, the field was moved from its primitive form to what has become modern science fiction, and most of the major writers were ones he had helped and instructed. No loss could have been greater. The field also lost August Derleth, who founded one of the first fantasy publishing houses, and Philip Wylie, whose *When Worlds Collide* and its sequel were landmarks of early science fiction.

Major changes within the field, however, were few and of uncertain importance. The British magazine *New Worlds*, which had been the major outlet for experimental writing in science fiction, ceased publication as a magazine; but it is to continue as a quarterly soft-cover book. Terry Carr resigned as editor of the Ace Specials, which were henceforth to be included in the regular Ace Books. And Donald A. Wolheim resigned to start his own line of DAW books. But Ace will continue under the able editorship of Frederik Pohl. Ben Bova has become editor of *Analog,* and early signs indicate that the magazine will continue on essentially its previous, successful course.

In previous years, a controversy had raged among writers and fans of science fiction over something called the "New Wave" or "New Thing." This began in the early sixties as a result of a small school of newer writers (centered around J. G. Ballard in England) who felt that the old form of science fiction was dead, and that newer, more experimental techniques must replace it. By 1971, however, much of this furor was forgotten. The expanded market had shown that there was room for all kinds of science fiction, and the tempest in a teapot had boiled itself out.

There is still a continuing argument about "speculative fiction" as opposed to "science fiction" (both, of course, shortened to "s-f"), but this seems of interest now largely to a few critics. By the end of 1971, most publishers and readers had decided that the exact name didn't too much matter, though there does seem to be some noticeable split in attitude in the different courses on science fiction writing. The Clarion Workshop, under the sponsorship of varying colleges or universities, seems to emphasize what might be called speculative fiction—a type of fantasy writing that attaches more importance to present relevance—while science fiction tends to be more future-oriented.

Academic interest in science fiction has increased remarkably. Literally hundreds of courses in science fiction are now being given. James Gunn, a well-known science fiction writer as well as educator, reports that his course at the University of Kansas has an enrollment of more than 150. The Secondary Universe Conferences are held regularly, attracting large audiences of academic professionals to serious discussions of the philosophy and significance of both fantasy and science fiction.

In sum, science fiction has never previously been as active, healthy or generally accepted as it is now. As an example, at the annual World Science Fiction Convention, held in Boston in 1971, there were about 2,000 attendees. This convention also received for the first time full recognition from a major newspaper; *The New York Times* had a reporter there, covering the entire four-day event, and the paper gave it an excellent spread, with none of the mocking attempt at humor that marked former reportage of science fiction events.

The Science Fiction Writers of America gave their annual Nebula Awards for best fiction published in 1971 to: Novel—*A Time of Changes,* by Robert Silverberg; Novella—*The Missing Man,* by Katherine McLean; Novelette—*The Queen of Air and Darkness,* by Poul Anderson; and Short Story (included in this volume) —*Good News from the Vatican,* by Robert Silverberg.

Judging by reports of contracts and activities at the end of 1971, it seems that science fiction may do even better in 1972.

—Lester del Rey

ABOUT THE EDITOR

Lester del Rey is the author of more than thirty books of science fiction for adults and younger readers. His most recent novel is *Pstalemate,* published in Fall 1971. He lives in New York City.